Book Cover by Enni Amanda at Yummy Book Covers

 Created with Vellum

*If you're far from your family
during this Christmas season,
this one is for you.*

HEAT LEVEL AND CONTENT WARNINGS

Before reading this book, I encourage you to first read this section to determine whether it's the right fit for your personal circumstances.

This book is closed door, which means there is innuendo, kisses are descriptive, and characters don't shy away from their attraction.

There is mild to moderate use of cuss words, particularly in emotional moments. However, there is no use of f-bombs, religious blasphemies, or known ableist terms.

There are mentions of bullying that the female lead experienced in middle and high school. The male lead suffered an injury that ended his career and the accident is described in moderate detail. Characters are adults and there are mentions of alcohol consumption.

If any of these topics are troublesome for you, please protect yourself and read a book that better suits your situation.

Visit my website mariloyal.com for general content warnings that apply to all my books.

CHAPTER 1
CONOR

Tis the season to be jolly. Unless your name is Sierra Fernandez and you've just glimpsed my face.

She uses her laptop as a tray for her coffee, her phone, plus notepad and pen—because apparently she can't just key her minutes on the device. As she pushes the door open with her shoulder, I catch the unmistakable notes of All I Want For Christmas Is You humming from her throat. The way they die upon sighting me would be offensive if it wasn't so funny.

"Oh." Her brow plunges, all the cheer bleaching out of her expression in a nanosecond. "Why are you here already?"

I tuck my tongue against my cheek and debate whether to dignify that with an answer. I've given up on trying to get on her good side after almost two years of Sierra one-sidedly hating my guts. I'm just not a hundred percent on the nice list, which is why I open my big yap.

"You don't have to act so offended about it when you're early too, you know."

She turns her little button nose up and makes a point of heading as far from me as she possibly can, even if that complicates managing a hot cup of coffee teetering very close to the edge of her makeshift tray. You'd think I poisoned her pet or something. But first, I don't even know if she has one. Second, I love animals. And third, I've never found out what I did to her that was so wrong that she dreads even sharing oxygen with me.

I relax a little when she makes it to her chosen seat without spilling a drop. Her big, dark eyes veer toward me for a second, like she's expecting some commentary from me. Instead, I focus on the work I was doing before she walked in.

I'm just about to send a pitch to Richard, our boss, for a campaign to promote our new line of activewear pants. *SPORTY* is a major sports gear brand that everyone—from little kids to elite athletes—recognizes and wears, not to mention the sponsorships and media we produce to increase the brand value as well. And who would know its products better than me, a former pro hockey player? That's precisely the angle that landed me this job in the marketing team, and I'll exploit it forever for every campaign I want to run.

Besides, I really love these damn pants. I have a pair on right now and they feel as if I was wearing nothing—which, hey, maybe that should be weird since I'm at the office. But I legit can't think of the last time I wore *pants*, not joggers or sweats, that didn't squeeze my hockey thighs or my ass in an uncomfortable way. Surely this experience proves I'm the right man for the pitch, right?

A hissing sound makes me lift my eyes. Sierra's face is scrunched up in pain. The steaming mug close to her lips makes me think she might've burned herself.

"Careful, it might be hot," I say with a heaping spoonful of sarcasm.

The ensuing glare makes me bite my lips. Laughing could potentially get me thrown off the tenth floor of this building.

"Gee. Thanks, smartass. I could've never guessed for

myself." She runs her tongue against the roof of her mouth a few times and for a second, I have a bizarre thought.

I wonder if there's anything I could do to make her mouth feel better.

I blink hard at my laptop monitor. A couple of ideas come to mind. The only feasible one that would also not get me fired or murdered, would be to offer her a drink from my water bottle. But I also doubt she'd want my cooties so I stay put and type even harder, hoping that my keyboard's noise drowns the very unwelcome thoughts in my head.

I might have limited vision in my left eye but I know Sierra's hot. I've known it since day one, even though that's also when she first directed a frown my way. Fortunately, her open hostility keeps me mostly immune—except for random moments of awareness where I truly regret forever being on her naughty list.

Like right now, after my ever helpful lizard brain just dumped the idea of kissing her into my logical brain like it's a present. Sure, I could soothe her burn with my lips. But she could also stab me with her sparkly little gel pen.

The door opens once more and I'm viscerally thankful for the distraction. Rachel Leon pauses at the entrance to cast a look my way and then to her bestie. "Ew, you guys are way too motivated this early in the morning."

I wouldn't define ten in the morning as early, but the aversion these two have to mornings is very well documented among the sales and marketing teams. They'd probably faint if I they found out I get up at five everyday, spend half an hour doing road work, another half hour on weights and chopping wood, shower, make breakfast from scratch, and still make it to work before seven. By now I've finished two reports, five invoices, and am almost done with the pitch.

"I owe my motivation to this, my third cup of coffee," Sierra says to her friend with a completely different tone of voice than she reserves for me. "Although it did burn me a moment ago. I hope that's not some sort of metaphor."

I snort.

Four laser beams point my way and I pretend like they're not intimidating at all, even though they could give lessons to professional hockey defensemen.

I hit send on my pitch right as some of our other coworkers walk into the room. Stephen, Kaylee, and Lewis are another little clique within the marketing department, just the way Sierra and Rachel are one. The difference here is that Kaylee's into Stephen, but Lewis is into Kaylee. It's not awkward probably because no one dares to bring it up. The three of them sit on the table across from me, starting by Lewis next to Rachel.

"Why's everyone sitting on that side?" I fold my arms. "Do I stink, or something?"

Sierra nods without hesitation, even though she's too far to really confirm that.

"I just want to be close to the door, in case this turns into a blood bath." Stephen casts a pointed look at Sierra's corner and then at me.

"Yeah, I mean, we all know how this is going to go," Kaylee says with a shrug. "You two are the only ones who have yet to organize a Christmas party from the team, so there's going to be a fight."

"Hmm." I lean back on my chair.

My opponent takes her sweet time firing up her laptop and arranging her things around it. She pushes a curl of dark hair behind her ear delicately, unbothered by my scrutiny. It was way easier to find flaws in the defense of an opposing hockey team than dealing with this woman. I'm sure she's come armed with a plan to nab this job and normally, I wouldn't give a shit about a one-time gig, except this is *the* biggest event of the year.

And it comes with a healthy ten thousand dollar bonus for the organizer.

Last year, we also had a team meeting the week of Thanksgiving to decide who'd be running the event. It was going to be my first Christmas party at the company, so I decided to not put my name in the hat and bide my time.

Well, guess what? My time is now. I need that money. The hockey dreams of almost sixty kids are counting on it.

"Good morning, team," Richard announces as he opens the door. He also brings a steaming mug, although this one is shaped like Santa's head. Festive but a bit disturbing too. He takes a sip of Santa-brain juice and pauses at the head of the table. "Where's Dave?"

Lewis is quick to respond. "Home sick."

And Sierra's even quicker to be helpful. "Oh, he must be joining online. I'll hook us up to the room."

"Excellent, Fernandez. Let's get this party started." Richard rubs his hands not because they're cold, but in glee. "Get it?"

I do a masterful job of resisting the urge to cringe.

Richard finally begins the meeting after Dave's hooked up to the room via Sierra's laptop. "We all know why we're gathered here. We're officially a month away from the most wonderful time of the year—bonus season." He laughs at his own joke.

I rub my hand across my mouth and beard, then adjust my glasses. I'll laugh when I'm wiring the bonus money to the hockey arena so it doesn't shut down in the new year.

In the background, Dave blows his nose loudly until Sierra presses the silence button.

"Anyway." Richard clears his throat after no one really joined in his laughter. "Last year we had a major skiing extravaganza at Aspen, but I received a lot of complaints from people who travel for work all the time because the last thing they want to do is also travel again for the holidays. That's why this year, I've decided to keep it local."

I check Sierra's expression from the corner of my eye and catch her inspecting me too. We both turn to our boss.

"Um, that poses a problem, sir," she says with her hand raised like this is a classroom. "It's not like our little town is too exciting during the holidays."

Ah, yes. Mapleton, Connecticut, isn't a sprawling metropolis. The small town's main employer is *SPORTY*, and the only reason headquarters are still here is because this is where the founder started the first product line of baseballs over a hundred years ago. We're close to New York but if Richard's saying we have to keep it local, it also means that the Big Apple is out of the picture.

"Since when do we run from a challenge?" I add just to antagonize her. The gnashing of her teeth tells me I succeeded.

"That's right, Mahoney." Richard points at me. "This brief is meant to push your creativity. I want this year's feedback to be that this was the best Christmas party *SPORTY* headquarters has ever had in its history."

I squirm, trying to contain the sudden rush of energy coursing through my veins. It feels very close to the seconds right before sliding onto the ice for a big game.

"Whoever brings the winning brief is guaranteed a ten thousand dollar bonus. But also…" We all lean forward, even the people who technically have no right to try this year. "A potential promotion."

Promotions always come with a salary increase. I don't need to be a math genius to know what that means. I lead a pretty cheap lifestyle, so any extra cash in my pocket will easily go to the maintenance costs of the kids's hockey program.

I open my mouth to fire a random half-baked pitch before Sierra can.

CHAPTER 2
SIERRA

Funny enough, it's not my biggest foe I have to watch out for right away.

"A concert!" Kaylee screeches so hard, her neck veins are about to pop. And it sets off pandemonium.

"Beyoncé!" Lewis, of course, joins in before she's even done catching her breath.

I have a brief, abnormal moment of camaraderie with the enemy. Conor's eyes meet mine and in them, I can see the same shock I'm feeling at the audacity of our coworkers. They had their turn and it's not our fault Richard didn't dangle a promotion in front of their faces when it was their respective chance to organize this thing.

Before Conor can recover, I bang my hands against the desk hard and bring all attention to me. More calmly, I say, "A fully immersive experience."

Every pair of eyes not already on me turns my way.

"That's the only way we can make this a success in a town as boring as Mapleton," I continue saying directly out of my ass. "Think about it. We have colleagues who come from all walks of life—blue collar, white collar, locals, expats, former athletes, fans. We all have one thing in common."

"What's that?" Richard asks when I leave them hanging for a second.

"We're all in *SPORTY* because it's exciting. So, whatever we do, it has to be something that stokes that need to belong and more importantly, to compete." I lean back on my chair, pretty damn smug that all throughout, Conor hasn't been able to get a single word edged in. I may or may not be smirking a little at him.

But he isn't cowed. He lifts his fist to hold his chin and says, "That sounds intriguing, but I don't hear a concrete idea."

I wouldn't say I hate Conor Mahoney but it's very close. The list of reasons why this man irritates me is long.

It started on his literal first day at the company. He was late and that's not really what triggered the avalanche, it's what happened before he arrived. Namely, our boss losing his ever loving mind about welcoming a recently-retired elite hockey athlete into our team. I didn't mind the fanboying, but when Richard decided right there and then that the best way to welcome the new teammate was to give him a cool project… and literally ripped one off *my* catalogue to give it to him… the seed of dislike was firmly planted in my mind.

I'm not a shitty person, though. I didn't assign the blame on the new guy who wasn't even around for Richard's great lightbulb moment. Except that was just the beginning of a near two-year saga that continues.

"I don't hear you offering one, either," I counter and fold my arms tight to keep my hands from making a strangling motion.

"Thank you for giving me the floor." His lips curve and he shifts his attention to our boss. "I have a simpler, sure-fire way of making this party succeed—guaranteed. And it won't cost us a pretty penny."

Richard's eyebrows take off like airplanes. "Color me intrigued."

"The first principle of marketing is knowing your customer, right?" Conor shrugs those big shoulders of his. "Well, *SPORTY* is a company for and by athletes. What we need is a sports event."

"Wow, that is *so* specific. We only have to narrow it down to one of the hundreds of organized sports that exist on this planet." The deadpan in my voice is perhaps a notch too obvious to be professional, but I can't help it. The stakes are really freaking high for me.

If you poll everyone in this office—or heck, in this room alone—about what Christmas is to them, you won't get the same answer twice. Some might say giving or receiving presents. Or the food that evokes memories from childhood and home. Also the drinks that make people forget precisely those things. Or the parties they attend to forge new memories. The music that brings a spark of joy to a year that feels old and tired, and reminds us of the promise that the new one brings.

For me, it's family.

That's the center of my life, even though it's a pretty small one. It's just my mom and dad, and everyone else is either back in my parents' home country, Venezuela, or all over the world. Being so spread out has made it so that I basically just have phone-cousins, phone-Aunts, and phone-Uncles.

Except for one person who is special. My grammie.

Grammie is Mom's mother and she also lives back in Venezuela. We've only been together in person once when I was a kiddy, but Grammie has always been there for me. She's the sole reason I learned actual Spanish growing up. My parents tried to make my life easier by only speaking English but then Grammie didn't understand me, so I studied hard to be able to converse with her. She kept me company in the afternoons while Mom and Dad were at work and I was out of school, thanks to Whatsapp. I did my homework while she cooked or sewed or cleaned. Basically, she brought me up from afar.

And she's getting older. *A lot* older.

"I got it." Lewis traces an arch in the air like he's painting a billboard. "Beyoncé singing while teaching a cycling class. Then the lights go dark and it's Post Malone singing while teaching a boxing class—and so on."

I scratch my head with the clicker end of my pen, wondering if he's serious. Except, pride beams out of his smile like he genuinely thinks this is the greatest idea since whoever came up with toasters.

"Well." Richard brings us back to what matters—his opinion. "I think both of these ideas sound promising. Unfortunately, they're equally half-baked."

Lewis glances around. "What about my idea?"

"Honey," Rachel says with a tone of voice that makes her sound sixty-years-old instead of late-twenties. "You had your chance to book Beyoncé last year and you took us to Aspen instead. It's Sierra or Conor's turn now."

I notice how she mentions me first. That's a good friend right there.

"Dude." Stephen leans over the table to look at his buddy. "Beyoncé's not even your favorite artist. What gives?"

But it's Kaylee's. I keep my mouth zipped, though.

"Well, uh…"

"We could do like a sort of Olympics-inspired event," Conor says, nodding to me. "It would definitely be the immersive experience Sierra suggested, while catering to our very unique target audience."

Mierda. Why didn't that occur to me? I basically served the whole idea to him on a silver platter.

I rack my brain trying to come up with an alternative that is at least just as fun, but Richard drops a bomb.

"That's it! An immersive Christmas sport experience." He snaps his fingers several times and humming in tandem. "You two have nailed the brief."

I pause. Even Conor shuts his mouth so tight that his teeth make a clacking sound.

"Um." I clear my throat. "I came up with the initial idea."

Conor chirps back. "But I fine-tuned it."

"Exactly, and that's why the two of you will work together."

"But—" We both start at the same time.

"You both challenged each other and came up with something really intriguing. I have no doubt you'll push one another to excellence for this event and that's what I want. An absolute banger."

Slowly, Rachel turns her head to offer me a full-teeth cringe. She's the only person in this room who knows what all is going through my head right now. Not only would I rather shave my glorious head of curls than work closely with Conor Mahoney, but also what this money means to me.

That latter is precisely what pushes me to challenge Richard one more time. "But does this mean we'll have to split the bonus? What about the promotion, then?"

"Yeah." A wrinkle appears between Conor's eyebrows. "I'll be honest, Richard. This doesn't make me super motivated."

"Me neither," I admit openly.

Richard throws his head back and releases a very Santa Claus laugh—all ho ho ho like. I guess he's channeling the inspiration for his mug or already getting into the seasonal mood.

"And I wouldn't expect you to, so I raise you this." He laces his fingers all villain-like. "It's ten-kay each, guaranteed, for organizing the event. But whoever impresses me the most gets the promotion. How's that for motivation?"

Oh, shit.

I swallow hard. Okay. If the money's guaranteed already

I'm definitely in, no matter how horrible it'll be to endure Conor's face up close. But if I also get that promotion, I could change the plan altogether. Grammie could come to America not just for a visit, but also to get some proper healthcare.

That's when I notice that Conor's attention is solely on me. His eyes roam my face like he's trying to read it for what I'm going to do. Odd. Why would he even care? This isn't the first project he messes up for me.

When I can't take the silence anymore, I say, "Fine. I'm in."

"Guess I'm in, too." Conor nods.

"Great. I expect a solid proposal on my desk in a week."

"Er, Richard… it's Thanksgiving in two days." Rachel now turns her cringey smile on our boss.

"And that's why I said in a week. That way they'll have all of tomorrow and Monday to put it together."

As if two nine-hour-long workdays were enough for that. Tomorrow and Monday aren't anywhere near enough, and there's no way I'm seeing hair or hide of this guy during the holiday break—no matter how pretty either of those is.

"Well, we have more or less a plan so this meeting is adjourned." Richard picks up his ridiculous mug and gets to his feet.

Dave regales us with one of those coughs that make everyone uncomfortable even though he's not in the room. I give him a polite wave of my hand before disconnecting the call.

Kaylee lets out a sigh that bleeds disappointment before leaving her seat. Meanwhile, Lewis huffs and pushes away from the table. Only when his chair slams back against the glass wall does he get to his feet.

"Good luck, Sierra." Rachel squeezes my arm. "I know this isn't what you were hoping for, but don't forget you're the one who took the initiative here. You got this."

"Thanks." I jut my lower lip. It sucks, but I guess I'll just cry my way to the bank.

"You coming?" she asks me when I don't move from my seat.

"Nah, I have a few minutes before another meeting in this room. I'll just stay and get some work done here."

By work I mean I'll make a flight reservation right away. This is going to be super expensive because it's so late, but I didn't have enough funds in my bank account to cover a cheaper ticket earlier. Now that I know the bonus is happening, I can charge the ticket to my credit card and pay it off later.

"Okay. See you later."

I respond without looking up from my screen. "Yep, bye."

"This is gonna be fun to watch," says Stephen just outside the door, no doubt referring to what could potentially turn into a shitshow. Best I can do is ignore him and focus on my renewed hope.

My browser pulls up the exact flight information I need once I type the first few letters. I've looked it up so many times that it remembers. My Christmas spirt returns with a vengeance and I start humming Mariah Carey's classic seasonal song. Mariah is Mom's and Grammie's favorite singer because she has Venezuelan ascent.

"Sierra."

I freeze. Apparently not everyone left.

Would ignoring him make him go away?

I close my eyes. Probably not. We're going to be in each other's grills pretty hardcore for the next three weeks. I swivel my chair and open my eyes.

Instant regret floods me. Conor leans his shoulder against the doorframe, arms folded and holding his laptop against his chest. The problem is that a strand of hair has escaped its pomade hold, arching over his forehead in a way that is offensive. He's all smiles and easy laughs with everyone but me, which is fine except for the fact that it earns me his most intense stares. Like this one. I wonder how his hockey opponents felt when his brown eyes were on them like this. Or if unlike me, they felt nothing at all.

See, that's another important item in the list of reasons why he irritates me. He has no right to be so freaking cute.

"What?" I grit the word out.

He narrows his eyes a notch. "Is this going to be an issue?"

I let the silence hang because making him slightly uncomfortable is the only way I can intimidate a guy who is like two hundred pounds of solid, very nicely shaped muscle.

"Not if you don't get in my way," I say at last.

"Hm." He straightens away from the doorframe. "I guess it'll be an issue, then. That promotion is mine."

I stretch my lips into a sweet smile that doesn't fool him, going by the way that little wrinkle appears between his eyebrows again. "You're going down, Mahoney."

CHAPTER 3
CONOR

ce has its own particular smell. I didn't notice it while I was a kid, skating before I could even walk properly. I certainly didn't pay any attention to it when I was a teenager or in college, rushing toward my dreams of a professional hockey career. I was too distracted by the smell of sweat and Icy Hot, body odor from a bunch of dudes, the distinctive stench of old equipment, or the glorious smell of new plastic gear.

I didn't notice ice's own scent until after the accident. In the year following it, the only thing that could get me out of bed was coming to this very rink. I'd sit on the stands on my own for hours, just sniffing the stuff like an addict.

Eventually, when I was able to pull my head out of my ass, I got a part time job here—which wasn't hard since I know the owner very well. I still spend my evenings and weekends either teaching kids, or leveling the ice, or cleaning the place. I don't care what, but I know I have to stay close to the ice to stay sane.

I open my eyes. The rink is empty except for me. It's Thanksgiving and every normal person is home with their family. Gramps and I worked all day prepping a meal that will feed us for two weeks, but we both had important plans after supper.

His, a little nap. Mine, a little skate.

He happens to be the owner of the rink, so I have VIP access twenty-four seven.

Pucks lay scattered around the surface. I bounce one with the end of my stick, the smacking sound echoing in the quiet around me. My skates slice the ice with a steady swooshing sound, harsher when I change direction abruptly just for fun. How many times did I do skating drills like this? Just skating around obstacles, pumping my muscles until they burn. It feels colder since I'm alone and my breath puffs faint clouds into the air. I don't drop the puck even as I zigzag across the expanse, just balancing the disc with my stick like a party trick. I bat it in once I'm close enough to the goal, baseball style.

The momentum takes me around the goal. I shoot a nearby puck into the back of the net in what would've been a wraparound goal. The crowd would be roaring right about now.

Taking a deep breath, I pump my legs even harder. That's the best medicine against the blues I get every time I viscerally miss playing. That and a little prescription pill I always carry in my backpack.

I repeat the drill from the top. This time I drop the puck once but I pick it up in a smooth swing and keep going. Ain't that the moral of the story? No matter what happens, you pick your ass up and keep going. At least, that's what I tell myself every morning.

"Knew you'd be here."

I brake hard enough to spray a frozen shower around me. "Hey, Gramps. I thought you'd nap all the way until tomorrow."

He grunts as he slides onto the ice. "Believe it or not, I was too full to fall asleep. Is that how pregnant women feel?"

"I wouldn't know." I snort and watch him as he finds his legs on the ice. He's the one I got the hockey obsession from. I swear that at his ripe age of seventy-nine-years-old, he's steadier on ice than on dryland.

"Now, let's see if you're still any good, kid." His stick is an extension of his body and he uses it to skate a wide arch that takes him right to a faceoff circle.

I sigh loudly. "When are you going to stop calling me kid? I'm twenty six."

"You'll always be a kid to me." He bends forward. "Are you going to keep an old man waiting?"

"Fine, you grump." I grin.

I glide over to face him and drop the puck with little warning. A better grandson would slow down and let him win, except that would piss Gramps off. He smacks the shit out of my stick and one of my legs, trying to get away with the puck. I'm faster and my body moves on muscle memory alone, even though everything on my left is mostly a blur.

Gramps takes off after me. His huffing and puffing follows me as I break away and fire the puck at the empty net so hard that my stick bends in the air.

"Damn, son. You still got it." He wheezes as he catches up.

"Never lost that, at least." I lift the corner of my mouth. "I just lost half of one sense, that's all."

His bony hand grabs my shoulder tight. "But I still have you, that's all that matters."

I groan. "Ah, shit, Gramps. Didn't we say we wouldn't get cheesy today?"

He ignores my every word. "I'm thankful that you didn't hit your head at a different angle three years ago, or there'd be no one to take me to my doctor's appointments now."

My face twitches. Too many things roil in my gut to possibly name them. I don't laugh or cry or scream. Instead, I take off my glasses and rub my eyes. They're wet and I'm going to pretend it's because of the sheen of sweat covering my skin.

"Is this your way of asking me to drive you somewhere?" I ask, trying for levity because I really can't take it when he gets sappy.

"Maybe." He lifts his white, bushy eyebrows. "I may or may not have pissed off my dentist and may or may not need a new one."

"I have no words for you, old man." I sweep a puck towards me and pass it over to him.

"What can I say? He disrespected me." He dangles the puck as if he hadn't stopped playing hockey way before I was even born. "Not everyone had a great grandparent like you to raise them well."

I shut my mouth because there's no point setting him straight. Him getting disrespected is code for he wasn't told what he wanted to hear. When Gramps gets something in his head, there's almost nothing in this planet that can pluck it out —and I have a bigger issue to focus on.

Namely, his decision to sell this place.

I already tried the route of convincing him against it with words. And for all of a dork I am, I'm actually pretty damn convincing. It's why I got a marketing degree. The problem is, that doesn't work against this stubborn oaf—especially not when he showed me a balance sheet I couldn't argue against.

However, coming home with a hefty bonus for Christmas will surely convince him otherwise.

I keep the conversation away from that elephant in the room. "We've basically burned through every medical practice on the west side of Connecticut. Can we keep it to a radius where I don't have to take PTO to drive you?"

"I worked so hard to raise you right and this is how you pay me?" He clicks his tongue and shakes his head in an exaggerated way.

I roll my eyes. "When's your appointment?"

"Monday at noon. That should work with your fancy job, right?"

"Sure," I say right away, even though it technically doesn't work. Sierra and I used most of yesterday brainstorming—separately. The idea is that on Monday we'll have some sort of armistice to pick one idea or mesh them, I don't know. I'm sure she won't be happy if I have to cut it short.

Or… on contrary, she'll be very happy to spend less time with me and this news will totally make her day.

"Great. And treat me to some pie after."

I cut a glare to him that makes him chuckle. He takes a puck and makes a big show of skating a circle around me and shooting at the goal.

"That's right, baby! I got it too." He throws his hands in the air and hoots.

I won't tell him because I'm not half as strong as I pretend, but I'm thankful to have him in my life too. I don't know what I'd have done without him, and it's high time I finally do something good for him.

I'll save this place, his legacy, if it's the last damn thing I ever do.

CHAPTER 4
SIERRA

"How's it going?" I pace back and forth across the living room, where I got exiled to after driving my parents bananas with my worrying.

"Let's see," Mom says with a sigh. "We have tried turning off and back on, unplugging and plugging, restarting the program, keying in the password again."

"And don't forget restarting the wifi router," Dad adds.

"Nothing?" The word comes out as a whine from my throat.

"Nope." Mom pops the P. "Sorry, Sierrita. The issue must be on Grammie's end."

I drop on the couch like a lump. "But it's Thanksgiving. Dinner's not complete without a chat with Grammie. She was going to tell me about the new crochet stitch she's been learning." Ugh, I know I'm being a brat, but I was really looking forward to casually breaking the news to the three of them at the same time that we'll be able to bring Grammie over for Christmas.

"Let me text my brother down there once more," Mom

mumbles this as she picks up her cellphone from the table. "But if it doesn't get through again, you have to give up."

Giving up isn't in my vocabulary, but we've been trying for an hour and it's almost getting to the time when I agreed to visit Rachel and her son, Adrian. I'll just try a quick chat with Grammie later tonight if the connection finally works.

Grunting, I pull myself up from the couch and head back to the kitchen. Mom looks up from writing a text and I give her a kiss on her cheek. Dad immediately points at his, and I have no choice but to drop him one too. "Thank you for trying, you guys."

"Is that all you're thankful for?" Dad teases.

"No, I'm also thankful for Nutella."

Mom shakes her head at me, her expression awed that she birthed such a little pest. "And here I thought you'd be thankful for having the best parents in the world, but no. Not only I have to be jealous that you love my mother more than me, but also Nutella?"

Her eyes twinkle with barely contained laughter and I keep a solemn expression as I say, "I'm sorry but the heart wants what the heart wants."

I don't really have to tell my parents that I love them, it's clear in a million ways. Like how I don't make fun of Dad's baseball team that keeps losing every season, or how I don't complain about Mom's rice even though it's always soggy. I'm busting my ass to fly Grammie over not just because I want to see her so bad, but also because I know Mom does too. She hasn't hugged her own mother in almost ten years. And if I make that earnest wish come true for Mom, Dad will be over the moon too.

That happiness is what I yearned to see on their faces tonight, but I've been foiled by distance again.

"I bet you like your friend better than you like us." Mom waves her hand. "Go to her. Go."

"I bet she likes her job better than us," Dad adds before taking a swig of his beer.

"Sure." I drawl the word as I leave the kitchen and start putting on my scarf and coat. "I'll be back in two hours, tops. Behave while I'm gone."

"As if. We're gonna thrash this place while you're gone." Dad chuckles.

Mom pops out of the kitchen for a second. "Drive safe! And also bring some of that pie Rachel bakes every year."

"'Kay, bye." I grab my keys and am out of the house before they can give me any more crap.

The whole street is lined by small one- and two-bedroom houses like ours, packed with working families that can't afford nicer digs, but still keeps theirs in tip top shape. Even though it's only Thanksgiving, we already have the nativity scene set up and glowing in the yard, surrounded by more lights than necessary. The whole block is populated by the same type of overly festive people, houses decked with tinsel, garlands, bows, snowmen, blown up gingerbread cookies, and more lights than an airport tarmac.

I turn on our trusty Ford pickup and the radio blares a Christmas classic from Nat "King" Cole. I raise the volume and sing off tune the whole way to Rachel's. She also lives on this side of town with the rest of us poors, so it takes all but ten minutes to arrive—and that's because I caught a long red light.

Rachel opens her front door before I'm even out of the car and shouts, "How did it go?"

"It didn't." I slam the door shut and stomp over to her, exhaling clouds of condensation out of my mouth. "Connection was bad so I'll have to save the news for next time."

"Boooo." She offers me a glass of wine the second I step into her house.

It's adorable just like her. Whereas outside is a dry winter landscape without snow yet, inside she has a cozy fire roaring, casting a warm light over boho chic decor she's been steadily collecting from garage sales for years.

Her son's sitting on the couch, and even though he doesn't pause from playing a football video game on the TV, he does say over his shoulder, "Happy Thanksgiving, Tía Sierra."

"Happy Thanksgiving, you football nerd." I rub his hair, which he normally hates. He's so engrossed in the game that he doesn't even notice, though. "What will it take for you to like a better sport?"

He grunts.

"Please, he doesn't even like proper football—the one played with the feet that we incorrectly call soccer here. Forget about your boring baseball," his mother says with a groan from the heart. After all, she once was on track for the US women's soccer team.

"Excuse me." I put a hand on my heart delicately, as if this wasn't the one topic that divides the three of us. "Baseball is *historic*. There's nothing boring about that."

She fakes a yawn.

I smirk against the rim of the wine glass and take a sip.

"Anyway." Rachel motions me to follow her to the kitchen and we take a seat by the counter. "I also have some news for you that I was waiting to tell you today."

I set down the glass slowly. "Am I finally going to meet your super famous professional soccer player brothers, who keep saying they'll drop by for the holidays and never do?"

"You know, you could just use their given names, they're a lot shorter than that spiel." She shakes her head and the straight hair of her bob bounces all pretty. "No, this isn't about Reid, Reese or River. This is about work."

"Oh, that's way less exciting."

"I'm doing it." She claps her hands at her chest. "I'm following my mentor's advice and applying for that position."

My joking mood evaporates and my eyes pop wider. "The talent campaign manager position?"

"Yes." She smiles and tucks her fists under her chin like they're necessary to prop up her grin.

I release a sound only bats can hear and throw my arms around her. "Oh my gosh! It's finally happening!"

"I know!"

"Mom? Where are the earplugs?" Adrian asks casually.

"Oh shush, child." Rachel chuckles and pulls away from me. "Ugh, I started working on my application but I'm second guessing everything."

"I'll look it over for you. And surely your mentor will, too?" I ask because I don't know for sure. Even though Rachel's been in the mentoring program for almost a year, her mentor, Camila Puig, is still a mystery to me. She's super intimidating and unapproachable at the office, but Rachel speaks about her so warmly that it almost makes me think they're different people.

"She will, but I'll feel so much better if you check it before I send it to her. You know…" She wrinkles her nose a bit. "I really don't want to send her a garbage application that will make her feel like she's wasted an entire year on me."

"Stop, I'm sure everything you've included in it is already awesome." I run my finger down the curved wall of the wine glass. "But I'm going to miss you so much."

"I'm not going anywhere." She bumps her shoulder with mine. "Well, I am. But it's just one department over."

"Who's going to give me moral support when Conor is being Conor, though?"

She cocks an eyebrow. "Maybe this is for the best. It's about time you let go of your grudge against him."

"It's not a grudge. You see, a grudge is all the negative feelings you carry some time after the wrong is done unto you, whereas he continually does new wrongs to me."

"Yeah, that's a grudge," Adrian chirps from the living room.

"Keep playing your game, child," I answer back with a scowl in his direction.

"If by wrongs you mean he took the last cup of coffee from the pot right before you walked in the kitchen, then I stand by my statement."

"Can we not talk about him? I'm already dreading Monday as it is."

I managed to avoid being in his physical vicinity yesterday and, of course, the long holiday weekend buys me a reprieve. But on Monday we're supposed to put together our ideas and I know for a fact that it's gonna be a whole mess. There's no way I'll put my best ideas on the table for him and I'm sure he'll take the same measure. So, we'll end up having to come up with something semi passable so we can get the green light from Richard, even though we'll be working on our own thing in the hopes to show up one another.

Who could possibly be excited by that prospect? I'm tired. I just want some holiday vacations with my family.

"Just try not to murder each other until I get my new job." She pauses. "Or after."

I grin. "I'm proud of you. No one has worked harder in *SPORTY* than you and you deserve to manage campaigns with hot, semi naked athletes."

"That's it." The noise from the TV draws to a halt and Adrian stands up with a huff. "I'm looking for those earplugs now. Hold the gross talk until then, please." We watch him pass us by on his way to the back of the house.

"How cute, he's still an innocent baby," I muse.

"Yes, I cherish every second I don't need to have the bees and the flowers talk with him." She props her chin with her hand. "You, on the other hand…"

"Me?" I blink fast. "Why is that relevant to me?"

"You're going to be working very closely with your extremely attractive nemesis whose shoulders make you salivate on your desk."

I drop my jaw. "That only happened once."

"That it happened at all means you're in trouble."

"It was before he made me look like a fool in front of Richard when I was on the tennis shoes campaign." I had made a glaring mistake in my presentation and not only I didn't notice, Richard didn't either. Instead of taking me aside to tell me, Conor pointed it out in the most gloating way. Richard fawned over him like Conor was the direct descendant of Einstein. The humiliation still burns.

"I'm just saying. If things get all hot and bothered between you both, I give you full permission to let go of your grudge and jump him."

I narrow my eyes on her empty wine glass. "Just how much wine did you have before I arrived, señorita?"

"Actually…" She looks up as if in thought. "Don't let it go. Just angry kiss him. Angry do more than kissing him. For both of us, please."

I snort. "Are you the one who's hot and bothered for Conor?"

"What? No. He's younger than me." She reaches over for the wine bottle to pour herself a glass.

"So?"

"I'm also more into the bad boy types."

This is when Adrian chooses to return but it looks like he's outfitted with earplugs. We don't get any further ew's tossed our way and the video game resumes.

I pat Rachel's hand. "Bad boys aren't good for you."

"Grudges aren't good for you, either." She takes a careful sip of wine, watching me from above the rim of her glass.

"Fine." I blow a raspberry. "I will consider being civil. Happy?"

"I don't believe you but I'll support you either way."

"Likewise, you clown." I throw my arm around her and squeeze her tight. "You just watch, you'll get that awesome position and I'll get the promotion."

"That's right, bebé." She clinks her glass with mine. "Cheers to the women making power moves regardless of the men in and out of their lives."

"Cheers!"

CHAPTER 5
CONOR

'm the biggest fool in this entire planet. I should've checked where the famous new dentist was located in advance. If I had known that it'd be a whopping forty minutes away, I'd have asked Gramps to shift the appointment to literally any other lunch break of the week.

But naw. Not only do we make it twenty minutes later than the scheduled time because I underestimated the drive, but also they've been seeing Gramps for over an hour. Basically, I'll get back to the office in the middle of the afternoon and Sierra is going to murder me in cold blood. I won't do anything to defend myself because I told her, and I quote, that I'd be back at one-thirty at most—un freaking quote.

That's not even the worst part. Since I thought this would be a quick thing, I didn't even bring my work laptop.

I sit in a much-too-small chair at the waiting area, my eyes trained on a TV screen showing a never ending reel of news. The arm rests are way too low, which means I'm hunched forward like a giant making itself small. If I stretch out my legs, I can reach the front desk where two receptionists keep sneaking glances my way. One of them leans closer to her colleague and uses her hand as a shield to whisper something.

They're on my right, so I can catch the whole thing from the corner of my eye without issue. The thing is that I can't for the life of me determine what their deal is. Did I put my clothes on backwards? Do they have holes? Stains? I run my tongue across my teeth, not feeling any food stuck between them. I comb my hair with a hand, making sure it's presentable. It's a bit too long at the top but I'm pretty sure I styled it this morning so… what gives?

The office phone rings and as one of them picks up, the other busies herself typing on the computer. I observe them openly for a second but I don't recall ever meeting any of them in the past. I wasn't the most prolific dater in college, and only had one girlfriend during the short length of my pro career.

My pants start buzzing and somehow that attracts both of their attention again. Great.

I pull out my phone from my pocket and my breath hitches. Sierra's name appears on the screen and I wonder whether it's possible to be physically killed through a phone call.

After clearing my throat, I open the conversation by saying a simple, "Hi."

"Where the hell are you?"

This is gonna get ugly fast. I pick myself up from the tiny chair and zip up my coat. I better take this call outside where I can get screamed at without an audience.

"Sorry, I—"

"You're more than an hour late, Conor. It better be for a good reason like you're dying in a ditch or something."

"How the hell would that be a good reason?" Outside, I pace back and forth across the entrance of the dentist office. "But no, if you must know, I'm very much alive and well."

"Isn't that a bummer." The heavy sarcasm actually makes me smile.

"I'm sorry—not that I'm alive. That I'm running super late, I mean." I push my glasses up the bridge of my nose and sigh. "I had to bring Gramps to the dentist and it's two towns over for reasons I won't bore you with, and I had no idea it'd take so long."

There's a very long pause where I even have to double check if the call has disconnected.

"You have a grandfather?" she asks with a weird thing in her voice. Like a sudden lightening that makes her sound like she's talking with literally anyone but me.

"I—yes?" I scratch my head. "Anyway, I don't have to teach lessons on Mondays so we can work until late."

That snaps her back to her usual lane. "Why should I have to work late to make up for you being late?"

"You're right." I cringe, if I could high stick myself I would. "I'm sorry. This is a hundred percent on me. I'll throw myself under the bus in front of Richard if I have to."

"I appreciate the sentiment," she says in what feels like a measured manner. "However, even if we tell him that we don't have a concrete plan because you bailed, it will reflect badly on me too."

I get it. This is like being forced to do a group assignment for a college professor, and shit's like half of your whole grade but no one else in your group shows up to the study session.

"Okay, give me one second." I prop the door open and the two receptionists zero in on me again. "Excuse me, do you know how much longer this may take?"

One of them stands up with a smile. "I'll go check for you."

"Thank you." I lift my phone back to my ear and say, "I have a proposal for you."

"I'm listening. After all, I literally booked my whole afternoon to listen to you."

"Thank you," I say as if she wasn't being a thorn on the side. "Anyway, I'm checking how much longer it's going to be and unless he's done right away, maybe we can start our meeting over the phone like this."

"That sounds reasonable." If anything, she sounds grumpier. Like maybe she was hoping to somehow rid herself of dealing with me while also not letting Richard down. If life has taught me anything, it's that we can't have our cake and eat it too.

The other receptionist returns. "The doctor says it should be about a half hour more."

I close my eyes and take a deep breath. I should've asked earlier. I might not have wasted the better part of the afternoon sitting at a cramped chair doing nothing.

"Thanks," I mutter the word before heading back out. "Sierra, you still there?"

"Ah, yeah."

"Okay, so…" I trail off, waiting to see if she wants to start.

The only sound coming from the other end is the shuffling of paper sheets. I check out my surroundings, looking for some inspiration from a quiet strip mall parking lot or even from the grey sky clouded over with tufts of white. The truth is that I came up with a lot of garbage ideas over the weekend and I was hoping that the pressure of one-upping Sierra in a verbal spar would inspire something better.

Sighing, I fess up, "I actually didn't come up with anything solid."

"Me neither," she quips right away.

Well, we're clearly off to a great start here. Someone's gotta really try, though.

I stuff my free hand in my coat pocket. "So… We said like Christmas Olympics, right? What if we do like a Secret Santa type of thing, except it's not for a gift exchange but to select teams people will be competing with for the event? We can give them two weeks to train and if we make it so each team has people from different departments, it's like an extended team building thing."

"And what would they be competing on?"

"A massive trophy full of eggnog? I don't know, help me out here."

Sierra sighs so loudly, I almost feel her breath against my ear. And for some reason I shiver.

"Actually, I think it'll be way easier for us if we keep it all a surprise. But also that way, if something doesn't work out then no one has to ever find out." She gives out an awkward laugh and it occurs to me for the first time that ultra confident, owns every room, can kick your ass and will, Sierra Fernandez, is capable of being nervous.

"What's your idea, then?" I ask, legitimately curious.

"Well…" There's hesitation in her voice that I can't understand. She has a prime opportunity to make me feel inferior, which has basically been her goal in life since I joined the marketing team. "The whole thing has to be Christmas centered more than sport centered. So what if we take some elements from certain sports, but make them Christmas?"

"I'm intrigued but I can't envision it," I admit.

"I don't know, swimming in a ball pit to find your Christmas present and silly things like that." Sierra huffs. "Do I have to do all the heavy lifting here, Conor?"

I surprise us both with a sudden laugh. "Okay, that actually sounds really fun."

"The *actually* was kind of unnecessary, I'm a genius."

"What else, Miss Genius?"

"I don't know. You come up with the next activity."

"Er… bobbing for apples but instead of water it's eggnog?"

"First of all, ew. Second, that's not an official sport. What's your deal with eggnog?"

"I really like eggnog, what can I say." I shrug even though she's not seeing me.

But then the door opens behind me and another female voice sounds. "Excuse me, Mr. Mahoney, but your grandfather is ready."

"Oh, thanks." I tell Sierra, "Hey, Gramps is waiting for me now. I'll give it a thought on the drive back and give you some ideas at the office, okay?"

"Fine." After a moment, she adds, "Drive safe."

"You too." I choke on my own saliva and shake my head hard. "I mean, sorry. Thanks?"

"Um, okay. Bye." She sounds confused before hanging up.

I press the corner of my phone against my forehead. What the shit was that? A small shred of civility tied my tongue in knots and that shouldn't have happened. Like at all.

My face probably glows like a red Christmas light as I walk back into the reception, and Gramps pauses whatever he was saying to motion at me.

"There he is, ladies, my former pro hockey player grandson —runner up to the Calder Memorial Trophy on his rookie season. Lost it to his best friend from college, funny enough."

"Gramps," I hiss as if that would get him to stop.

"I knew it." One of the women snaps her fingers. "I recognized him from somewhere. Thought he might've been someone I dated in college."

"You have good taste." Gramps smirks. "And he's single, too."

"'Kay, that's the cue for me to wait in the car." I swivel around and head back out. I must be the epitome of pathetic if I need my grandfather to find me dates.

I unlock the door and climb on the passenger's seat of the Dodge Ram, purchased with my very first pro hockey paycheck as a gift for Gramps. I happen to be the one with the best vision in the family, so I'm the only one who drives it now. I turn it on and ramp up the heating because I have no desire to make myself even more uncomfortable than I already am.

A few minutes later, Gramps joins me by climbing onto the passenger's seat with a hefty grunt. "That was rude, kid. There I was talking you up and you ran like a coward. Now I'll never be able to show my face in this place again."

I groan. "Gramps, you're killing me."

"What is it? Are you planning to never date again after what happened with Nikki?"

Hearing the name of my ex wasn't in my bingo card for today.

"Let's go, I'm late for work." I put on my seatbelt, which prompts him to do the same.

Unfortunately, that distraction isn't enough to make him change the conversation. "They were both nice, single, *employed* young women. Besides, they're both hockey fans, to the point that they recognized you."

"They probably saw the accident video on replay a million times, just like everyone else," I mutter. That was one of the worst things about the whole shitshow. Every time I tuned into a sports channel, the clip was there. And every time I watched it, I could feel the blow that ended my career all over again.

"Although one of them said she likes you better when you're shaved," he parrots, ignoring me altogether. "And honestly, you deserve someone who likes you for your facial hair as well."

I blow a raspberry. "Can we please drop this topic?"

"But it's fun."

"Not for me." I prop my elbow on the door handle. "Gramps, whenever I'm ready to date, it'll be someone I choose. Not you."

"I have better taste, though. I did warn you there was something off about that ex of yours."

I squeeze the steering wheel a bit tighter. This is the biggest reason why I haven't dated anyone seriously since that whole mess. Nikki was a walking red flag from the beginning. A super hot blonde bombshell singling me out from a professional team with at least a handful other single guys—even though this is *me* we're talking about—should've given me pause from the beginning.

The more goals I scored the more she acted like the most doting G of the WAGs, but if I played badly she pulled away. It was no wonder she broke up with my ass the second I retired. It wasn't me she was after. It was for the fame or status, I don't know.

And yeah, she also didn't have a job like Gramps reminded me a second ago. Maybe she was just looking for a ticket to a leisurely luxe life, and once it was clear I wouldn't be able to provide that anymore, she bailed.

"Gramps, sorry to cut this riveting conversation short, but I actually have to do some brainstorming for work while we drive. Let's talk about women later, preferably while I'm unconscious."

He snorts but drops it. For now.

CHAPTER 6
SIERRA

One of the many reasons why I don't vibe with Conor Mahoney is that his desk is right across from mine. No one can understand how annoying it is to constantly have to see the face of your nemesis, especially when said nemesis is one of the most attractive guys you've ever seen in person.

Right now, he's giving one more pass to our presentation for Richard, due in like twenty minutes. The glare of the monitor light reflects off his glasses, so I can't see his eyes. But he's spent like five minutes tapping the clicker of his pen against his bottom lip without saying anything. Either he's engrossed or bored and I need him to be neither so he can stop drawing my attention to his lips.

They're surprisingly full. The upper one's slightly thinner with a shapely bow, which is infuriating because my own lips aren't that pretty.

Ya va, I tell myself. Where in the heck did that come from? Since when do I wax poetic about Conor freaking Mahoney's lips?

I duck my head and fix my eyes on a *SPORTY* magazine in my hands. This has been going on all morning. Earlier, I fixated on his eyebrows. I wish I could say they're ugly and make him look like a creepy clown but… no. They're strong, dark, and with a slant that make him look intense when he's serious even though he rarely is.

This all started yesterday when he returned from taking his grandpa to the dentist. Like, just learning that he has a non evil side softened me. I really wish I could keep the bonus money and get the promotion without working with him, because I'm starting to suspect that Rachel is right. My grudge might be in a bit of danger here.

"I thought you weren't going to work until late last night."

It takes me a moment for his words to register. "What do you mean?"

"Clearly, you put a shit ton of work into this presentation." He lifts his attention from the screen and cocks an eyebrow. "Almost as if you wanted to look *real* good in front of our boss."

Oops. I got caught.

I deflect by saying, "I'm just taking this very seriously."

"Sure…" He elongates the word to an obnoxious degree. "But anyway, Richard's gonna love it. You did great."

"Are you being sarcastic?" I frown.

"What? No. I mean it." Conor cocks his head as if confused.

"Oh." I squirm and readjust the skirt of my cable knit sweater dress. For the first time, I want to offer an olive branch. "Any, uh—any suggestions for improvement?"

He hums. "I could offer a few but there's barely any time left for changes. Let's just roll with it."

I gnash my teeth, immediately regretting the olive branch. He has *a few*? But won't even bother? I bet he's going to yeet them at Richard right in my face to make me look like an incompetent fool.

"Fine." I snap the word so hard that even Rachel, sitting in a Zoom call next to me, turns to give me a look like something's wrong with me. "I—I have to go make a call. See you in Richard's office."

"Okay…"

I jump to my feet and when I'm five paces away, I remember that I didn't grab my phone. I look everywhere but at Conor or Rachel as I return to grab it. But I don't have to call jack squat. I lock myself up in the women's bathroom to wash my face, hoping the cold water helps me get over myself.

*

Twenty minutes later, I feel slightly less like a shitty human being while I sit with Conor in Richard's office. We're on the same side of the conference table at the front of the office, sitting in perfect silence as we wait for our boss to return from a bio break.

My laptop is hooked up to the screen on the wall, showing the first slide of the presentation and of course I'm doubting everything. I thought I was being clever and cheeky when I put one snowman holding a glass of eggnog on one side, another snowman on the other with a baseball, and some mistletoe above them. Now, looking at it while seconds away from starting the meeting, I feel like a little kid who drew her fever dream with Crayons.

I wish someone would tell me that my ideas aren't childish —and for a second I contemplate asking Conor for more validation. Except that he'd immediately whiff my insecurities.

Best I keep pretending I'm the second Camila Puig, the company's top female manager who has been dubbed as the Ice Queen.

Rustling catches my attention and I turn to Conor. He's rolling up the sleeves of his grey flannel shirt and I get a heart attack.

His arms are a weapon of mass destruction that needs to be regulated. It should be obvious by the healthy beard but I'm surprised to see his arm hair from up close. Muscles bunch as he turns his arm one way or the other to fix up his shirt. But the worst part is the veins running under his skin toward his big hands. I am weak.

Of course, that's when Richard waltzes in.

"All right, what do we have here?" He pulls up the chair right across from me and turns to the screen.

I freeze, my brain turned into complete mush incapable of thought, only of existing.

"Sierra?" Conor whispers beside me.

Slowly, I turn to him. Where I expect gloating in his expression if he caught me salivating over his arms, what's actually reflected in it is concern. Like maybe he thinks I'm panicking over the presentation.

That snaps me out of the haze. I'm nothing if not professional. And I'm not going to show *any* weakness in front of my rival.

My pulse spikes. I tuck my hands under the table so neither of them can see them shake. I hate this. I hate that I feel this visceral need to be the best, to prove I know more than anyone else, which makes the possibility of that not being the case feel so much more terrifying than it makes sense. It's why I snapped at Conor. It's the real reason I can't stand him. For some reason, his presence alone has the power to make me feel inadequate. And if Richard says something to critique my presentation and Conor joins him… I'm a raw nerve right now—it wouldn't be pretty.

"Are the snowmen drunk and about to make out?" our boss asks.

Conor seems to find this funny by the way his mouth twitches, but stays suspiciously quiet.

"Yes," I respond with fake bravado.

"Sounds like a good party. Go on."

Conor's grin stretches wider. Is he genuinely amused or making fun of me?

"Right." I click on the next slide. "So the brief is called *SPORTY* Christmas. We decided to hold a series of competitive events fueled by spiked eggnog and assorted alcoholic beverages, each one celebrating an organized sport but with a Christmas twist."

I launch onto the basic idea, a circuit of different activities where people can get progressively jollier while also burning the previous station's alcohol by playing something. We couldn't come up with a lot of activities in the course of a day, but the gist is there. We even managed to comb together a semblance of a budget.

I finish the presentation and sit back, waiting for them to rip everything to shreds and laugh in my face.

Instead, what happens is worse. Richard says, "While I really like the direction, I'm still disappointed."

I feel Conor stiffen next to me as well.

"I gave you four days, so I expected a crystal clear plan. This still feels very brainstormy."

"Four days?" Conor shakes his head to snap himself out of the shock. "You gave us two. Last Wednesday and yesterday."

"But you're two people, so realistically I gave you four days." Richard gyrates on the chair and leans his elbows on the table. "I'm going to be straight. I had high expectations of this event and raised them even more when I decided to put you both on it together. That's how boss math works, FYI. If you let me down, I'll remove the promotion from the table and will reduce your ten-thousand bonus accordingly. Is that clear?"

"Yes, sir," we both answer at the same time like the well trained former pro- and college-athletes we are.

"Now, like I said, I do like the idea a lot. But when you give me next week's update, I expect an impressive amount of progress."

"Right."

"You got it."

Conor and I scramble to stand up before we're even dismissed. I hug my laptop against my chest as we walk out.

We take a few hasty steps away from Richard's office until Conor suddenly grabs my elbow and pulls me into a storage room. The door clicks shut behind us and for a moment, there's only dark. After some kind of scratchy noise, the light turns on and Conor turns to face me with wide eyes.

"I can't lose a single cent of that bonus," he says.

I nod super fast. "Me neither."

"I think we need to pull all-nighters and weekends to make this thing a smashing success."

"I agree." I swallow hard.

"We have to take this as if it were the playoffs of our career."

"I—sure. That's one way to look at it."

"So… truce?"

I glance down at his outstretched hand.

I must be taking so long to react that he drops it and expels a heavy sigh. "Sierra, I'm with you on this thing. Why are you acting like I'm your enemy?"

"Aren't you?" I lift my eyes to his. "Are you really telling me you're not just waiting for the right moment to stab me in the back and get the promotion and the glory?"

"What?"

"It's what you do, Conor. You always point out everything I do wrong and throw it in my face right when it's going to be the most embarrassing for me. I'm surprised you didn't share all your *suggestions* for my presentation in front of Richard just now."

He scrunches up his entire face. "When the hell have I ever done that?"

"The tennis shoes presentation?" I start, hugging my warm laptop tighter. "How about the TV commercial pitch? Or the radio jingle."

"You critiqued my ideas in return."

Heat creeps up my neck because that's true. "Maybe but there's a big difference between us, Richard always sides with you. He worships the ground you walk on and if you truly don't know it, you're a fool. Having to work so hard at competing against a fool would piss me off even more."

"Oh, so that's it. You'd rather keep up this nonsensical cutthroat competition with me and screw us both over just to prove your—by the way, completely wrong—theory that I have it out against you?"

"It's not wrong—"

"Yeah, it is." His brow darkens. "You're conveniently forgetting that I critique the others just as much as I critique you, and they do the same in return."

"You're so much nicer to them, though!"

"Yeah, because you intimidate the shit out of me!" He, a 6 foot 2 wall of muscle who used to be a professional hockey player, releases this collection of words from his pretty mouth that make no sense. "You glare at me like I hurt your puppy. I breathe and you snap. You sit as far from me as you can as if my smell were nauseating, or something. How the hell am I supposed to treat you the same way as I do everybody else? What if it makes it worse? What if being nicer to you just makes me seem weaker enough so you can go for the jugular?"

It's as if a donkey had kicked my chest. Suddenly I can't breathe and it's hard to stand up straight, yet all I can do is stand there gaping at him.

Conor throws his hands in the air. "Fine, keep hating me. I'll plan this damn party on my own if I must."

He yanks the door open and leaves me standing in the storage room as still as the shelves. They keep me company as I examine my own actions and find myself very firmly in Santa's list of people who only deserve coal.

CHAPTER 7
CONOR

have no plan for how I'm going to tackle the work day or even the Christmas thing with Sierra, which is shitty after spending the better part of last night agonizing about it. I stretch over to grab my backpack from the passenger seat and catch a glimpse of my face in the rearview mirror.

"Whoa." I do a double take.

Is that a zombie or is it me?

Dark circles frame my eyes and speaking of them, they're red. Apparently, I also forgot to comb my hair this morning. At least that I can fix relatively easily with my hands. It's straight but springy and since I didn't put on any product, it's going to spend all day with weird cowlicks all over.

Whatever. It's not like I'm part of *SPORTY*'s calendar of hot athletes.

Sighing, I drag myself and my backpack out of my pickup. It feels drastically colder today, like maybe it could snow soon. Closing my eyes, I inhale deep and feel a faint note of ice. Or I could be hallucinating because I'm running on little sleep and lotta coffee.

I hoist my backpack and weave through the parking lot

toward the entrance of the building. With one hand, I fish through my pockets until I locate my ID in my joggers' left pocket. The stream of employees narrows at the entrance where everyone has to badge. I recognize one of the sales guys and tip my head in acknowledgement.

"Dude, you look like you either had a great night or a really bad one."

I offer a Mona Lisa smile. He can think whatever he wants. I don't have to broadcast to the whole company just how truly uncool I am.

"How's Linda?" I ask about his wife, to direct his attention away from me.

"So pregnant, dude." He shakes his head in something like awe. "Due around Christmas."

"That's awesome, man. It's going to be—"

"Conor?"

A different voice sounds behind me and I snap my mouth shut. Slowly, as if this was a horror movie and not a random Wednesday morning, I turn to face the scariest person in the entire building. Except Sierra's in a brown coat and a beige beanie that matches those chunky boots women love in the winter. Not really axe murderer material.

More importantly, her expression looks normal. And by normal, I mean everyone else would think she's glad to see me.

That's weird.

She tips her head like she's asking me to head over to her. It's not some creepy dark corner but the opposite end of the reception desk, and I'm pretty sure there are plenty of security cameras around the lobby. Besides, her hands are busy with two hot drinks and not with sharp knives. Should be safe, I guess.

"Uh… I gotta go, but send my regards to Linda, yeah?" I tell the sales guy.

"Not unless you want her to set you up with her cousin. She still talks about you, you know?"

I give an awkward laugh and wave my hand at him. Sierra's eyes study me as I approach and my self-consciousness skyrockets. I should've made an effort this morning. Maybe I should've worn something sharper than one of my old St. Cloud U sweatshirts. Or the same joggers I wore yesterday. When's the last time I trimmed by beard? And is that a finger smudge across my glasses?

After standing at a safe distance from her, I say a very awkward, "Hi."

Instead of responding, she offers one of the cardboard cups to me. I blink at it.

"It's hot chocolate. I know you have a sweet tooth," she says.

"Um…" My eyebrows twist in confusion as I accept it. "Is it poisoned?"

Her expression flashes to annoyance. "You know, I considered it, but then if I go to jail there won't be anyone to take care of my parents."

"All good points." I wrap both hands around the warm cup and bring it against my chest. "However, I'm still confused as to why you're giving me this."

"It's a token of my apology." After a quiet beat, she adds, "I'm sorry."

My eyes pop wide open.

She shifts her weight to another leg. "Say something."

"Hold on, I'm processing."

Sierra releases a big sigh and drops her head a little, only to take a sip of her own drink. "I know this probably makes no difference but… what you said yesterday made me think a lot. And you're right, I've been horrible to you."

"No, I—That's not what I meant. It's just—" I stop when she raises a gloved hand.

"It's true. I don't know if it's the first generation American or the only daughter thing, or the fact that I was a former gifted child who isn't being bullied anymore but still constantly struggles with an adult world that doesn't just work out every single time I make the smallest effort." Sierra fills her lungs with a big breath and adds, "You've been the main reason I've had to grow up."

"Huh?"

"I had it relatively easy at work until you showed up. Like, Rachel and I are a unit. We work together like a well-oiled machine and produce results just like it. And the others are good, but they're not as good as us. Then you came in and you became my… competition. And I didn't like it." She shrinks. "See? I'm horrible."

My head's spinning. I run my hand through my hair just to make sure my head's still in its place. "I… don't know how I feel about getting a compliment that comes along with insulting yourself."

"I'm not saying I'll start being your bestie now, so don't get too excited."

"Ah, now we're talking." I smile a little as I raise the hot chocolate. The scent envelops me in the comfort that was missing until this very moment. "So, truce?" I ask for the second time in less than twenty four hours.

"Truce." Sierra nods.

I shift my cup to my left hand so I can offer my right. "You have to shake on it. That's how it works."

"Fine, let's make it fully legal." Her brow scrunches as she bites the tip of her finger gloves and pulls it off. She grabs my hand without hesitation and gives it two solid pumps before releasing. "There, happy?"

That's not how I would describe it. The problem is that I can't. I take advantage of sipping the peace offering so I don't have to speak.

Her hand fits perfect in mine. It's so much smaller but strong nonetheless, like the physical manifestation of her personality. The big difference is that her skin is so soft it made mine tingle. As we walk over to the elevators, I open and close my hand, trying to rid it of the sensation.

We fall to the back of the elevator as three other people hop on and I don't feel any less nervous because we signed a peace treaty. The littlest wrong move could push us to war again.

Even then, there's one pressing concern. Clearing my throat, I ask, "So, what are we going to do about this thing?"

"Well, if you don't have any meetings this morning we can brainstorm."

"I'm clear. I'll book us a meeting room," I offer.

Sierra nods and it's silence after that. I decide not to push it and add nothing further until we reach our floor. We take a moment to set up at our desks and, while she chats with Kaylee, I find us an open meeting room one floor below ours.

A few minutes later, we're armed with hot chocolates and laptops, sitting across each other in the meeting room. Sierra alternates between looking at me and at her screen, but doesn't open the conversation like she normally would. She's a take-charge kind of person and this is uncharacteristic. Like maybe she also can't find her footing in this weird new dynamic.

"Um…" I push off the table and stand up. This room has a smart whiteboard and maybe that's a better way to go about it. "How about we just start by throwing some keywords about what we each think makes Christmas special?"

"Sure. Let's start by the basics." She glances down and says, "Hot chocolate."

I jot it down on the board, followed by eggnog.

"Mulled wine and gingerbread cookies," she says next.

"Peppermint anything," I say and add it to the list.

"Snowmen. Which, by the way, I've always wondered why they can't just be called snowpeople."

"Good point. It's not like you can see what's between their legs." After a pause, I add, "They don't even have legs."

Sierra snorts. I turn over my shoulder and I find an amused smirk on her face. I face the board again and bite my lip. Making her smile for the first time shouldn't feel momentous and yet, here we are.

"Reindeer," I say in a thick voice.

"Garlands."

"Elves that are never on shelves."

"Gifts."

"Trees."

"Lots of lights. I'm pretty sure the space station can see my whole street right now." Sierra laughs lightly.

"Are you big on Christmas?"

"Oh, yes. We do the religious Christmas and also all the silly stuff too. It's my favorite time of the year." She claps her hands. "Oh, music! Can't forget the classics."

I lift the corner of my mouth. "Like Mariah Carey?"

"*The* classic."

Once I've included music on the list, I say, "Ice skating. That's a very Christmas thing for most people. What else?"

We speak in unison. "Santa."

"Although to be clear, in my house the one who gives us the Christmas gifts is Baby Jesus."

"Really?" My eyebrows rise.

"Yep, that's the tradition back in my parents's home country. Apparently in Spain, it's the three wise men."

"Huh."

"I think this makes it pretty clear that we need to have food, drinks, decorations, and gifts in whatever we do."

"Right. The question is how to incorporate this into fun,

sporty events." I rub my jaw and realize my beard's wild enough that I probably look like Sasquatch. "And I think we need to really nail down the events before we even look for venues."

"Ugh. I almost forgot about that." Sierra puts her face in her hands. "This is ridiculous. Why do we have to start organizing this so late? Like, I'm sure all venues in town are already taken."

"It's supposed to be a challenge, I guess." I read through the list on the board again and start noting down basic event planning stuff. Venue, catering, decorations. It'd be great if we could work backwards and just book all the logistical stuff first, but what if we end up needing a bigger place? Or smaller?

"Well, I've been giving myself headaches from thinking so hard but other than gift ball pit, I haven't come up with anything else that sounds good. You?"

I cringe a little. "Would you kill me if I tell you I got nothing?" Especially when I've been thinking more about our rift than this project.

Sierra sighs and leans back on her chair. "Clearly we need inspiration."

"Should we go talk with a mall Santa?" I joke but she tilts her head like she's considering it.

"Hmm, not a terrible idea."

"You can't be serious." I snort.

"Well, no that." She sits up straight and types up on her computer. "My mom is a nail tech and one of her customers was talking about this Christmas fair she's organizing. Maybe we can try that."

"My brain's not braining so I'm down."

"Okay. Should we take a field day to the fair?"

With her? Just us? No coworkers nearby to keep us civil? Or to keep me sane?

"Let's do it," I agree, as if I wasn't triggering a whole existential crisis within myself. Because it makes no sense that I'm feeling something close to excitement when just an hour ago I dreaded being around her.

CHAPTER 8
SIERRA

Life's weird. That's the only way I can explain how I find myself in the passenger's seat of my work foe's pickup truck. Or former foe? I don't know. It's not like I can shake two years of feeling sour about the guy just like that, which is why I find this moment so strange.

The first thing that made me kind of record scratch when I hopped on, is that his truck smells good. Like aftershave and man. I have no right thinking that anything Conor Mahoney adjacent is good and yet, here I am, inhaling the stuff like it's giving me a high.

The next thing was the sheer size of him. Clearly, I kept him at bay enough that I knew he was a tall guy, but didn't have a real concept of his size until we sat in a vehicle cabin together. These trucks are made for giants like him because where I have plenty of room around me, Conor is just snug. His knees almost bump against the dashboard. Meanwhile, my seat is at level with his and there's still so much empty space between my legs and the front of the car.

But the one thing that snags my attention the most is how he drives. Namely, super slow, always under the speed limit.

Even grannies pass him. And he bodily turns to the left a lot as if he expecting a freight train form that side or something.

I wait until we're at a red light to call his name. "Conor."

"Hmm?" He turns to me. Today his hair is a messy halo that would make him look boyish if it wasn't for the lumberjack beard.

"Why do you keep turning to one side? Isn't that uncomfortable?"

He blinks slowly. "You don't know?"

"Know what?"

Turning back to face forward, he says, "I have very low vision in my left eye."

"What?"

"Don't worry, I passed all the driving exams thanks to my glasses."

"That's not what I mean." I scratch my head through my beanie. "I mean, weren't you a hockey player? Then how…"

"So you haven't seen the video either?" Conor rubs his beard in a way that almost makes him look uncomfortable. "I thought everyone who knew me knows what happened."

"Sorry, I've spent two years trying to not think about you. Stalking you online would've been the opposite."

"Makes sense." His lips stretch into a little smile for a second, but then the light changes and he sets us in very slow motion again. "The eye injury is what ended my career. Or technically, the brain thing."

"Brain thing?" I shrick.

He's nonplussed. "Severe concussion and an exudative retinal detachment. Super fun. Thirteen out of ten recommended."

My jaw drops. I bodily turn to face him, checking for signs of I don't know what. Except there's nothing in him that tells me he's gone through something so traumatic. The Conor Mahoney I've known these past two years likes to joke, gives me crap, is sharp in meetings, and clearly still works out. I knew he'd had some sort of injury that cut his career short, but no one talks about it and I assumed it had been a bad torn ligament or some knee issues—the more common stuff that forces athletes to retire.

"But like… are you okay now?"

Conor turns to glance at me, openly surprised that I even ask. "Well… I guess so. I just can't get another blow to my head because it could be catastrophic, but no biggie."

"No biggie? What if you're walking down the street and something hits you in the head by accident?"

"That would really suck."

"I'm being serious."

"Me too. No one would like that." His laughter dies off when he catches sight of my glare. He checks his left side again before merging to the left-turning lane. Sighing, he says, "It really sucked back then. The recovery, the delusional hope that I could play again, the depression that followed right after… Let's just say I'm okay *now* and leave it at that, okay?"

"Okay," I mutter and shift in my seat, trying to get comfortable in my own skin. There's a block of ice lodged in my throat that I can't explain.

"Oh, I think this is the place." Conor slows the truck down even more as he points to the right. There isn't a trace in his voice that he's remotely as upset by the conversation as I am to have brought it up.

The modest convention center in downtown Mapleton is decked in Christmas paraphernalia until it almost looks like a blown up gingerbread house. There's enough tinsel hanging from its roof to wrap around the Ecuador line, and I'm pretty sure the lights are spending half of town's electricity. A massive sleigh with a Santa and reindeers hangs from the slant of the roof. Firs on sale flank the entrance and take a good portion of the parking lot.

We end up parking a block away and walking in what I feel like an awkward silence. In comparison, Conor appears relaxed with his hands in the pockets of his bomber jacket.

"Um, give me a moment. I need to use the restroom," I say the second we walk into the venue and before he can respond, I mix with the throngs of people in the direction of the restrooms.

Inside, there's a little old lady who looks a lot like Grammie just washing her hands. She doesn't seem to mind that I pace back and forth, instead of actually using the facilities.

What would my grammie say if I told her all of this? That I'm today years old when I find out the guy I've been hating on at work is actually… a person? Someone who's been through some shit?

I fish my phone out of my pocket and find Youtube, where I type a hasty question. *What happened to Conor Mahoney?* I hit play on the first video that shows up.

The old lady looks up at my gasp.

The video didn't even give me a chance to brace myself with some short introduction or something. Literally one second, Conor is in his uniform skating furiously in the middle of a game, the next second someone else's stick slams against his legs and sends him sliding at full speed against the board, where he slams his head at an awkward angle. Then he doesn't move. Like at all.

People rush to the ice to check on him and I speed forward, waiting for the moment he gets up or even moves. But the video ends with him being taken away on a stretcher, and one of his gloves falls on the ice and stays there.

. My lungs work in overtime as I click on another video but it just shows the blow from a vantage that makes it look worse, almost as if he'd sustained a neck injury even though he didn't mention one while on the car a few minutes ago.

I change to a different video. This one must be from sometime after he underwent some procedure. There's a patch on his left eye, at odds with the sharp suit and tie he's wearing. His hair is shorter here than on the man waiting outside for me, and he's fully shaved too. His right eye is devoid of life as he stares into the camera and announces his retirement.

I finally understand what I started feeling in the car. Horror. At myself.

What does it say about me that it takes knowing *this* to see him as a person, and not the asshole I built up in my head because I was intimidated?

Because that was what made me snap out of it—when he said that *I* intimidated him.

"Shit, I'm such a terrible person."

"Are you, dear?" I whirl around. The old lady's drying her hands with paper towels. "You seem pretty normal to me."

"No, I'm so not normal." I shake my head hard and bite my trembling lower lip. "I've been really, really mean to this guy who maybe isn't so bad."

"Have you apologized?"

I pause. "Yeah, this morning."

"Then you're not so terrible after all. Truly bad people never admit their wrongs." And with that, she glides out of the restroom, leaving me to my existential crisis.

"Maybe I should apologize again," I tell my reflection in the mirror. She has glassy eyes and her chin trembles like she wants to start crying. I take a deep breath and immediately cough at the stench of a busy day's worth of bathroom yuck.

First, I need to step back out of here and face him. But then what? I already apologized for being an ass, what would be the point of doing it again? I have to just… stop being one. Treat him the same way I treat Stephen or any other coworker. That's literally the only way I have to atone.

I smack my cheeks to snap myself out of the funk, and finally walk out.

CHAPTER 9
CONOR

know. My stomach roars like a monster merely upon reading the text message. Problem is, I think we'll be at this fair a while. And not just because Sierra's taking a long time in the women's restroom.

My eye twitches.

ME

> What was that? My fave homemade dish as thank you for taking you to the dentist and pissing my coworker off because I was so late coming back to the office? Hmm?

GRAMPS THE GRUMP

> Would you look at that.

> New grandsons on sale on this here website I just found.

I can't help chuckling at the cheek on the old man. I'm typing back another smartass response when I feel two laser beams drilling into my head.

Lifting my eyes, I find Sierra studying me like she expects me to drop into a dead faint all of a sudden. I take a deep breath and expel it through my nose. This happens a lot after the injury, people treating me like I'm fragile.

And okay, I kind of am. But it doesn't feel great to have it rubbed on my face when that's precisely what I try so hard to forget everyday.

Now that I think about it, until this weird day, she was the only outlier.

I return my phone to my pocket and make my way over to her. "Ready to get seriously festive?"

"I'm always festive." She runs those dark eyes of hers all over my face, the seriousness in her expression not reflecting any of the cheer around us.

"Okay, stop."

Sierra reels back. "What?"

"Stop that thing you're doing. The pitying all over your face." I point at her face with my finger and run eights in the air. "That right there is what I hate the most in the entire world. And if you truly meant what you said this morning, feeling sorry for me isn't the way to make us get along."

She turns her frown away from me. "Fine, I'll try. Just watch where you're going. You're too tall for your own good and you might run smack into something and keel over in front of me."

"So that wouldn't make you happy?" I dare to nudge her with my elbow.

"No." She smacks my arm away. "It'd be too messy and with our history, I'd be suspected of murder."

"True. Aren't you regretting hating me now?" I can tell that was the wrong joke to say the second her entire body grows as stiff as a plank.

"Let's go." She walks almost robotically to the ticket booth.

I'm still trying to figure out why that comment sat so badly with her when she slams a ticket against my chest. Sierra doesn't wait until I grab it before pulling away, and I end up having to catch it midair.

"Can we find something to eat first?" I ask both to change the mood and also because, thanks to Gramps, my stomach is doing the twist and shout.

"Best idea you've had all day, Conor Mahoney."

We sweep our eyes across the place. The expanse of the convention center has been transformed into a maze of booths advertising everything from recycled wrapping paper, hand-carved elves, and glitter-covered garlands that in my opinion should be outlawed. There are so many people it's hard to see what's in the stalls beyond the entrance and no one thought of hanging high enough signs for my benefit.

But then I catch whiff of something wonderful. It's cinnamony and sugary, and I shift gears to head that way.

"What the—"

"Follow the scent, Fernandez." I point to the left. "That way."

I act as an icebreaker for her, though at some point we have to pass through a big crush that makes me slow down. Sierra runs into my back and I pause to glance over my shoulder. She's rubbing that button nose of hers that she typically has upturned in my direction.

Damn, she's cute.

I clear my throat. "You doing okay down there?"

"Not if you brake like that, no."

"Sorry. Grab onto my jacket, or something."

A second later, I feel the tug of her hand grabbing a fistful of my jacket. I resume the trek, pretending like my pulse didn't do a weird thing just now.

We make it to the goal and I spread my arms wide like I'm the one responsible for the existence of a food stand. "Voilà."

Sierra steps out from behind me and gasps so loud, a bunch of people nearby turn to us. She clasps her hands at her chest and screeches, "Churros?"

I double check. Honestly, I didn't really care what the food was but there's a sign hanging over the stand confirming what the goods are. And even better, it looks like they sell hot chocolate.

"No," I say gravely. "*Heaven.*"

I recognize the look she's giving me. It's the same one I used to get from opposing team players right before a faceoff. She stands no chance against me as we race towards the end of the line for the churros, which is probably why she tries to play dirty. *Tries* being the keyword there, because it doesn't matter how hard she pulls at my jacket, I'll still run even if the thing comes off.

My clothes are all askew when I get to the line before her. "Geez, woman. It's churros, not the promotion."

"You're right, you get the churros and I get the promotion. How about that?" Her lips stretch into a wide grin and something in me unwinds. This is a bit more like the Sierra I'm used to. No more pitying glances or awkwardness.

I shake my index finger. "Nuh-uh. I'm getting both *and* another cup of hot chocolate."

"Whatever." She gives me the cold shoulder in favor of studying the menu hanging from the top sign. I guess she doesn't know that I'm still looking at her, because she runs the tip of her tongue across her lips, already tasting the goodies.

I face forward and smack my hand against my own lips. They're tingling for no reason at all, whatsoever.

We walk away with cups of the thickest hot chocolate I've ever seen, and baggies of churros. Hers is a normal size but I got a triple because ya boy's hungry. I tuck my mutant churro bag inside the pocket of my hoodie and pluck one churro out as we walk. I bite into the hot, fried dough powdered with sugar and cinnamon and stop when I see Sierra dip her churro into the chocolate.

"What?" She asks as she chews. "This is how it's done."

"Oh." I also dip my churro and put it in my mouth.

A groan tears out of my throat once the explosion of flavor hits my tongue.

"Geez, Mahoney. This is a Christmas fair, not your bedroom."

I duck my heating face. "Sorry. I just wasn't expecting perfection on my tongue."

Sierra snorts. "Anyway, now that we have secured snacks, we should start actually working."

"Right." I take another churro from my hoodie pouch and check our surroundings out. "Let's just walk for a bit and see what catches our eye."

I let her lead the way, happy to take my time dipping churros into hot chocolate. I almost want to cry because I've been having both things wrong my whole life.

We pass by a booth with oversized tree ornaments and one with crystal reindeer in all sizes. Someone's selling Christmas trees made out of all materials, leather, velcro, even pieces of silverware. I grab the sleeve of Sierra's coat to make her stop and find my phone to take some blurry, one-handed pictures.

Up next is a booth selling candy, and this time she makes me wait so she can buy a baggy of peppermint candy canes. She seems to like those, judging by the way she smiles as she tucks them into her purse. Or maybe they're for a gift. And actually, Gramps likes these. I should get some as well.

"Can I have a bag as well, please?" I ask the seller.

"Of course, gorgeous," says the woman who could be my mother. "It'll be eight bucks for you."

"Hey! You charged me ten," Sierra grouches.

"Sorry, darling. He's my type. Tall, hairy, and with pretty eyes."

My face burns as I give her ten dollars and refuse the change. "Hairy?" I ask as we walk away. "Maybe I should shave it all off."

Sierra huffs. "But then you wouldn't get free stuff from single women."

"She wasn't single." At her look, I add, "She had a wedding ring on her finger."

"Oh, wow. You checked? Was she *your* type?" Sierra chuckles and I don't know why, but it annoys me.

"No, I have one eye that still works better than average. And she totally wasn't my type."

"Sure."

I scrunch up my face. "C'mon, my type is people my age."

"Hmm." Sweeping her attention around, Sierra suddenly points behind me. "Someone like her?"

I don't know why I turn. There's a blonde woman just outside a stand, dressed in the sexy version of Mrs. Claus. Actually, I think my ex wore something like this four years ago, complete with the micro mini skirt and the gaping cleavage. It had been fun back then, but being reminded of my ex by this random woman makes my mouth taste sour.

"No," I say with a shake of my head. "That was my type once but not anymore."

"Huh."

I tilt my head. "Why do you sound disappointed?"

"Not disappointed. Surprised." She shrugs. "I guess I really don't know you at all."

"Of course you don't. Today's the first time we actually had a civilized conversation."

Her teeth scrape against her lower lip and it occurs to me that right now, her lips must taste of Christmas—sugar, cinnamon, and hot chocolate.

I must've lost my mind somewhere along the way.

Shaking my head heard, I shift my focus away from her and onto the merchant stands. There's one with themed jewelry that looks like something out of a high end store. Then one with illustrations depicting realistic nativity scenes and snowy houses decked in decorations. I take pictures of some oversized gingerbread cookies that would take a whole family to eat, and in that process I lose track of my coworker.

I spot her a moment later chatting with an old man dressed in full Santa outfit, who seems to be trying to push an elf on the shelf on her.

"Um, thank you, but I really am just looking."

The man shifts his attention to me once I join them. "How about you, young man? Would you adopt one of my children?"

From the corner of my right eye, Sierra gives me a warning look. I put my hand on her shoulder to steer her away. "Sorry, I was just looking for her."

"A young couple such as yourselves should adopt one of these elves, so you're ready for when you have children of your own."

What the—My brain glitches and I say, "We're not a couple, she's my sister."

"Oh." Santa-look-alike drops his jaw.

"Haha, see ya!" Sierra all but runs away and when we're a few paces away, she hisses at me. "Your sister? Excuse me, but we couldn't look less alike."

"I know but it worked. He was so shocked that he couldn't keep peddling his creepy little creations." I grin.

She twists her lip in a grouchy way. "Good point. Maybe we should dress as creepy elves for the party so everyone leaves us alone."

"Damn, that's a solid idea." I trail behind her and mull it over for another moment. "Actually, we should have a ridiculous but very festive dress code for the whole thing."

"Like, we dressed like elves and Richard as Santa because we're his minions?"

I snort a laugh. "That'd be great if we can convince him."

"I'm sure that if you pitch it, he'll be—Stop!"

I freeze.

Sierra's eyes are wide as saucers and she puts both hands up as a barrier, even though one still carries a steaming cup and the other one a half eaten churro.

"What?" I whisper, looking down at myself to find something offensive.

"Don't move a single step."

"Sierra, what? You're freaking me out."

She swallows hard and slowly looks up.

I do the same and find a big sprig of mistletoe hanging right above her.

"Oh." I relax.

"Don't you dare take one more step, Mahoney."

I take out another churro from my pouch and dip it in my chocolate. "And why's that, Fernandez?"

"Don't play games, you know why. There's no way I'm going to—"

"Kiss! Kiss! Kiss!" Someone shrieks off to my left. I turn and it's the same chick in the sexy outfit from earlier. She's looking at us like we're the most entertaining thing that's happened all day.

"Shush, you." Sierra casts a mean glare her way and the woman smiles sweetly. But then my coworker sets her laser beams on me again. "And you, stay where you are. I'm going to walk away carefully and then that way neither of us will have a chance of standing under this cursed plant at the same time."

"Would it be so bad to kiss me?" I ask, chewing on my snack.

"I'm not even going to dignify that with answer." She starts walking backwards, away from me.

I swallow my snack and say, "By the way, the elf peddling Santa is right behind you. I guess you'll have to kiss him instead."

With a yelp, Sierra launches herself forward and since I don't move away, she slams against my chest. I tilt my face down just as she does the opposite. Her eyes are as wide as they can be when she checks over her shoulder and finds a grand total of no one. Not a single person or elf.

"Ugh!" She pushes against me so hard that I stumble.

"Aww, bummer," sexy Mrs. Claus pouts at us and steps back into her stand.

I'm chuckling as I follow right after Sierra, but I pause alone under the mistletoe and inspect it. I take a picture, not because I don't know what it looks like, but because I want to remember.

After I catch up to her, I mention, "We forgot to put mistletoe on the list."

"There's no way we're putting mistletoe in the venue. That's an HR issue waiting to happen."

"I don't see the big deal. There was mistletoe at the Aspen inn last year. Didn't Karl from legal and Mindy from HR get together because of it?"

"Really?" She pauses. "I thought they got together before the Christmas party."

"I don't really know. My point is that Christmas is also a season of love, so we should put mistletoe everywhere."

She whirls around and plants herself in front of me. "Not everywhere."

"Some places."

Her frown intensifies. "One place."

"Two places."

"One and that's final."

"Fine, right at the entrance."

"So if you walk in at the same time as Richard, would you kiss him?"

I shudder. "Okay, somewhere at the back."

"That's a good boy."

I bite my churro. "Are you comparing me to a dog?"

"Hmm, someone did say that you're hairy and with pretty eyes." Is it just me, or are her cheeks darkening? But then she clears her throat and I figure she really is embarrassed at giving me some sort of compliment. "Anyway, I think I'm having a few ideas now. And you?"

Oh, yeah. A few ideas around mistletoe all right.

It takes me a second to figure out that she's referring to the Christmas party, and not about mistletoe kisses.

"Right, yeah. A few. That velcro Christmas tree we saw got me thinking."

She cocks an eyebrow. "Yeah?"

"What if we get that thing, wrap some baseballs in felt, and make people throw them at the tree to decorate it? Whoever gets more balls to stick wins a prize or something."

"Like a twist on a fair booth?"

I shrug. "It's not the Olympics theme but it might be fun, especially if people are drinking spiked eggnog."

"I love it." My jaw drops but then she repeats, "No, I love that idea. It sounds super fun."

"Like your ball pit gift idea."

"Right." The word comes out softly from her mouth, all her energy going to her brain that I can practically see whirring. "Those massive gingerbread men cookies. What if we have a bunch of those lined up and people have to throw something random at them? Again, winning a prize if you destroy the cookie."

"Yes. A little violent and a lot de-stressing." I rub my chin. "Okay, we've mentioned prizes twice. What kind?"

"I don't know, especially if we're really going for the ball pit idea. Individual prizes would compete with that."

"But not if the booth prizes are points to be able to get more gifts from the ball pit."

"Oh!" Sierra inhales sharply. "Yes, like an arcade. You earn tickets for every game you win, then the tickets translate into more time in the pit to fish for more gifts."

A slow grin takes over my face. "So basically, we sell the idea of possibly infinite gifts."

"Except of course, they'll have a hard time wading through the ball pit because of obvious reasons, and also because they'll be drunk off their minds."

"Which also means they'll have to cycle the booths several times, which will get harder the drunker they get."

"And that sounds absolutely not boring at all!" She lifts her hand for a high five and I comply, but she latches onto my hand with surprising strength. "We've finally nailed the brief, Mahoney."

I fixate on her smaller hand grabbing mine like it's a lifeline, her fingers twined between mine. "Uhh."

But she still doesn't notice and even shakes my hand. "This

is going to be the best Christmas party *SPORTY* has ever had. Those bonus checks are in the bag." Finally, she drops my hand and skips down the aisle.

I glance down at my hand, open and close it.

Well, I guess I'm glad we didn't kiss under that mistletoe. If grabbing her hand twice in one day has me so damn tingly, I'm sure I'd embarrass myself if I kissed her.

CHAPTER 10
SIERRA

Conor doesn't get nervous before presentations, probably because they're nothing compared to playing in front of thousands of fans and haters. But for me, they're a big stinking deal. He answers some emails while we wait, and I'm doing breathing exercises that actually make me progressively freak out even more.

I let out a particularly shaky breath that makes him lift his eyes. His glasses sit a bit low on the bridge of his nose, which means I get the full blast of his pretty eyes. Not my own words.

"Are you really Sierra Fernandez or five shaky rabbits in a trench coat?"

My mouth twitches but I refuse to smile. "It's been five shaky rabbits all along. How are you so calm? If we don't get Richard's green light today, we can probably kiss the bonuses goodbye, forget the promotion."

"Oh, I'm not calm at all," he says in an even tone of voice, his hands deftly working the keyboard as he speaks. "I went to the barber and put on a legit dress shirt for this shit, what do you think?"

I blink slowly. To be honest, he usually dresses like such a jock for work—which is fine, this is a company of sports people. But somehow it hadn't clicked with me that he'd made extra effort today until this moment. His hair's a tad shorter and combed to perfection, with a nice little wave at the top and all. His beard's trimmed and edged; I can actually make out the shape of his square jaw now. I'm pretty sure his pristine white shirt is tailor made because they don't possibly make them for such wide shoulders and tiny waists.

I go as far as pulling away from the table and check out his legs. He's in maroon trousers that match his socks and dress boots. Turns out Conor Mahoney knows how to match his clothes.

"Wow."

"Right?" He smirks, attention still on his screen. "I figured if I look like a businessman, I can fool everyone into seeing me as one."

"Dress for the job you have and not the college you went to, and all that," I tease.

"Hey." He lifts his face to give me grumpy expression.

It makes me chuckle but the tension returns to my shoulders once the amusement ebbs away.

"Hey," Conor repeats in a different tone now. "Seriously, why are you like this? You're always so self-assured."

"The five bunnies are very good at manipulating the robot." I lean back against the chair and fold my arms, not caring if it wrinkles my red blouse. My logic wasn't too far from Conor's, except I figured if I looked festive I'd be able to more cheerfully deliver this pitch. "I think… I think I'm going to let you in on something about me."

His eyebrows rise. In a second, he's closing the lid of his laptop and pushing it aside.

"Never mind, I changed my mind."

Conor groans. "Oh, c'mon. I was excited to be part of the exclusive circle of trust."

I bite my lip, completely thrown by that groan. Does he know how he sounds when he does it?

More importantly, that old woman at the fair was right. Conor's eyes may not seem special at a glance. Light brown and deep set, framed by unfairly long eyelashes. But they have a light in them that I haven't been able to face in the past. They're searching, which I took to mean he wanted to dig deep into my soul and carve out all my secrets. Now that I'm not running away from them, I wonder if he's just a naturally observant and curious person instead.

"I have this like, core hurt that I carry like a chip on my shoulder everywhere I go," I start saying, wringing the hem of my blouse under the table. "I mentioned I used to get bullied as a kid, remember?"

"Apology, hot chocolate." He smacks his forehead and squirms. "Wow, I'm absolute garbage. How did I gloss over that fact?"

"You didn't, *I* did—on purpose. I didn't want to dwell." I glance out the window at the gloomy landscape. The sky is grey with charged clouds that refuse to break apart, even though the bare tree branches below are rising up to embrace the onslaught. "But kids were pretty brutal about the fact that my dad was the school janitor, my mom a nail tech, and that I had an accent. So I made proving I was smarter than them my whole personality. It's why the concept of failing at the smallest thing turns me into an insufferable jerk."

His brow crashes like thunder and he starts cracking his knuckles. "Who hurt you? Just say the names and I'll drop by."

I yelp a quick laugh that devolves into blowing a raspberry. "Well... thanks. But I bet I'm the only one who has to work through this stuff."

"They should work through my fists." Conor sighs and drops his hands on the table. "But, Sierra, failure isn't so terrible. Trust me, I would know."

For the first time, I note the self-deprecation in his expression and something in my chest twists painfully enough to make me gasp.

"Conor, you're not a—"

Of course, that's when the door to the conference room opens. Richard strides in, whistling Deck the Halls in an extra jolly way.

"Alright, folks. Let's get the ball rolling, I only have fifteen minutes today." He takes a seat at the head of the table.

Conor tears his attention away from me and grabs his laptop again. This time he's the one hooked up to the system and he pulls up the new and updated presentation. *SPORTY* Christmas Olympics is no more, and is instead replaced by *SPORTY* Christmas Fair.

This time we give the presentation together. It was a natural byproduct of having spent all Wednesday together at the fair downtown, and then yesterday working on the package. Am I nervous that I'm not getting the full marks on my own? Yes. But I truly didn't do this by myself.

Besides, a single presentation won't make or break my case for the promotion. I suspect that the day of the event will be the decisive factor.

Whenever it's Conor's turn to talk, I observe Richard for any negative signs, but the man is a vault. It works great when he's faced with customers or suppliers, but it's driving me up the wall right now. My voice wavers a bit when I mention words like *nostalgia* and *competitive spirit* as I deliver the closer for the pitch.

"And that's it. What do you think?" I stretch my lips into what I hope is a happy smile, and not an I'm-barely-containing-my-barf cringe.

"Hmm." Richard swivels in his chair to face away from the screen and back to Conor and I, sitting side by side across from him. "I'm a bit disappointed—"

I'm dying. This is what dying feels like.

"—That the Olympics theme isn't there, but this does sound fun." Slowly, Richard's mask cracks to let excitement through. "Oh, man. It's almost a shame it's only going to be for adults. My kids would *love* this idea."

I'm alive again. I can breathe.

Conor leans forward. "So we're a go?"

"Well, almost. There's just one thing I wasn't clear about." I grip the edge of the table as Richard makes a pause. "What about the venue?"

"Right." My coworker taps his fingertips against the table surface. "There's a bit of a problem about that."

"Money's not an issue." Richard shrugs.

I bite back what I really want to say, which is that maybe he shouldn't have tasked us with this so late in the year. I keep quiet because the actual problem isn't even that.

"Ice skating is a big activity in the event," Conor says with his business voice. "And there's only one ice rink in Mapleton."

Richard asks, "Is it booked already?"

"No, I know for a fact that it's not booked because it's my grandfather's."

When the issue doesn't seem to be computing for Richard, I explain, "It could be seen as a conflict of interest."

Richard hums while in thought. "But it's also a single-source option. Let me talk with Martin and see what he thinks. If he doesn't go for it, you'll have to eliminate the ice skating activity from the event."

"Roger that."

"In the meantime, you have the green light. Full press court. The whole nine yards. If you need to work remotely to organize everything and keep the secrets, do it. And use your corporate credit cards if vendors aren't setup already." He smacks the table once and stands up, leaving without further ado.

The stress leaves my body and I deflate.

Conor elbows me. "See? We nailed it."

"Well, not quite. We haven't solved the issue of the venue yet."

"But at least we can start spending." He closes his laptop and grabs his coffee mug with the logo of his former pro hockey team.

I push off the table. "But where are we going to put all the stuff if we have to keep it hush hush from literally the entire building?"

"I have a big shed," Conor says as he pushes the door open with his shoulder. "I'll text you the address and you can start dropping stuff over whenever you want."

With that plan, we split off to start collecting all the junk we'll need.

*

Something about filling the back of my truck with assorted Christmas stuff has finally let it sink in. This is happening. The ten thousand dollar bonus is sure-fire now. Even if I don't get the promotion, it means I don't have to cancel the reservation for Grammie's flight over for Christmas. All I have to do is break the news now.

I honk from the parking lot of the wretched high school I attended, which is still Dad's workplace. This is as far as I get every time I have to drop him off and pick him up after work, and Dad knows the routine. Not even a minute later, he's walking out at a hurried pace and gets in the passenger's seat.

"How was work today, mija?" Dad asks as he puts on his seatbelt.

I dance a little in my seat. "I have great news."

"¿Sí? ¿Qué pasó?"

"Nope, you have to wait until we're home and call Grammie too."

Dad huffs. "Unfair. You shouldn't have hinted at it if you weren't going to share."

"It's because I'm so excited! But first, let's get out of this horrible place so I can be properly happy."

Fortunately, the drive home from here is pretty short. Unfortunately, Dad spends the entire time trying to get what the big news is out of me.

"Did you get a big project?"

I crank up the volume of the music even higher.

He dials it back down. "Is it a boy?"

I look away because hell no.

"Are they finally making you CEO of the whole place?"

I snort because I wish.

The lights inside the house are on, which makes sense because Mom's shift at the salon ended like half an hour ago and she takes the bus back and forth. I'm the one who usually drives the truck because *SPORTY*'s building is clear across the other side of town.

"Susana," Dad calls out when we walk in. "Break out the champagne because Sierra has a big announcement to make."

"Dad, please." I laugh as we wrestle with removing our winter wear at the entrance together.

"There's no champagne," Mom says back from the kitchen while banging some pot or pan. "We might still have some Cacique, though." That's the favorite brand of Venezuelan rum for the Fernandez family and I'm not opposed to a sip.

"Okay but first, we need to call Grammie. And let's hope the connection works this time."

I rush into the kitchen with my work bag and take out my laptop. It smells like Mom is working on some stew and I fire up my laptop as my stomach croaks.

I wrinkle my nose at the kissy sounds behind me. "Ew, your daughter is here, you guys."

"Don't be jealous." Mom drops a quick kiss on my head. "I promise I won't say *ew* when you bring a guy home and kiss him."

"No, I bet you'd say worse things," I mumble too low for her to hear. In the meantime, I click on the messaging system and start to call Grammie.

After a first attempt that fails, Dad asks, "Did you give her a heads up that you were calling? It could be she's not available."

"I did. I texted her on Whatsapp earlier and she said she'd be around." I press the call button again with a bit too much strength. It makes my finger hurt.

I lean forward, glaring at the calling logo until it changes. It goes green for a second and then there she is. My grandma.

"Sierrita," she says in a choppy voice. Her face is wrinkled but smiley, and her eyes have that arch they get when they're happy. "Que Dios te bendiga." Every conversation with an elder starts that way, with a blessing. I can't wait until she gives it to me in person.

"Grammie, tengo noticias." I can see my parents leaning over me through the tiny thumbnail that shows us. Our image is crystal clear compared to how grainy Grammie's is, but it doesn't matter. In three weeks she'll be crystal clear and 3D.

"¿Qué?" she asks, leaning closer to the phone until we can see her ear.

Dad chuckles and I elbow him to stop. "Que tengo noticias," I repeat, take a deep breath, and finally spill the beans. "Me están dando un bono en el trabajo y te voy a poder traer para acá para navidad!"

I open my hands in a *surprise* gesture and look up at my parents. They're both looking at each other.

"¿Qué pasa?" I ask, confused when no one is bursting into cheers and hollers.

"Ay mija," Grammie says with a sigh. "Me encantaría pero es que estos días no me siento muy bien."

"What do you mean you don't feel well?" I shake my head to shake my cables back in place.

"Grammie's hypertension has been getting worse," Mom explains to me, caressing my hair.

"But she can get treatment here."

"Honey, that would be too expensive for us." Dad presses his lips tight. "We can't afford it."

"Well, I can. The bonus is ten thousand dollars." When they grow silent, Grammie asks for a translation and I comply.

Only for her to throw an unexpected curveball at me. "Sierrita, no quiero que uses to dinero en mí."

My eyes bulge. From the beginning, this money has been labelled as to be used for Grammie, and not for me.

"Didn't you say you want to rent your own place?" Mom asks with a little smile. "That way you don't have to keep putting up with your yucky kissing parents."

"No." I blink at her, at Dad, then at Grammie. "No. All along I've been working so hard to see Grammie. This is happening. I'll fly her over and pay for her treatment. Case closed."

"But—"

"Grammie, ya hice la reserva de tu ticket. Te lo envío por email en la noche," I say to her. To my parents, I mumble. "I'm going to go change."

My heart hammers in my throat as I walk out of the kitchen, and not in the way I expected this night to go. Both of my parents knew about Grammie's worsening condition and hadn't told me. I knew she wasn't doing well in general and that's why I hatched this whole plan. But for the first time I start really contemplating the possibility not just of not being able to see her this Christmas, but of not being able to ever again.

CHAPTER 11
CONOR

"It's a great day to split you up." I rub my gloved hands together and grab my Stihl ax, hoisting it on my shoulder as I consider the massive block of wood that took me all morning to saw out of a tree, and then haul to my chopping block. I probably sound like a horror movie villain with the laugh that escapes from my throat, but I'm just excited to use all my strength without restraint.

This is literally my favorite thing to do away from an ice rink ever since retirement. It's a great workout and it also helps me work through whatever is occupying my mind. And right now, it's a certain event I have to pull off with a certain woman.

I plant my boots at a good distance from each other and from the wood, and drop my ax with the power of my entire body. The hilt buries itself with a satisfying thunk and I already see the first crack. With a jerk to the side, I free my axe and repeat the process.

My plan after this is taking a shower to wash off the sawdust, dirt, and sweat from the morning run and the tree felling. Then I'll have the world's biggest breakfast—I have bacon in the oven that is calling my name. Then I'll bundle up the chopped wood and take it to Gramps and some of our neighbors. After that, I'm hitting the town to scout some potential venues if Conrad's Rink doesn't work out. And after that, I'll watch tonight's game that will feature Max's team versus Nate's—should be fun.

Tomorrow is Sunday, so it's not like we'll be able to schedule any visits, but having a finalized list of vendors should help us make all the calls we need starting Monday morning. And once I send it to Sierra, I'll ask her if she wants to get together tomorrow after church to get started on all the manual work this whole thing will require.

I've offered my cottage as headquarters for the operation, since it turns out she lives with her parents. Needless to say, I spent all last night cleaning and making sure the place doesn't look like a frat house.

Besides, it'll be cozier with freshly split wood burning in the fireplace.

After three more hacks, the wood splits in two and I shove one half off so I can work on turning the other one into decent sized logs. The more I split, the easier it gets until I can drop the ax down one handed. I rest the ax against the chopping block and walk around it to haul the other half back on top. It's damn heavy and tears a series of grunts out of me.

"Whew." I make a pause to remove my glasses and pull up the hem of my shirt. The outside is all grimy and so is the shirt's neck area, so all I have left to clear the sweat off my eyes is the inside of my shirt.

A cough echoes around me.

I lift my head.

Am I hallucinating? Why is Sierra Fernandez standing some three yards away from me? And also why is she looking down—

Oh. Right. Lifted shirt.

"You have abs."

"So have you," I return like a clown. "Everybody has abs."

She snorts and folds her arms. "Well, mine don't look like that."

My lips twitch and I make a show of looking down at my stomach. "You mean other people aren't as hairy?" It's not like I'm covered in a thick carpet of hair, but there's no doubt I'm healthy on the testosterone.

She doesn't respond right away and instead squints, still giving her full focus to my stomach as I wipe my face with my shirt. "Eight? Who the hell has eight abs? And why do you even need all of those?"

"To split wood?" I suggest, finally pulling my shirt down and putting my glasses back on. My muscles complain as I bend down to pick up my ax. "What brings you here this early?"

That said, I get back to work on the last half. I think she tries to talk but gives up against all the noise. This time it takes three good thwacks to split the massive chunk and I make a pause just to gather my breath.

"Well?"

Sierra shuts her mouth tight and blinks fast. There's something in her expression that I like. A lot. It's almost enough to wipe off any trace of exhaustion in my muscle fibers. As if my body were priming me for something I have no business thinking about with my coworker.

"Um." She clears her throat and it makes her cough. "Right. You said we could use your shed to store stuff and I have a loaded truck..."

"Oh, yeah. Let me help you." I bury the ax into the wood and pull off my gloves.

"You should just finish what you're doing."

I pause. "I don't want you to waste your time standing there, though."

"It's not a waste, trust me." Is it just me, or is her voice raspier? "Watching you is giving me an idea."

There's no way she's hitting on me because basically until a week ago, she hated my guts. So, the only way I can deal with this sudden desire for her to actually hit on me is by joking.

I place one arm across my chest and the other hand to hide my crotch. "Are you objectifying me?"

"What?" The question comes out shrill and her face reddens. "No! I was thinking about ax throwing, you dork."

Well, that's disappointing. I drop my hands and walk over to her, pretending like I'm not a bit hurt.

"What do you mean?"

"We should have a ridiculous booth like throwing an ax to a row of gingerbread cookies."

"That sounds weird enough that I'm sure Richard will love it." Our boots scrunch against the dry gravel. As we head to the driveway, I ask her, "How many axes are we talking about?"

"I guess two if we're pairing everyone up."

"Then I got it covered."

Sierra looks up at me. "I knew you had a lumberjack look but I didn't know you actually were one."

"It's kinda new." I shrug. "I bought this land after retiring because I wanted to be far from all the eyes, and ended up surrounded by trees instead."

"So you decided to kill them?" Her voice is teasing so I don't take it too seriously.

Yet, I still give a serious answer. "Hey, I'll have you know I'm the sole provider of firewood for five families plus myself."

"That's actually cool, not gonna lie."

I put a hand on my chest. "Two compliments in one day? My heart can't take it."

"Two?" She frowns.

"This plus all the admiration to my abs."

"I wasn't—" She splutters and coughs. "I wasn't admiring them."

"Sure…" I drag the word out and it fades not because I'm done teasing her, but because I've set sight on her truck. "What the hell, woman? Did you cram the whole store in there?"

"Kind of?" She all but skips over to lift one end of the tarp that protected everything from the elements, and it's almost like opening Pandora's box. There's an explosion of tinsel, garland, and some oversized candy canes underneath. "Ta da! I got everything I could and it's not just decorations, there's also crafts stuff. The only thing I couldn't get was that big velcro tree, some asshole bought it before me."

I laugh. "I'm the asshole. It's in my shed."

"Oops." Sierra grins at me.

"Okay so, if you want to start bringing in a few light stuff, the shed's in the back."

"I saw it," she says. "It was behind this lumberjack chopping wood like it's the eighteen hundreds."

I ignore her. "I'm gonna go get some baskets to get all this stuff."

"Roger that." She opens the trunk and hoists herself on it with her arms until she sits on the popped door. I watch in amusement how she swivels around and stands up to push some shopping bags toward the edge. Then she repeats the process going down.

This will take all day if left to her own devices.

Shaking my head, I walk ahead of her to open the shed. I pull up the two rough hewn baskets I use to cart around the wood logs. I'm sure something will fit in them.

Sierra pops her head in, curls falling all over her shoulders. "Is this where you keep all the dead bodies?"

"Sure, if by dead bodies you mean more wood, tools, and hockey equipment," I answer with a deadpanned expression.

"Surprisingly boring for a man cave." She huffs as she puts

the shopping bags right beside the massive velcro Christmas tree.

"I don't know what you were expecting and I won't ask." Snorting, I turn around and head back out to her truck. I don't need to do the whole process she executed earlier. Rather than that, I toss the baskets in and just hoist myself up with one hand. Unless Sierra had help, it must've taken her an hour to load all this junk in.

"Huh. Since you're there, just pass me stuff," she says from a distance still.

"Sure." I test a few of the bags and boxes to find the lightest stuff and pass it over to her. While she's on her way to the shed, I grab the heavier stuff and fill up one basket with bags, and haul a box over my shoulder.

I'm pushing everything against a wall in the shed after our second trip, when I hear the noise of an engine. I figure it's not Sierra leaving, since we have more shit to offload. But then I walk over to the driveway and freeze, torn between horror and amusement.

Gramps is getting out of his neighbor's car and spots the lonesome woman right away. "What do we have here? A female in my grandson's property? Are my eyes deceiving me?"

Something like a mewl comes out of my throat. I'd be open to the idea of a black hole swallowing me whole right about now.

"Oh, hi." Sierra leaves the shopping bags on the ground and straightens up. "Grandson, you said?"

"That's right." Gramps offers his hand for Sierra to shake and she returns the gesture. "Conrad Mahoney, but call me Gramps. And that's Frank behind the wheel, my neighbor."

Frank is an even more sour old man than Gramps, and he's glad to ignore the rest of us from his car.

"Lovely to meet you, I'm Sierra Fernandez. I work with your grandson."

"Just that? A bummer. He's single, you know?"

"Gramps," I bark the word to try to stop him. It doesn't so I hurry the hell up.

"Has been for three years," he keeps saying, "ever since that awful Nikki."

Slowly, Sierra turns to cock an eyebrow at me. "So awful, am I right?"

I finally reach them. After waving my hand at Frank, I turn to the other two. "Gramps, why are you here at this time? Is everything okay at the rink?"

"Very pretty, I'll give her that," the old man says, ignoring me as if I didn't exist. "But a real succubus, if you catch my drift."

Finally, I grab him by the shoulders. "Can we please not talk about Nikki—ever?"

"Bah." He shrugs himself off my hold. "You're always can we not this, can we not that. Let an old man live before life takes him."

I'm whining now. "Gramps. You're killing me here. Is there something wrong?"

He folds his arms. "Nothing wrong. I came to bring you the casserole and cornbread leftovers you were supposed to pick up."

"Crap." I run a hand through my damp hair. "Sorry, Gramps. This week has been so intense working with Sierra that all I could do every night was just come home and crash."

"Just worked?" He looks between us.

Sierra nods with shocking seriousness. "Just worked."

"Boo. When I was your age, I misbehaved some. Enough to get me a son out of it."

"Where are those leftovers?" I take to ignoring him now.

Sierra bursts out laughing. She clutches her belly and lets out a loud, hearty laugh that fills the air with feminine notes. Even Gramps is as enchanted as I am.

That is, until he finds me about to drool and smirks. I duck from his view and open the passenger door of Frank's car to grab two massive containers. The blast of country music inside is all the greeting I get from Gramps's neighbor.

Straightening, I shake my head at my old man. "Gramps, this will feed an army. Did you leave some for yourself?"

"I'm tired of eating it already. Besides, now you can share with Sierra here." He gives an exaggerated wink that makes her chuckle again.

I hope she just thinks he's kidding, because he's not. If I don't separate these two as soon as possible, he's going to start babbling who knows what incriminating pieces of Conor Mahoney trivia to this woman in a misguided attempt to make her fall for me.

"Great, can you please put this in my fridge and go?" I push the containers against his chest. "I'm afraid Sierra and I still have some work to finish so…"

Gramps lowers his voice, which doesn't mean much when he has megaphones for lungs anyway. "Conor, how can you be so filthy when you have female company over? I thought I taught you better."

I can't stand the burning in my face anymore so I give up. "Fine, keep embarrassing me. I'm going to finish chopping wood for all I care." With one last glare at the two of them, I walk back to my chopping block.

CHAPTER 12
SIERRA

ME

Mierda mierda mierda

You were right

I'm in deep shit

RACHEL HOT MAMA LEON

????

ME

He's so cute Rachel

How was I immune before?

RACHEL HOT MAMA LEON

Who

Oh. You're talking about Conor

Girl, I don't think you were *ever* immune

You were just fooling yourself

glance up at the back of his head. His brown hair is combed but a few strands still defy gravity, and his neck is a thick column of muscle just like the rest of him. Dude has an *eight* pack, and he's not even a professional athlete anymore. I really fooled myself into thinking he was some dorky weirdo these past two years.

Since he's walking ahead of me as he chats up the employee showing us this venue, I take another moment to observe him. And by him, I mean the bubble butt in Conor's *SPORTY* brand joggers. And the massive thighs underneath.

Okay, no wonder he doesn't wear a lot of dress pants. It must be hard to find something that fits all that muscle.

I grab my phone again.

ME

Cute? Scratch that

He's smoking hot

Have you ever seen his butt?

RACHEL HOT MAMA LEON

Yes. I may be a single mother but the operating part is *single*

ME

Why did you never hit on him?

Because if I were you without any weird grudges I would have

RACHEL HOT MAMA LEON

Qué va

You would've killed me

Tho I did debate whether it was worth dying for

I snort. That momentarily catches Conor's attention and

he glances back at me over his shoulder. But then the woman says something that pulls his attention again.

> **RACHEL HOT MAMA LEON**
>
> Does this mean you're going to start hitting on him or that he's game for me? Inquiring minds need to know

> **ME**
>
> Neither? Lol
>
> It'd be too weird either way

> **RACHEL HOT MAMA LEON**
>
> I was kidding btw
>
> I'm not really interested in your man

> **ME**
>
> He's not my
>
> Wtv

She sends me three laughing emoji and I stuff my phone back in the pocket of my coat.

"—Love to host *SPORTY*'s Christmas party," the woman says in this way that tells me she's been gushing this whole time.

Meanwhile, I haven't been paying any attention. Or at least not to her.

I take a moment to check my surroundings instead of my project partner. Right now, the event room of this hotel is half-finished for a wedding that's happening this weekend. The theme seems to be winter wonderland, which I guess is apropos. Frosted garlands and tinsel, silky white fabrics, and white Christmas lights everywhere.

What matters the most, though, is that it's pretty small for what we need. And not just because it's crammed with tables and chairs except for a dance floor by the stage out front. It'd be hard to make different sections for the activities without causing a crush with all the headquarters employees and plus ones.

Obviously, Conor knows because he keeps the conversation nice and non-committal. "Thanks! Are you a big fan of *SPORTY*?"

"Absolutely. Best tennis shoes ever. I may or may not be gifting a new pair to each one of my kids this Christmas." She whirls around and spreads her arms. "Well, what do you think?"

"Could you give us a moment to walk the place on our own?" I ask with a polite smile.

"Of course! Take all the time you need. I'll be at the reception desk." Her eyes positively glow as she backs away from us until she's out the door.

I still whisper just in case there are microphones or something. "It's gonna suck to tell her the place doesn't work. Tag, you're it."

Conor blows a raspberry. "Listen, I've been keeping her distracted while you fiddled with your phone. You should have the decency of being the one who lets her down."

"I'm the one who let the previous guy down." I fold my arms. This is the second place we've visited already and they've both had the same issue.

"Fine." He casts a grumpy look around. "Is there really no way we can make this place work? It's slightly bigger than the other one."

"Let me show you all the ways it won't work." I glide around him towards the stage. "See this? I'm not even sure a whole band would fit in here."

"Oh, shit." Conor's eyes widened. "We haven't thought about sound. Hold up." He plucks his phone out and taps furiously at it as he walks this way.

My own phone buzzes in my pocket and I ignore it, thinking it's another text from Rachel that I definitely wouldn't want him to see.

"I just emailed us both with a reminder to figure out music for the event," Conor says and stands beside me, tucking his phone back in his pocket.

"Cool. So, anyway." I clear my throat, trying not to get distracted by the scent that clings to him. It's nothing super fancy, just freshly showered man, and apparently that's enough to make me send weird texts to my friend. Back to work, I say, "We'd need about that much space for food and drink. Then about the span of those three tables for the ax throwing booth, which would literally leave us with enough space for only one more booth and a small standing area, but no ball pit or other activities. Pretty boring fair. And pray tell, sir, where would we stuff a thousand people in this place?"

"Okay, okay. It doesn't work." He huffs and puts his hands on his hips like some old man. Which immediately makes me think of his Gramps and all the embarrassing things he spewed out about his grandson. "Now what?"

I shrug. "I guess we go to the next place."

Conor throws his head back with another one of those groans that sound R-rated. We both grow still. Me, while I observe the tension of his neck tendons. Him, looking up.

Wait, why?

I lift my eyes too. "Oh, no."

"It wasn't me," Conor says, as though there was a smidge of suspicion in my mind that he was somehow behind the mistletoe hanging above us.

He is solely responsible for the way my pulse takes off like a rocket, though.

"Um…"

"We don't have to kiss." Conor tilts his head back down so our eyes meet. "There's literally no one else to know."

Wait, so he's trying to get out of kissing me? Does he not want to? Am I the only one who finds him attractive now?

I don't know how it didn't occur to me until this literal moment that he may not feel the same way. Like, I'm cute and I know it. Medium height, medium build, pretty face, even better hair. I have no problem getting guys's attention. The challenge is in keeping it, because I'm more intense and driven than they tend to prefer—as said by my college ex and a couple other guys I dated later.

And I guess that's why. I've only ever shown Conor my bad side. I have no right being shocked if he doesn't find me attractive.

That rankles.

I fold my arms in what I hope looks like a disinterested way and say, "Well, I don't know about you but I'd rather have no bad luck."

"Hmm." Conor rubs his beard and I wait. "That would definitely suck."

Oh.

My heart starts hammering against my ribcage. "Yeah, I think we've both had enough bad luck to last us a lifetime."

"Right. Okay. So." He turns enough to face me even though we're still two paces apart. "Tell me how you want to do this."

"Huh?" I blink hard, not registering a single word he's said because he's taking another step forward and oh my goodness, he's *tall*. I don't think I'll be able to reach him even when I put my arms around his neck.

Wait. A. Moment. Am I about to put my arms around Conor Mahoney's neck? The guy I've hated on for two years?

Moreover, am I really going to put my mouth on his?

I double check and sure enough, there's still mistletoe hanging right above us. A whole ass bushel too, in case anyone tries to miss it.

"I mean…" His voice lowers and I steel my body against the shiver it threatens to produce. "I have no idea what you like. Soft or hard?"

"What?"

His mouth twitches. "Soft or hard kisses, Sierra?"

Right now, either or. Both. As long as there's at least one.

I take a final step closer until our chests touch and I look up. Up. Amusement glints in his pretty eyes, like he thinks this is all a joke. Guess it's time to show him this is serious business.

I put my hands on his chest and slowly slide them up. His face transforms first into surprise that we're doing this, and then his eyes lower to my lips. I lick them slowly, sweeping the tip of my tongue softly across my bottom lip. Now I feel his heart beat hard against my hand.

"Go big or go home, Conor," I say with a raspy voice that shocks even me.

His eyes lift to mine, searching for something I guess he must find because the next second, Conor splays his hand on my lower back and pushes me against him. I gasp, worried that I'll lose my balance, until his other hand sneaks through my hair to hold the back of my head.

And then his mouth is on mine.

Duro, I think in the quiet of my mind. He definitely chose the right option.

I do the same to him and run my hand through his hair to push him closer. His lips suckle my bottom one with intent, his beard scratching softly against the skin of my chin. One quick sensation of his tongue against my lip has me gasping and that's all Conor needs to deepen the kiss.

Coercing my mouth open with his gets him full access. Feeling his tongue caress mine tears a guttural groan from deep within me. I feel so hot all over that I'm sure he'd never need to chop wood again if he keeps kissing me like this, I'll become fire myself.

He pulls away for a breath and I scratch at his neck to bring him closer. But then our noses bump and he's kissing the other corner of my lips, starting all over. Sighing against his lips, I let my hand roam from his chest to his shoulder, feeling the coiled strength there as he holds me from melting into a puddle on the floor.

"Still hard?" he asks against my lips, his voice almost choked up.

It takes me a second to figure out what he's talking about and then I remember he means the intensity. "Try soft now."

"'Kay."

Oh. I'm gonna die.

It's even better when he takes his sweet time savoring my lips like we have all day. Every lick and gently applied suction travels all the way down to my curling toes. I've never been kissed like this. It's always been a means to an end—one that is definitely not going to happen on the stage of a hotel's event room. This was basically a dare that will just end in a *gotcha*, but I'm sure as hell going to enjoy every second of it.

I tilt my face until I capture his upper lip between my teeth, scraping them softly. His hot breath fans against my skin carrying the scent of the coffee we drank on the way. I can still savor it when I run my tongue across his lips and this time, he's the one making that sound that immediately transports me to a dimly lit room.

"Conor, you need to stop making that sound." I pant against his mouth. "Or at least don't make it in public."

"What?" He sounds confused or in pain. Maybe both.

I pull away slightly and it takes him a longer moment than me to open his eyes. His glasses have slid dangerously low and I raise one hand to push them up the bridge of his nose.

"Don't moan, Conor. You sound way too sexy to be in public."

"I—" He swallows hard. "Okay. Thank you?"

My lips tingle as I smile and the gesture attracts his attention again. His look bruised and wet, and I'm sure the woman waiting for us outside is going to know what we were up to right away. Especially if his beard has irritated the skin of my face.

So, I guess if I kiss him again it's going to get even more obvious, huh?

My voice also doesn't sound fit for the public as I say, "I think we've secured our good luck, don't you think?"

Slowly, he unwinds his hand from my neck and trails it down. The calluses in his hand against the skin of my neck release a traitorous shiver from me. His eyes are dark as he continues deliberately running that hand down my spine, until it meets his other one at my waist.

"To be honest…" Conor takes a deep breath in and as he releases it, he takes a step back until his hands drop at his sides. "I'm not sure I can think right now."

I choke and cough. If the color of his face is anything to go by, the kiss affected him just as much.

"Um." I clear my throat. "Here's the deal, I'm not as bad a blusher as you are so I'll go tell the hotel employee that we have an emergency and you sneak out the back, okay?"

His chest works harder for oxygen even than mine. "Good idea. I'll, uh, wait for you in the truck."

"You do that." I turn quickly and hurry down the hallway in the middle of the tables, but something makes me stop. I glance at him over my shoulder. Conor's still standing in the middle of the stage, his glasses on one hand and the other one running down his face. When it's visible again, it somehow seems redder than before.

I did that. I kissed my former foe under the mistletoe and made it impossible for him to walk out in public.

I slam my hand against my aching lips to contain a squeal.

CHAPTER 13
CONOR

"Well, this got out of hand," I whisper at my reflection in the rearview mirror where half of my blood has collected.

As agreed, I'm waiting in my pickup and no matter how I sit, I can't seem to cool my face down. Or the rest of my body. And okay, she saw how into her I was, so whatever. It happens. I'm a man who is into women, with a special focus on the complicated ones. The real problem is that I need to make the drive back to work as comfortable as possible, because otherwise she's going to freak out.

And with reason. We're just coworkers after all. That kiss shouldn't even have happened.

I turn the heating off and roll the windows down. Surely the cold will help. Hopefully.

I drop my head back on the headrest and close my eyes. Sierra felt so perfect in my arms, like a lock and key that are an exact match. It doesn't matter that I almost had to pick her up from the floor to kiss her properly—she gives back as good as she gets and shit, she was really into it. Just as much as I was. The sounds she made, the taste of her mouth…

I groan and then choke in my own saliva when I remember what she said about that.

"Conor, you asshole. You're not helping yourself."

I rub my forehead. I better get my shit together real quick because she'll get in my car any second now.

"Think about bad things," I tell myself. "Stepping on a puddle in your socks. A puck to the teeth. Not getting a ten thousand dollar bonus and the promotion…" It almost feels like it's starting to work until Sierra's figure appears in the parking lot.

She's fully decked in winter gear and all I can see is her pink nose above her scarf, her dark eyes fixed on my truck, and a mass of wild—and extremely soft—curls that escape from under her beanie. That's it. And it's enough for my hormones to go *hello again*.

Quick, I take off my glasses and close my eyes tight because maybe if I don't see her, I can stop fantasizing. But then she opens the passenger door and her scent invades my nose again. I casually prop my elbow on the door and rub my face as she hoists herself into the car.

"Okay, I decided to put on my big girl pants and told the clerk the truth. She took it surprisingly well." Sierra twists on the seat to buckle up. "But as I was talking with her, I had a horrible realization."

"Huh? What."

She was able to think about anything other than the fact that we just ate each other's mouths?

Sierra takes what I feel is too dramatic a pause before speaking. "Wait, why do you have the windows down? It's freezing here."

I mumble something incoherent because I'm not about to explain when clearly I'm the only one who is still hot and bothered. Maybe this kiss wasn't a big deal to her, which—fair. It was just mistletoe, not like I took her on a date with the intent of starting something. Shit, even if I had, it's her prerogative whether she feels anything for me or not.

And who do I think I am? For a moment there my head really took off by itself, huh? Why the hell would Sierra get all shaken by me? I'm the most awkward turtle I know. I sure didn't rock Nikki's world enough for her to stay with me, and Sierra's a far cooler woman. She's hardworking, honest even if it hurts, and decisive. The entire opposite of my ex.

Snorting softly, I crank up the heat until Sierra stops shivering. I don't need the cold anymore. I just cooled my jets without help.

"So, what's the horrible realization?" My voice comes out raspy, as if that part of my anatomy had yet to recover. I clear my throat slightly.

Sierra picks up the conversation without missing a beat. "Well, you know how we keep talking about booth this, booth that?"

"Yeah?"

"Conor, we don't have any booths."

I stop firmly at the stop sign, partially because I have to and also so I can look at her. "Shit."

"Right."

"Uhh, how many do we need?"

After pausing to count with her gloved fingers, she says, "At least six but maybe more. It depends on how many food and beverage stations we need."

"And they'd be pretty big too, so I'm not sure how long each would take to make."

"Yeah, pretty big." But she says this while looking out of the window. "Tell you what, divide and conquer. I'll look for the DJ and you take care of the booths."

"Why do I feel like I got the short end of the stick?"

Sierra sighs. "Fine, whoever finishes first can help the other one. Besides, we'll both have to put equal elbow grease into the props."

"Are we, uh, still working on those at my place?"

Silence.

Great job, sucker, you just made it real awkward.

I'm about to repeat Richard's words that we have to keep everything a surprise but remix them with the new tune of and-there's-no-mistletoe-in-my-cottage-so-no-shenanigans-will-happen, which I'm *sure* is going to reassure her and not make this silence heavier at all.

"Yep." Sierra pops the p extra hard. "No way we're doing this at my parents's." I feel her laser beams turn to me.

"That's okay, we definitely don't want to inconvenience them."

"How come you're not weirded out that I still live with my parents like everybody else?"

I shrug. "I moved back in with Gramps right after the accident and only bought my property after I started working at *SPORTY*. Everybody has their circumstances."

"It's a culture thing. My parents will only let me leave the house when I'm happily married to someone they approve of." She chuckles under her breath. "Joke's on them, I don't have enough money to rent out on my own either."

"Eh, being on your own isn't what it's cracked up to be." And since that makes me sound a tad too pitiful, I add, "You have to clean and cook all by yourself, and even have to chop your own wood, you know?"

"Oh, I've already been doing that since I was a kid, both of my parents work like horses. It's why that promotion would really make a difference for me... I'd go from doing chores in one house for three people, to one apartment for one."

We're pulling into *SPORTY's* parking lot and I wait until I park the truck at an available spot before opening my mouth.

"Yeah, sorry. I'm not giving up on the promotion. I have my own plans for the extra pay."

She lets out that throaty laugh of hers. "Fine, I thought I'd at least try."

I turn off the car and welcome the freezing cold air outside, inhaling it into my lungs. It still doesn't smell like ice, though, so we'll have to wait some more for the first snow.

Sierra's already walking ahead of me through the parking lot and I catch up quickly with my longer strides. "So…" I trail off for a moment. "Are we starting this weekend, then?"

"We should." Sierra nods. "Which means we have to get the equipment from Camila Puig ASAP."

We both cringe.

Listen, I'm all for powerful women. Heaven knows how attracted I am to the one walking beside me in this frozen parking lot. However, Camila is a step over that. She's fear in stilettos—as in she induces fear and could stab you with her stilettos for saying the wrong thing in her presence. I have no doubt that she'll be CEO in a couple of years, and make *SPORTY* the top athletic brand in the whole galaxy in just as long.

My plan of a long and happy career is to not incur her wrath.

"Tag, you're it," I say.

"No way. We're both doing that one toge—" But she finishes the word in a yelp.

My body reacts before I even realize what's happening. Or I guess I saw the signs during the walk and my amygdala's taking care of the rest.

I pivot on my heels and stretch out my arm. Sierra lands on it instead of the hard asphalt, as she would have if she'd been all alone when she slipped. I wrap my other arm around her to fully stop her momentum. Her face's scrunched up, waiting for a painful impact and when it doesn't come, she cracks one eye open to find my face right above hers.

"You okay?" I ask.

Her other eye pops open too. She blinks hard. "Um. Thank you. Yes."

I hold her tighter against me to avoid any chance of slipping again and haul her back to her feet. "Careful, it's slippery," I say with a chuckle.

She smacks my chest.

Still grinning, I pull away and this actually puts us in the same position as when we were about to kiss under the mistletoe. Maybe Sierra's realized the same because her eyes catch on my mouth and my muscles tense. But then she's stepping back and checking the ground.

"Well, hopefully I make it to the building in one piece now." Another laugh, this time an awkward one.

"Right. Yeah."

I hang back a pace or two to watch out for her, and also because I don't want her to see that my face is flaming up again. Is this going to be my life now? One kiss from the woman and now every time she's near, my face is going to give me away?

"Hey, I have something to do. You go ahead," I mumble once we're in the lobby.

She casts a glance over her shoulder and nods. "Sure, take your time."

I do. I take as much time as I need to behave. It includes washing my face with freezing cold water three times and taking a walk around the whole building. By the time I make it to the marketing team, I'm no longer at risk of being pulled into the infirmary.

Richard calls out from his office. "Ah, Conor. We were waiting for you."

We? And then I notice Sierra standing beside him, and

they're the only ones in the office right now. She motions at me to hurry with her hand, which makes me think this must be about the event. I jog the rest of the way and stop before our boss' desk.

"Sierra here was telling me that you guys still haven't found a decent venue, which works out with the news I have."

She and I exchange a glance and I say, "Oh?"

"I explained the situation to Martin and we definitely can't set up your grandfather's rink as a vendor in our system because it's a conflict of interest."

I can feel Sierra still looking at me but I don't know how to react to this.

Richard keeps talking. "However, we found a loophole."

My heart kicks a little, just like it does when I'm starting a morning run. Or like it did when Sierra pulled me down to kiss her.

"Yeah?" I stuff my hands in my joggers, aiming for casual disinterest and probably fooling no one.

"We can use the community contribution payment category, and it'd be well justified. I did a little research and Conrad's Rink has been a landmark of this town's history, even produced our very first professional hockey player here present."

"Former," I mutter.

"Anyway, Martin thinks it makes it extra special around the holiday, so congratulations lady and gentleman, you have found yourselves a venue."

"Great, I'll just use my lunch break now to talk with the owner." I try my hardest not to smile but fail.

"You do that. And get a fair price out of him too."

I'm not sure if he means fair to my grandfather or to the company. Although I guess the definition of fair would be both ways.

That doesn't matter. I do my best not to vibrate with excitement as I trace my steps back to the elevator. Even if it's a one-time thing, I'm sure this will make Gramps rethink closing down the place.

*

"No."

My eyes bulge. Gramps stands by his desk and I do the same opposite to him, which is probably a good thing because he looks like he may wring my neck otherwise.

"What do you mean *no*?"

"It's the easiest word in the planet, kid. That particular letter combination means it's not gonna happen."

"Gramps." I lean over his desk and rest my hands against it. "A large sum of money will fall right on this desk. It will help us work through a good chunk of the overdue bills. It'd be a great start to a new revenue stream of private events, which in turn will help us hire more temps so you don't have to do everything by yourself. We might even"—I take a deep breath—"replace the geriatric Zamboni that makes a whirring sound when it runs."

"That Zamboni belongs in a junkyard, just like me. I want to retire."

"But—"

"No, you try working for sixty four years and have a young buck come tell you that you can't retire."

"I'm not saying you can't retire, Gramps. I'm just saying the place doesn't have to close down when you do."

"I want to close it down!" I reel back because Gramps never yells, and yet that's exactly what's happening. "I'd raze it to the ground if I could and then pour kerosene on every damn pile of debris and burn it to ashes."

My mouth opens. "What?"

Huffing, he lowers himself slowly until he plops the rest of the way on his chair. "This is where I taught you everything about hockey and made you dream big, and it's no replacement for the dream I put in your head. It's best if it disappears altogether."

"So this is my fault." I bark the words and it makes him look up. "You closing this place and ruining a bunch of little kids's dreams because I lost mine is *sure* to make me feel better, huh?"

And there it is, the ugliness that had been brewing between us that neither wanted to face.

I pick myself back up and shake my head. "I don't care if this makes me a coward, but I'm going to remove myself from this conversation before I say something a lot damn spicier than that. Call me when you change your mind."

Gramps doesn't stop me on my way out. And he also doesn't call me back.

CHAPTER 14
SIERRA

I freaking love my job. *SPORTY* is literally paying me to listen to music right now—and not just any good jam trending on Spotify, but Christmas music.

So far I've found two solid candidates who make the wildest remixes to Christmas classics that sound like club bangers until you pay attention. One's Boston based and the other from New York, and I've already emailed them asking for rates and availability. But no matter who pans out, they just secured themselves a new fan.

I'm shimmying my shoulders when Conor walks into the office, and two bizarre things happen at the same time. First, that even though I'm partying at my desk, I somehow light up like a Christmas tree at the sight of his face. I'd argue it's because I'm excited to hear news about the venue but I'm not in the business of gaslighting myself. I can confirm that Conor Mahoney is officially out of my naughty list, and I never thought that would happen.

But then I notice the other thing. And that is his face. It's not arranged in the normal way.

Okay, his nose is still in the middle and all that. But

normally Conor's face is the textbook definition of happy, all shiny eyes and easy smiles that I used to take as a personal attack. The man plopping at his seat across me looks like he's about to punch something. Or cry. He's definitely screamed, at least.

I pause my happy music and remove my headset. How do you ask the guy who was your former work nemesis if he's okay?

"Yo, dude. You look like you fought a bull," Stephen says casually while munching on chips from a crinkly bag in an annoying way. Or maybe I'm just annoyed that he could get straight to the point without overthinking.

Conor doesn't answer right away. Sighing, he pulls at his red scarf from one end until it unwinds from his neck. After tossing it on his desk, he removes his glasses and rubs his eyes with the most exhausted sigh I've ever heard from him.

What the heck happened?

First he gets the kiss of his lifetime from yours truly, and I'm not exaggerating. I know he was into it because that heavy blush didn't lie—I've never seen him do that. Then after that, he got the great news that we can use his grandpa's rink and he went on his way to get the sweet old man on board. Nothing in his expression right now would make me infer any of these things actually happened today.

Conor jams his glasses back in place and pins a hard stare on me. "Sierra, can we please have a word?"

"Ohh." Stephen puts a handful of chips in his mouth and crunches loudly, watching like he expects a MMA fight.

One by one, our colleagues turn their attention to us. Lewis is on a call but you'd think someone stripped naked in the middle of the office with the way his eyes sparkle at the poten-tial drama. Next to me, Rachel stops scribbling something on her planner and scrunches her nose at me in that way I know means she's wondering if I'm okay. From the opposite corner,

Kayla glances between Conor and I like this is a tennis match, even though no barbs are being exchanged. Dave is still home sick.

Meanwhile, I'm racking my brain to figure out what I could've possibly done wrong—today, I mean. He wouldn't randomly get upset at the million ways I've wronged him in the past two years.

Well, whatever it is, we don't need an audience.

I push away from my desk and say, "Let's find a conference room."

"Yeah, good idea."

I try not to focus on how his muscles flex while he removes his jacket. Thankfully, I have to keep walking around him towards the meeting rooms hallway, or else the gossipmongers would catch me drooling over Conor.

Man's more than fine, what can I say. I wasn't even immune when I thought I hated him.

He sighs behind me several more times until we lock ourselves in a meeting room. I whirl around to face him with my arms folded. "Okay, what's wrong?"

Is it the kiss? It has to be the kiss. He probably regrets it. My mouth goes dry at the concept and I have to work my throat several times until I'm able to swallow.

If he does regret it, it's going to be real hard to pretend like I'm cool about it. Because I'm not. In fact, it's the entire oppo-site—I'm still very hot about it. If he wanted to kiss me again right now I wouldn't care that the meeting room walls are iced out glass panes.

"Gramps doesn't want to do it."

"Huh?" What? Kiss me? I also don't want to—*Oh.* "Oh, shit."

"Yeah." Conor rubs the back of his neck and avoids my gaze like it burns. "He just won't listen, old curmudgeon that he is."

Ugh, I can feel things rising to my head. Embarrassment at what my previous train of thought was, and also a headache.

As I massage my temples, I say offhand, "I don't get it, he doesn't seem that bad."

"Yeah, well. Maybe you should've been the one to ask him." Conor hangs his head and leans back against the glass wall. "I had a feeling this could happen and yet… So basically, it's all my fault."

"Wait, wait. I need you to backtrack and like, fill in all the blanks for me."

Another extremely pained sigh and then… "Gramps wants to close the rink."

You could hear a pin drop.

"Um, why?" I cringe because his body language screams that this is personal. However, this is also about our project—our bonuses. Grammie being able to spend Christmas with us, getting medical treatments and quality prescriptions. Me being able to hug her with all my might and giving her all the presents she deserves.

He runs a hand through his hair and it gets all spiky and messy. "It's complicated. The finances haven't been working out for a while but he refuses to do something about it. Like this kind of event could be a legit new revenue stream, you know?"

"Absolutely. I'm pretty sure I've watched only a million holiday movies with skating dates and family events at skate rinks, and all that. Why not corporate parties too?"

"Right. Thank you!" He gestures with his hands before slumping again. "But that's not the real reason. *I'm* the reason."

When all he does is frown, I say, "Words, Conor."

"He thinks it's a constant reminder of… you know." He waves a big hand around the air. "The career I lost and all that."

I suck in air.

Conor starts gesturing bigger the more he talks. "But it doesn't, and that's what he doesn't get. I *love* teaching kids how to play hockey. I want them to succeed way past what I ever achieved. Why do they have to get their dreams destroyed so early because of me? Like, how would that ever make me happy? Make it make sense."

His speech ends in him huffing and puffing, his cheeks pink and eyes flashing with temper.

Um. As we say in Spanish: adorable.

"I have a proposal for you."

"I'm all ears." He lifts a hand to rub his stomach. "And frustration."

I press my lips against the smile that starts to form, because he's still so wound up about this and I don't want him to think I'm mocking him.

"What if I try talking with him?"

Conor's eyebrows rise a notch. His lips part another notch —and I zero in on them. I wonder if they'd still taste of coffee.

Wait, he's moving them.

"You'd do that?"

"I mean…" I clear my throat and wrap a hand around my elbow, squeezing hard enough to remind me that maybe kissing him again, ever, especially here, might not be such a bright idea. "At least about the event. I can't promise I'll convince him to keep the rink open forever."

"Right. Of course." Then one corner of those perfectly shaped lips of his rises. "Joke's on him, though. With the bonus and the promotion money, I'll save the rink."

"Ah, so that's why you're doing this?" I shake my head. "It's very sweet, but I have my own list of reasons for getting that promotion."

"I know. But if there's no venue, then there's no event, and no one's getting a promotion."

"And that's why I'm going to get your Gramps on board, nothing else." I poke him in the chest.

I freeze as he wraps his hand around mine and grins down at me. "Thanks, partner."

"Ah, yeah. Sure."

I walk back to my desk on shaky legs. Someone should tell him that he has a lethal one-two combo between that smile and his touch.

*

Conrad Mahoney, or Gramps as he prefers to be called, is stunned to find my head popping in from his office door. He opens and closes his mouth, eyes squinting up at me like he thinks I'm a mirage.

"Is this the pretty miss I met at my grandson's?"

Who can resist this charm?

Grinning, I straighten myself and stand by the door. "The one and only. How are you doing, Gramps?"

"Well, certainly much better now than a second ago. Please come in and pull up a chair." He gets up from his with enviable agility I don't even have now, and starts fussing about. "I'm just sorry the place is such a mess. I'd have tied it up if I knew you were coming."

There's a worn sofa pushed up against a wall, but every surface of it is covered in books, magazines—and I spot a *SPORTY* one with his grandson's handsome face on the cover—and paper sheets of different sizes and shades of yellow. The actual chair across his desk has a stack of binders that he tries to pick up at once. His huffs tell me they're heavy, so I rush over to help.

"Now, take a seat and tell me why you're brightening my dinky office."

I snort a laugh.

Gramps is funny. His voice has a harsh quality to it, as if he were permanently stuck in annoyed mode. But his eyes are bright and his wit is quick. I can see where Conor got his own sense of humor that he uses to diffuse every awkward situation with.

The chair creaks under my weight, which just serves to remind me of what Conor revealed earlier at the office. He's doing all this to save this place, that's how much he cares about it.

"I hated Conor for two years," I say, realizing a second later how that would make no sense to Gramps. "Or, okay. I didn't *hate* hate him. I was just generally very annoyed by his presence and how our boss basically bent over backwards for him from the beginning. I was jealous."

He lifts up his gray beanie and scratches the top of his head through a mass of white hair. "I'm not following, pretty miss."

"But then," I continue as if there hadn't been a pause. "Our boss forced us to start working together to organize the Christmas party for the company. It's only been what, like two weeks? And that's literally how long it's taken me to undo two years worth of resenting him for no reason.

"Your grandson's a really good person." I shrug. "I couldn't imagine a better teacher for little kids and I haven't even seen him in action."

He grunts. "Did he send you over to give me this pitch?"

"No, that's just a freebie for both of your sakes. Here's my real pitch." I smile. "We really need your help to make this company event happen. A nice bonus for each of us, and a promotion for one of us, is on the line."

"How nice?"

"Nice enough that I'll be able to fly my grandmother in from Venezuela for Christmas and maybe pay for some of her medical treatments, too. She has hypertension and it's been getting worse."

I bite my lip. Crap, it may sound like I'm laying it too thick but it's all the unvarnished truth.

A few days after breaking the news didn't go as well as I expected, Grammie and I had a chat. She had to think about it really hard, because flying to another country—one where she doesn't even speak the language—sounds stressful enough to drive her hypertension through the roof. But losing the chance to see us would be much worse for her heart.

So it's a done deal, she's coming for Christmas. And even if we fail at putting together this event, I'll carry the credit card debt for a year if I have to. But I'd rather not, so here we are.

"Well." His chair croaks even louder as he leans back and laces his fingers over his belly. "Did he tell you why I refused?"

"Yes."

"And what do you think about that?"

"Not my business, really," I respond honestly.

Gramps barks a hacking laugh that startles me. "I like you, pretty miss. You're a breath of fresh air."

I tilt my head and offer a sweet smile. "Does liking me mean you'll let us use the place for the *SPORTY* event, at least? It's up to you two to hash out the rest, not me."

"Yes, but on one condition."

"Oh?" I fold my hands neatly over my lap, trying not to scratch my head through my own beanie as if that could help me figure out the condition in advance.

"That you join my hardheaded grandson and I for dinner tonight."

Funny, Conor called Gramps a curmudgeon. Gramps calls him hardheaded. Clearly they're cut from the same cloth. And clearly they'd kill for each other.

How sweet.

"Hmm." I tap my chin. "What if I already have plans?"

"Then no *SPORTY* party."

"Good thing I had no plans." Chuckling, I stand up and offer my hand. "Deal."

Gramps shakes it with surprising strength, and that's when I notice the particular glint in his eyes. Like somehow he's the one who has won the bargain, and I can't figure out how.

CHAPTER 15
CONOR

Two texts and a phone call to Sierra have fallen into a black hole. Fortunately, I'm a man of some sense—not a lot, let's not go overboard—and guess that I have no right to blow up her phone just to satisfy my curiosity. But she's the only one right now who could tell me whether this event will live or die, because it's not like Gramps and I are on speaking terms right now.

It's when I'm driving home at the end of the day when my phone finally buzzes. I'm stopped at a red light so I take a quick peek, and it's not Sierra. It's none other than my grandfather himself texting me.

Be home for dinner at seven sharp.

Huh?

I check the time on the dashboard and snort. How can he text that when it's five minutes till?

Once the light turns green, I take a right and change course for Gramps's neighborhood. He still lives in the house I grew up in, not too far from Sierra's. I hope she's okay. Like, I don't really have a significant baseline since, well, we've only started communicating a few weeks ago. But after we legit started working together, we've had a timely back and forth and this is odd.

What if she got into an accident? What if she never even reached the rink?

I park haphazardly by the curb of my childhood home and walk in the door exactly five minutes after the hour. "Gramps? Did Sierra come see you at the rink? She's not responding and I'm worried."

"You're late," he grouches from the kitchen, followed by the sound of pots banging.

I round the corner and freeze at the entrance to the kitchen.

It's only in this moment, as I take in the strangest scene I've ever witnessed with my own three eyes, that I realize I'm huffing and puffing and that my heart beats a mile per second. I can finally rest assured that Sierra's fine because she's in my Gramps's kitchen. And I can guess this is also why she couldn't respond earlier, because her hands are busy stirring the contents of a pot.

What's more shocking is that she's wearing matching Christmas aprons with Gramps, emblazoned with two merry snowmen drinking what appears to be cups of eggnog. And they're frilly, too. The ruffles don't look half bad climbing up Sierra's shoulders, but Gramps's face is almost getting drowned in the things.

I'm not even conscious of plucking my phone from my pocket and snapping a picture. Or ten.

"Hey—"

I interrupt Gramps. "Can someone tell me what the hell is happening here?"

"Watch that mouth of yours, kid." Gramps places his hands on his hips.

I press my lips hard to not laugh but some of it escapes. Sierra glances at me over her shoulder with the most curious smile. It makes me forget what I was thinking about. "Sorry, I looked at your texts but I haven't been able to answer. As you can see, I'm more than okay."

I turn away and hope my beard and scarf hide the blush creeping up my neck. "Good. That's—No worries. So, I suppose it went well?"

"Yes, I accomplished what you couldn't in a matter of seconds." Her dark eyes twinkle with competitive spirit.

Gramps grunts. "It helps that she's much easier to talk to."

Or to look at? Because if so, yes. If she really set her mind to it, she could scam me out of the clothes off my back. I definitely wouldn't mind that.

Clearing my throat, I unzip my jacket and start unwinding my scarf. "What can I help with?"

"Wash your paws and set the table," says Gramps, but since he's taken over the sink washing something, I change tack toward my bathroom.

I need a moment to process this bizarre twist, so I take my sweet ass time washing what Gramps described as paws. My glasses are foggy from a day's worth of dirt, so might as well wash them too. Not because I'm avoiding seeing Sierra and Gramps be all happy and familiar together, or all the weird things that's making me feel. Like I could get used to that sight. Like I want it to be a normal occurrence.

Nah, not at all. No one's freaking out here or anything.

I dry my hands with a towel and snatch a couple of tissues from the box to lightly pat my glasses dry. My first year with glasses taught me a lot. First, that you can't treat prescription glasses like they're hockey helmet visors, or they break. Second, that those fancy cleaning cloths they come with take too long to dry compared to how frequently glasses get dirty. Third, that rubbing them with paper will scratch them—but patting is okay. Just have to be gentle.

I'm in the middle of this operation when I walk back out

into my childhood bedroom and find my coworker standing there.

"Whoa!" I startle and jump back, which makes my glasses slip. I catch them mid air, sparing myself from an uncomfortable drive home with bad vision. "Um, Sierra. What are you doing here?"

"Gramps sent me. He said it'd be interesting to see where you grew up, and you know what? He's not wrong." She's still wearing that funny apron and it just serves to stress how none of this makes sense.

"Uh…" I ball up the damp tissue in my hand and put my glasses back on. "Anything interesting, then?"

"So many things. For example, this. When was this?" She points at a picture tacked onto a cork board that hangs over my desk, where I used to half-ass my homework. I step closer behind her and a big sigh empties my chest when I see which one.

"First grade." I wrinkle my nose. I'm six years old in the picture, grinning up at the camera like I had no concerns in the world, even though I was missing the entire front row of my teeth. Both of my parents held each of my hands, and although you can't see him, Gramps was there too. He's the one who took the picture.

Sierra chuckles and it's like bells and twinkling lights, hot cocoa with marshmallows and a snuggly blanket, all in sound version. "That's a lot of teeth to be gone at the same time."

"I stopped a puck with my mouth, it's how I learned that I didn't want to be a goalie," I respond with a thick voice. Will it be weird if I clear my throat? I'll just try to swallow down the weird feeling.

"Um." She turns her face to me, biting that perfect lower lip of hers. "Can I ask you what happened to them?"

I'm close enough to feel the heat of her body radiating against my arms. I can inhale the scent of her shampoo and the smell of food that clings to that damn apron. Sierra Fernandez is in my childhood bedroom, asking me personal things like she's curious about what makes me *me*.

"Traffic accident," I respond after a moment. "Just a couple of months after that picture was taken."

"Oh, Conor. I'm sorry." She lifts her hand to find mine, and gives it one squeeze before dropping it.

Shit. What if I want her hand in mine for longer than that?

"Thanks. It was a long time ago and I uh, don't remember them very well." I rub my neck just to get rid of the feeling of her hand squeezing mine.

"You really look like both of them though." She studies them for a moment. "You have your mom's hair color and her smile—with teeth, of course. But adult you looks so much like your dad."

"Yeah." I smile a little, because I hadn't laid eyes on this picture in a long while. But she's right, I have both of my parents faces in mine. "I guess that means I'll look just like Gramps when I'm old."

"Not a bad prospect." Sierra snorts. "You wouldn't believe the amount of old ladies I caught checking him out when we went to the supermarket earlier."

"How did that even happen?" I shake my head. "Actually, how did you even get him on board?"

Sierra clasps her hands at her back and pivots to face me. "It wasn't hard and I'm not bragging. I just explained what's riding on this for both of us."

I scratch my beard, analyzing her. "Clearly, my reasons weren't the ones that convinced him. What are you doing all this for, Sierra?"

"My grandmother." Her eyes soften, lips stretch into a soft smile. "She lives back in our home country and her health isn't getting any better. I want to share at least this Christmas with her, if only once."

"So it's not because of an apartment?"

She has the decency to turn sheepish. "No."

"You lied." I narrow my eyes.

"Kinda? I'd like to have my own place one day, but it's not the main reason why I'm after this bonus and the promotion."

"That makes sense," I say softly even as I fold my arms. "But you still lied. Why?"

"I didn't trust you." Sierra admits this openly. "I didn't know you."

"And now?"

"I'm getting to know you." Her eyes sweep around us, to the faded posters of Gretzky and Dryden, the medals and ribbons nailed to the walls without order, the bookshelf leaning under the weight of books, gear, and old toys, to the tiny bed I hated during my teenage years. "And very closely, at that."

I swallow hard. I want to ask her if she wants to learn more. If she's liking what she's found so far. But something holds me back.

I've never been the smoothest talker with women. That kind of talent comes from self-confidence, and I've always lacked something in that department. Whether it was my upbringing, or the fact that I was a good player but not the cream of the crop, also not the most good looking guy in the room, and smart but not about to win awards for that either. In just a few short weeks, Sierra has seen everything about me, all of my shortcomings and everything I've lost. Not to mention that we've been cat and dog for two years. I can't imagine she'd want anything with me.

So, I clamp my mouth tight and don't ask, even if curiosity will be gnawing a hole through my stomach later tonight.

But it's like she's gone and read my mind, because all of a sudden she says, "You're a good person, Conor Mahoney. I'm sorry I didn't see that before."

My mouth opens.

"Hey, are you up to no good in there, or why is Conor not setting the table?" Gramps yells from the hallway, as if he didn't dare approach any closer.

Sierra and I jump away from each other as if we had been, in fact, up to scandalizing shenanigans.

"I'm—Um. Can I just use your restroom for a second?" Sierra pushes a curl behind her ear.

"Yes, of course. I'll—I'll go set the damn table."

"Hah, yeah."

"Yeah…"

We both pivot in opposite directions at the same time. I make a whole racket as I stride toward the kitchen, hoping Gramps knows who exactly is coming.

"Gramps," I hiss anyway. "What the heck was that?"

"Well, you never know. Two attractive young people alone in a room?" He starts chuckling in his usual raspy way and then stops. "You do find her attractive, right?"

I frown. "What kind of question is that?"

"Well, she's very different from that ex of yours."

"Whoa, okay. My head's spinning here." I lean a hand on the table and massage my forehead with the other one. "Are you by any chance trying to matchmake me with my coworker?"

"I knew there was a brain in that thick skull of yours."

I growl. "Gramps, she's my coworker. It would be inappropriate to—"

"Not if she also wants to—"

"Not to mention," I say a little louder to drown his voice. "She all but hated me for years."

"Past tense. You did learn what that means in school, right?" He blows on a spoon loaded with stew and takes a careful bite. "Besides, she cooks really damn well. You should've seen how fast she chops vegetables."

"Yeah, well. I think she said both of her parents work so she grew up pretty self sufficient."

"Sounds leaps and bounds better than that spoiled Nikki of yours."

I lower my voice. "Can you please stop comparing them? It's just not gonna happen."

"Not with that attitude. Listen to me, kid. If you don't want to grow into an old lonely bat, you should open your eyes and really see what you have standing right in front of you."

I clench my jaw and run a hand through my hair.

I see it, alright. I have three eyes that combined work pretty freaking well. Sierra is amazing—smart as a whip, true to herself, hotter than the center of the sun.

"Let's just drop it, okay?"

"You can't keep running away when things get hard, Conor." And with that, he's turned it around to our earlier fight. "You have to try and it's okay if you fail. That won't kill you, will it?"

"What are we talking about right now? Sierra or the conversation from before?"

"Both." He jerks a thumb towards the hallway. "That girl didn't beat around the bush to get what she wanted. Learn from her."

I frown. "Even if what I want isn't what you want?"

"Yeah." Gramps sighs heavily. "If that will make you happy, then fight me tooth and nail. We wouldn't have reacted so big before if you hadn't avoided the topic for so long." He pauses for a second. "But then, I wouldn't have met the future mother of my grandkids."

I groan. "Gramps, if you say anything weird in front of her over dinner, I will kick you out of your own house."

"In this weather?" He puts a hand on his chest, as if offended.

"Gramps…" I growl his moniker in warning.

"Fine, but move a little faster. I don't have decades for you to waste gathering your nerve to ask her out."

That's when steps echo down the hallway and a second later, Sierra appears. "Whoa, why is the table not set yet?"

"I'm coming." I give Gramps one last warning look, and pull up a drawer to collect utensils.

CHAPTER 16
SIERRA

Conor's hair is silky soft. I could run my fingers through it all day long and in fact, am considering it in the middle of the office because of a strand that's arched over his forehead. It's been tempting me since the start of the phone call I'm in, discussing terms with the DJ we're hiring for the event. The good news is that our desks are pretty wide. If Conor was sitting closer, I'm pretty damn sure I'd have embarrassed myself already.

His beard's surprisingly soft, too, not at all what I'd have expected. I looked up potential reasons online and concluded that Conor must oil it up and maintain it with way more effort than most guys. Which checks out—guy has a fine work ethic and I appreciate that. I'd also appreciate the feeling of his beard against my skin again.

"—So excited to work with you," the DJ from New York says into my earpiece.

"Yes, likewise!" My voice sounds so shrill that half of my coworkers turn to look. I duck my face and lower my tone. "Well, I'll email you the contract in a minute and once you return it, we'll be all set."

"Fantastic. Thank you so much for the opportunity. This is gonna be bomb."

Being bomb, bueno. Bombing, no bueno. There's no room for error here.

After some more pleasantries, we hang up and I take a moment to gather myself. It's like dinner last night with Conor and his grandfather has unlocked something in me. I already knew I was attracted to the man because I'm not in the business of lying to myself, but now it's something else. I can't stop looking at him. Purposely keeping myself at a decent distance feels like nails on chalkboard. I want to spend more time with him—but without the prying eyes around us.

Sighing, I take out my earpieces just as a notification pops up on my screen. Fifteen minutes for our meeting with Camila Puig, Rachel's mentor.

I look up and find Conor's attention already on me. "Ready?" he asks.

Nope. I'm not ready for all of this. It's not like I planned on being single forever or anything, but my priority has been work, work, and more work. Dating won't make me money or help my family—that's all on me.

But that was easy to say when I didn't have anyone in my sights. Conor has been sitting in front of me for two years and I didn't *see* him. I pretended like he wasn't even there. I think Rachel was right that it wasn't simply that I disliked him because I was professionally jealous of him. I was afraid of him. That this could happen. That I'd develop a crush on him.

Well, it's happening, all right.

"Sure," I answer with an airy voice and grab my coat from the backrest of my chair.

"Say hi to Cam for me," Rachel says without pausing a beat from typing an email.

"Cam?" I ask.

"That's how people close to her call her."

Everything in Conor's expression screams *no way*. I doubt Camila Ice Queen Puig has anyone that would fall under that definition too.

"Right..." I elongate the word with a healthy dose of skepticism.

Clear across the office, Richard stops minding the copy machine to say, "Good luck, guys. Don't let her intimidate you."

"Ha ha." Conor stuffs his hands in the pockets of his joggers and murmurs, "Easy for him to say."

"Remember," Kaylee says in a teasing tone. "Showing any weakness to predators is a sure-fire way to die."

Clearly, we shouldn't have asked Richard for help in getting an audience with Camila during the staff meeting earlier. But Conor and I have been trying with her assistant for one week and it just wasn't happening, yet our timeline keeps getting tighter and we really need the gifts that go in the ball pit. Logically, the next step was securing some goods fresh from the factory, for which we need Camila's help. She's the lead factory manager, after all.

Conor and I drag our feet toward the elevator. He presses the button and as we wait, says, "We need a game plan."

"I'm open to suggestions."

"A keyword for when we should just quit and run."

I snort. "Maybe I'll just trip you and escape on my own."

"That's fine. At least one of us should live to tell the tale."

The elevator dings and we step in. I reach over to press the ground floor button, but again he's faster and beats me to the punch.

"No, but seriously. How the hell are we going to succeed bypassing the purchasing process with Camila Puig?" he asks and I watch with such hyperfocus that it almost feels like he's moving in slow motion as he lifts a big hand of his, and combs his fingers through his silky soft hair. The skin between my fingers itches.

"Well, we just don't have time to put a normal internal order. It should be fine if we just buy a crate with the company credit card. The question is whether she'll even agree."

"It's Christmas, the season of giving, of being jolly—surely we can appeal to that?"

Slowly, I give him a side eye. "Does she seem the most festive person to you?"

Last year, Camila didn't go to Aspen with the rest of the company. Apparently, she worked the entire holidays through. The year before, she also didn't attend the annual bash although for a different reason. She was going to get married and then it didn't happen. Gossip ran rampant for weeks but no *SPORTY* employees had been invited anyway, so no one really had any idea why she didn't get hitched. I remember that the year before she did go—it was at a fancy hotel in downtown Boston and she dressed to the nines. Hollywood starlets would never. But she spent the whole night arguing with suppliers over the phone. I got too drunk for my first one, so I don't even know if she was there or not.

"My left pinky's more festive." One corner of Conor's lips rises and then he elbows me gently. "Tag, you're it."

I gasp at how my entire body flares to life just with that friendly touch, and pass it off as something else as I say, "Conor Mahoney, are you scared?"

"Oh, yeah. Big men feel fear, too."

I cock an eyebrow. "But you look strong enough to face a bear."

"I'd rather protect you from a bear than face Camila Puig."

Cálmate, I scream to my heart.

"Well, the good news is that you won't be alone," I say, pointing at myself. "Which also means I'll kill you if you abandon me to her."

"Hmm." Conor narrowing his eyes at me as he rubs his beard is doing things to me. "How about this, I just stand beside you looking pretty and you do the talking."

"So I do all the work?"

"And I give moral support."

"On one condition." I pause strategically and it reels him in, going by how he leans forward ever so slightly. "You deal with the carpenters for the booths on your own. I'm really not looking forward to that one."

"Deal." He stretches his hand out.

I wonder if I'm too eager because Conor startles at how quickly I grab it. Just as fast, I try to pull it away and he stops me.

"Hey, has no one told you that a business handshake has a specific duration?"

"Huh?" He could be saying the earth is flat and it wouldn't register in my mind right now.

"You always remove your hand too fast." Conor keeps my hand trapped in his without even pumping it. They're just frozen together midair. "It kinda makes the other party wonder if you're nervous or hiding something."

Yes and yes. And I'm obviously not about to admit it so if I can throw him off the scent, I'll happily let my hand live in his for as long as it takes.

"Fine, handshake master. How long is an acceptable handshake length?" I ask with sarcasm I don't feel at all.

He hums from deep in his throat and I find myself breaking into goosebumps all over. I don't know what is it about this guy's throaty sounds that immediately get me going.

"I'd say about twice as long as your usual."

"At this point, I'd say it's been about ten times that and it's starting to get awkward," I mumble, because I'm this close to using the link between us to pull him down for a kiss that would scandalize the security guys checking the cameras.

"I will release you now, since I believe my point has been made."

I steel myself against the delicious friction between the calluses of his hand against my skin, and let my hand fall limp at my side. "Thanks for the lesson, I guess."

"Sure, any time."

Does he mean it? I hope so. I'm sure there are so many other lessons he could teach me.

The elevator dings again and I realize this was simultaneously the slowest and fastest ride of my life. I almost wish for an electric outage just so I can accidentally get stuck with Conor for longer.

Alas, we march to the security desk where we sign up for an impromptu visit to the factory and receive yellow safety vests in return. We momentarily leave the warmth of the main building and take a very snippy walk outside to the converted hangar that is now *SPORTY*'s main factory.

"Oh my word, it's too freaking cold for there to be no snow."

"It's going to snow soon," Conor says from behind me with the calm of someone who is comfortable with this horrid weather.

"What? How do you know?"

"My nose." He taps it, as if I didn't know what one looks like. "I can smell the ice in the air."

"Huh, that's interesting. Could you also smell an abandoned bag of money laying around?"

Conor laughs. "I wish. That would solve both of our problems."

Instead, we have to face Camila. We make our way through the factory floor using the walking paths, checking this way or that for forklifts or hanging loads like we were instructed in the safety class that every *SPORTY* employee has to take yearly, per Camila's command.

Her assistant is in a phone call when we arrive to the office area and she waves us right in, like her boss is doing nothing but expecting us. I check my watch because if we're actually a second late, I'll run off on my own and leave Conor to deal with the consequences. But we're a few minutes early so, after exchanging a glance of mutual reassurance with him, I knock on Camila's door.

"Come in."

I take a bracing breath at the sharpness of her tone but promptly open the door. "Hi, Camila. May we come in?"

"I just bid you to do so."

Shit, she did. This is already going wrong.

Clearing my throat, I walk in and am glad to confirm that Conor does the same. "I'm Sierra Fernandez and this is Conor Mahoney, we—"

"I know who you are," the woman responds without looking up from her iPad. "You work with Rachel in Richard's team. Your email said you're organizing the company's Christmas party and want to talk about that. Get to the point."

Conor peels his eyes open and his shoulders rise as he tries to shrink. That reminds me that I can't do that if I want to get this manager's attention.

"About that. As you know, we received the assignment with a short lead time, which leaves us unable to follow the normal channels to purchase some goods from the factory. We would be extremely thankful if you approve the purchase of a crate of baseballs via company credit card rather than by purchase order."

She has surprisingly pretty eyes. They're a light brown that almost looks yellow, striking when paired with her dirty blonde hair. They're also striking fear through my heart as she asks, "And why would I do that?"

I'm so stumped that Conor decides to take over. "You're the only person who can approve this and save Christmas."

Short, sweet, maybe a bit too Hallmark for an audience so heartless.

Camila folds her arms delicately and leans back on her plush chair. "Now try that again with a business reason."

"Company morale," Conor spits out right away. "This is the top event every year and we can't put out something that feels incomplete."

"Sounds like your problem and not mine. Try again."

"We'd be forced to buy baseballs from the competition instead," I say, a bit embarrassed about how my voice shakes in the end.

"Now we're talking. We definitely can't have that." She picks up her iPad again, her long, perfectly manicured nails making tapping sounds as she types something. A second later, my phone buzzes in my back pocket. "There, approval sent. Now get out of my office."

"Thank you, ma'am," I say, and Conor salutes her but she's already focused on her screen and doesn't notice.

We're rushing out through the factory when I say, "Did you seriously just salute her?"

"Ugh." He cringes. "I couldn't stop my body from moving. She just gives eau du drill sergeant."

I bark a laugh but he's not wrong. "I don't know. I think I want to be like her when I grow up."

Conor scrunches up his face at my words and not at the gust of chilly air that's stabbing mine. "Why?"

"There aren't many women out there doing the thing and being taken seriously the way she is."

"I take you seriously," he says as he holds the door to the main building open for me, and the only reason I'm able to keep moving is to run from the cold. Otherwise, his words would've stopped me.

"Well, thanks," I mumble as I pass him, but my heart beats

so fast I'm sure that not only Conor can hear it, but the security guys all the way across the lobby too.

We do quick work of returning the vests and signing off from the factory visit, and the elevator trek back upstairs starts quiet. From the corner of my eye, Conor seems relaxed and not like he just said the sweetest words a guy has ever uttered in my direction.

And then something changes. He grows as still as a statue.

"What?" I ask.

He's blinking up at the ceiling. "We have a problem."

"Oh no. Did we forget something? I thought all we had left today was contracting the carpenters and starting the crafty part."

"It's not that. This problem is wrapped in a red ribbon."

"What?" I look up… and groan. "Not again." There's a handful of mistletoe hanging from the elevator ceiling, the ribbon pressed between the ceiling panels. "I'm sure HR will be *so* pleased about this."

"Was this even here a minute ago? I don't recall."

"Great, what if we got bad luck already because we didn't kiss before?"

"Shit, we don't need that before the event but…" Conor takes a step back—the opposite of what I expected. "We can't kiss again."

No barb Camila Puig threw my way hurt anywhere as much as this moment.

Conor all but fuses himself to the opposite corner in an attempt to put as wide a berth between us as possible.

Like, I get it, he can't fathom the idea of putting his mouth on mine again and that he'd rather earn a thousand years of bad luck or whatever. He doesn't need to be so theatrical about it.

A small wrinkle appears between his eyebrows as I also take a big step back until my back hits the wall and fold my arms.

"You're right, we absolutely can't. It's just not gonna happen again in a million years."

Self-preservation, baby. I'll deal with the crack in my heart later.

The elevator dings and as the doors open on our floor, I find Rachel waiting on the other side. She takes one look at us, frowns in confusion, and then glances up.

"Oh, you guys. It won't kill you to share a little peck."

A little peck?

Conor doesn't kiss like he doesn't mean it. In fact, he even asked me how I preferred to be kissed, which is a first. And I'd *never* prefer a peck. But knowing what I now know about him, even that would be enough to do me in.

"Did you put this thing here?" I grouch as I step out of the elevator and hold the doors open by keeping my hand on the sensor.

"No, it was Lewis. I think he was hoping for a different outcome."

Reaching up, Conor grabs the offending plant and tears it down, ribbon and all. "Fool, he should just use words instead of tricks."

"Totally." Rachel steps into the elevator and presses a button in the panel. Looking at Conor, she says, "Nothing sexier than a man who knows what he wants and goes for it."

As I move away and the doors start closing, a thought strikes me like a lightning bolt. Does that mean that if Conor isn't using either words or tricks on me, then it's a sign that he doesn't like me that way?

And fine, that's his prerogative. He's free not to reciprocate my feelings. But I'm also free to wish he did.

Mierda, what do I do now?

CHAPTER 17
CONOR

Something's not right, and it's not just because I can't get this damn felt wrapped around a baseball properly. Who came up with this garbage idea?

Ah, right. Us.

Sierra and I sit in my living room, or the disaster zone it has become. The coffee table between us is piled high with felt sheets in festive colors that we cut out to the size we need to wrap the baseballs with.

She makes a lot quicker work of it than me, just dropping a baseball in the middle of a felt square, gathering up the corners, and wrapping them with twine. Then she glues a strip of golden felt around the mess to make it look like the top of a Christmas tree ornament and you know what? It looks damn near perfect, whereas my creations look like a drunk kindergartner tried crafts for the first time.

But that's not the issue, I'll get the hang of it eventually. What's making a bead of sweat form on my forehead is Sierra.

It's like she's avoiding me, which is hard to do when she's at my house and there's literally no one else in a three mile radius.

"Hey, Sierra."

She flinches.

What the hell? Was my voice too loud?

I lower it to ask, "Can you please slow down for a second? I need to see it again."

She sighs, but starts from scratch slower. Snap, that's the part I was missing. I was just gathering up the felt corners and tying them, but she makes a quick twirl that really brings the felt together at the top. That trick I can definitely adopt. I can't mimmic the deftness of her smaller hands for this kinda stuff, though.

"Cool, thanks." I better pick up because she has a much bigger completed pile than I have.

For a while, the only sounds are the crackling fire consuming the logs in the fireplace, and the rustling of felt against our hands. I keep checking on her from the corner of my good eye, but she's so focused on what she's doing that it's almost like I'm not here at all. A little wrinkle appears between her eyebrows as she concentrates on tying up the twine. She bites the corner of her lip ever so slightly as she works and I have the most feral urge to lean over the coffee table and bite it for her.

I should've kissed her earlier in the elevator. The problem is, I was deathly afraid of my face not hiding consequences from our coworkers.

Focus on your baseballs, asshole, I say to myself.

"How many of these are we making?" I ask when I can't stand myself any longer.

Sierra hums from deep in her throat and I don't know why suddenly that sound makes me boneless. I have to make a conscious effort to keep sitting upright.

"I'd say we should fill that whole box. With use, the felt will start peeling off and making the balls too hard to latch onto the velcro tree."

"Makes sense. We do want people to win sometimes for it to be fun." I lean back against my couch. "How do we know this even works, though? Should we test it?"

Finally, for the first time since we started working on this, Sierra lifts her head and blinks up at me. "Oh, you're right. That's a good idea."

"Okay, to the shed." I smack my thighs and shift myself to stand. I pause at the door, grabbing my full winter gear because I'm pretty sure my nose hasn't lied to me. It's going to snow tonight and if not, pretty soon. The last thing I want is getting sick and leaving Sierra to pick up my slack so close to the freaking event.

Bundled up in scarves, beanies, gloves, and thick coats, we trudge through the gravel with the help of my camp flash-light. The frigid wind howls through the branches of the pines around them. Ahead of me, Sierra shivers and my free hand twitches. I stuff it in the pocket of my jacket to prevent it from reaching out again. I don't think she'd welcome me putting my arm around her, even if it's not for nefarious purposes.

"Hold this." I pass along the lantern to her so I'm the one working the latch and pushing the big door open.

Standing at the threshold, Sierra says, "Wait, this is kinda creepy. You didn't bring me here to murder me, right?"

"No, this isn't my murder barn. That one's deeper in the woods," I respond with a hefty dose of sarcasm.

With the weak light of the lantern, I locate the light switch and flip it on. The inside bathes in bright yellow light. There are a bunch of bags and boxes blocking the way to the massive velcro tree, and I push some of them out to the corner.

Meanwhile, Sierra turns off the lantern. "I admit it looks a lot less creepy now, thank you very much."

"Please, as if I'd ever hurt you." I'm only a teeny tiny bit hurt that she'd remotely consider that notion.

Her eyes flash to me for a second. "You do routinely kill trees, though."

"That's only because I can't shoot pucks at someone's face anymore." I sigh and stretch out my hand. "Pass a ball."

She fishes around the plastic bag hanging from her hand that carries some of our creations, and lobs one at me. After catching it, I take a glance around to see what the best distance would be.

Earlier in the afternoon, I finally contracted the carpenters who will build the booths for our event in record time—thanks to paying them double for the effort. That included sharing a blueprint of their dimensions and look that Sierra and I put together last weekend, so the measurements are still fresh in my mind. I walk around the tree and all the debris around it and it checks out with what I expect the size of the booth to be. Next, the booths will be propped up against the wall in the hallway bordering the ice rink, and people will basically have to use the remaining width for the throw, which is about where I stand now.

I throw the ball and it slides off the curvature of the tree, falling to the floor without mercy.

I stand there, blinking, heat rushing up my neck.

"Wow." Sierra sucks her lips in, as if to stop from laughing. "I thought you were an athlete, what the hell?"

"Of a different sport, okay? Watch me shoot a puck and see if you laugh." I fold my arms. "Why don't you try instead?"

"Fine." She takes another fake ornament and steps up closer to me, pushing the bag against my stomach until I grab it. "Step back."

"Good idea, I don't want to be pelted when you throw the ball backwards."

She sticks her tongue out at me, which is the most life I've gotten out of her since this morning. I make a point of standing as far to the side as I can, which gives me perfect view of Sierra shutting me the hell up.

Because she makes a perfect windup, the kind a professional baseball pitcher would do complete with leg raised high, torso twisting around, and her arm coming forward like a whip. The ball—I mean, the ornament—flies off the tip of her fingers as if she were controlling it with string. It smacks right into the tree with enough force for the impact to echo around the barn.

And of course it latches onto the velcro tree with no issue.

It all happens so fast that a microsecond later is when Sierra's foot falls back to the ground.

"What the hell just happened?"

Her shoulders start shaking with a quiet laugh. "Sorry, big guy. I was an athlete too."

"What? Why don't I know about this?"

"It's not a big deal. There was no pro future for me." She shrugs like it's no big deal. "I played softball up until college with a scholarship. Now the only action I get is the spring beer league at my neighborhood."

"But… that's amazing. You're amazing." I can't seem to close my mouth after that.

Even more shocking, her face warms up. "It looks cool but that was a really slow ball, just for the record."

"Who cares? You could probably kill someone with how heavy it is." I lift a hand to rub at my chest, right where my heart is throbbing harder than it ever has. One thing is finding my coworker attractive, quite another is to find her spectacular.

And that's what she is. Just the most outrageously hot woman I've ever met.

"Wanna throw again?" she asks, and everything about her glows right now. I don't know if it's because of the thrill of showing me up or if it's because I'm officially done for, and I don't care. I just want this moment to last forever.

"Yeah." I sound choked up and try to swallow it down. "But apparently you'll have to teach me how."

Sierra jerks her head at me to join her and I have to force myself not to run over like a lapdog wagging his tail. "Okay, all you have to do is throw with your legs instead of your arm."

"What?"

Her mouth opens and closes as she utters more words, and none of them get through my addled brain. The only things I can think of are how Gramps is right, and I can't let this woman pass me by. And second, I have no idea how I'm going to win her over. Should I just find excuses to flash my abs more? How did I ever date before?

"Conor, are you going to try?"

"Yes," I say with firmness. "Yes, I'm going to try very hard."

"Okay…" Her eyebrows twist as she steps away from me.

Right, the baseball. She wasn't talking about me trying to ask her out on a date. I'll do both, but for now only throwing a baseball well matters.

I don't do the fancy windup she did or anything, but I'm more conscious of my leg placement and how that propels the ball forward. It thwacks against the tree, teetering for a second while I hold my breath, but it stays put.

"Yeah!"

"That's what I'm talking about!"

We high five each other and I get the gift of her eyes crinkling at the corners with joy. Right now, she seems happier that she taught me something than a moment earlier when she left me in the dust.

Maybe she's warming up to me just a bit. Maybe there's hope.

Something catches my attention from above her head. Slowly, my lips stretch into a smile. "Look." I point behind her.

Sierra turns to face out of the barn door and as her eyes

adjust to the dark outside, she gasps. "Oh, wow. You were right."

"What did I tell you? My nose doesn't lie."

I follow after her and we stand at the threshold, watching the delicate flurries of the first snow making their winding descent to the ground. The light from inside the barn makes them glint in an almost magical way.

Sierra's dark eyes are wide with wonder as she takes in the sight. "It's so beautiful."

"Yes." I'm staring at her instead, mesmerized. "Yes, it is."

I don't know if wishing on the first snow is a thing or not, but I send a wish up to the heavens that I get the chance to experience this with her again. And again.

CHAPTER 18
SIERRA

"Cheers to your new job!"

We clink our glasses, braving the sloshing champagne that now trickles down my hand and down Rachel's arm. Giggling, she grabs a napkin from the table and gives it to me, even though she has the bigger mess now soiling her blouse. And I know her, if I don't grab it, she'll just hold it up for me until I do, further delaying her own cleanup process.

I grab it and shake my head. That's Rachel in a nutshell, the most giving person I've encountered in my life. A lump rises in my throat and something presses behind my ears. I don't know if the previous champagne flute is to blame but I suddenly want to burst into ugly tears, that's how much love I'm bubbling with for her.

"I'm so, so freaking happy for you." I sniffle into the napkin. "You deserve this and the whole rest of the world. And the universe too."

"Oh, geez. It's just a job offer, Sierra. Don't make my floodgates open now." That's when she finally plucks a napkin for herself and yep, she blots her blouse first before taking care of the trickle of tears down her face.

I reach over for a clean napkin and not so gently dab at her face. "Look at us, we're mess. We're supposed to be happy and celebrating, so what the hell is this?"

"You have no right to ask when you're the one who started it." At least a laugh comes out as she says this.

"I'm sorry, I just love you so much, pendeja."

"You have weird ways of showing your feelings, Sierra."

Grinning, I lean back against my chair. We came to this fancy downtown bar straight from work, ditching our responsibilities the second we read the email from HR offering Rachel the position of Publicity Talent Manager. Starting January, she'll transition to taking care of publicity accounts for the *SPORTY* brand, which in simpler terms means she'll manage campaigns with celebrities hired to promote our brand and products. How freaking cool is that?

If anyone deserves it, it's Rachel. She's worked twice as hard to get here as the rest of us, all while raising a son as a single mother. All she's missing is a cape.

"And here you were, freaking out that you wouldn't get it."

She shrugs. "You just never know with these things. They said they had several candidates in mind, including external. And you know how they can lowball externals a lot easier because they don't know better."

"But you got it." I smile. "And I told you so. Now, pay up."

Rachel snorts at my extended hand, but still makes a big show of fishing for her wallet to take out a five dollar bill. That's what she gets for betting against herself, the fool.

"Excellent." I snatch the crisp bill. "Next round's on me."

"Hah, that won't even cover half of it."

"Whatever. Just stop betting or you'll lose money for the Operation: New House."

"You're right." She rubs her hands. "I'm so excited for that, but even more that moving to the next school district means Adrian will enroll in a much better sports program."

"Yep, I can feel my tears coming back up." I pat my eyes dry, not even kidding because I'm genuinely feeling so emotional right now. I guess it's the season of miracles, after all.

"Fine, let's change the topic then." As she props her bent arm over the back of her chair, Rachel asks, "What's the deal between you and Conor?"

Of course, this happens at the same time as I'm taking a sip of bubbly—and it goes down the wrong pipe. I hack horrible coughs that make half of the patrons turn our way.

"What are you talking about?" I sound like a chainsmoker with pneumonia as I ask.

"You guys don't seem to hate each other, but you were all weird in the elevator the other day." She offers my glass of water to me. "Here."

I take it and swallow water down in big gulps, both for relief and for stalling. "Any chance we could talk about literally anything else? Environmental policy? Politics back in our home country? How your famous brothers are doing this season?"

"Hmm, none of those sound appealing to me and I thought we were here for me?"

"I fail to see how that sentence is a fully strung thought." I sigh, though. Rachel has determination in spades and she won't drop a bone when it's already clenched tightly between her jaws. "Fine, the answer is I don't know. And I'm not being cheeky here, I really don't."

Rachel leans her elbow on the table and props her chin on the heel of her hand. "Was it my fault? Were you about to kiss under the mistletoe when I interrupted?"

"No." I fold my arms and melt a little on my chair. "If anything, he seemed extremely reluctant to kissing me again."

We both stare at each other, neither of us reacting to what I just admitted.

The soft jazz music wraps around me like a fake safety

blanket. Any moment now, one of us is going to explode with sound and movement and drastically change the atmosphere of this bar. Not sure if for the better.

Rachel tucks her tongue against her cheek, still quiet as she watches me sweat through my cardigan across from her. Clearing my throat, I pick up my glass water again and take an elegant little sip.

"*Again?*" She shrieks the word. Next thing, she smacks the table. "And you weren't planning to tell your best friend?"

"Well, in my defense Grammie's my best friend and she doesn't know either, so why should I tell you first?" I pretend to check my nails.

She ignores all that. "You kissed Conor Mahoney? *You?* How was it? I demand every minutia right this second."

Groaning, I lower my face to my hands and run them up and down my face. "Oh my gosh, Rachel. It was the most incredible kiss of my life—and he doesn't want to do it again! Ugh."

"Backtrack, please. I beg." She snaps her fingers several times. "And give me all the details too."

"There's not that much to it, to be honest," I say and launch into the story of that venue visit. In retrospect, I was already crushing on the man before the kiss—otherwise, I'm pretty sure I'd have ignored superstitious threats. That was just the device I used to negotiate acquiring a kiss.

When I tell Rachel about how Conor asked me how I wanted to be kissed, her eyes all but pop out of their sockets. She leans forward, hands on the edge of the table as I tell her what I can of the kiss. It's not like I'm a writer and can use pretty words to describe something that was transcendent.

I explain as much with a shrug. "What can I say? The man knows how to use his lips. And tongue."

"I imagine he knows how to use the rest of his body too, huh?" Rachel's lips curve into a sneaky smirk because, unfortunately, a lamp hangs low over our table and easily lights up my reddening face.

"Probably."

"And you want to find out." Her smirk deepens.

"Maybe."

"Which from you means heck yeah."

"But what good is that when the man contorted himself to get as far from me and that mistletoe as he could?"

"Have you considered—oh, I don't know—asking him directly?" Rachel lifts her hands and gives an exaggerated shrug.

"What's the point? He said with his own mouth that it wouldn't be a good idea to kiss again."

"He could've meant at the office."

Crap, I hadn't considered that. One thing is kissing at that hotel, with no one we know to bear witness. Quite another would be making out in the elevator and have it, say, open its doors right in front of Richard's face. Or worse, in front of someone like Camila Puig who would immediately march us to HR.

"Oh."

"So, what are you going to do now?"

I pull at one curl and twirl it around my finger. "Nothing, I guess."

"What?" Rachel drags the word in disappointment. "You mean to tell me there's a hunk of a man you're into, and you won't take a bite?"

"Rachel, please use that amazing brain inside your beautiful head. If you were him, would you give me a chance after I consistently treated you like crap for two years?"

"Oops, that's a conundrum."

"And that's on top of my less than stellar trajectory with men." She knows all about it. Dates I ditched because I'd rather be studying or working, and then them ghosting me in return. Or worse, in high school, where I couldn't even find someone to go to prom with me because the popular kids got everyone thinking that the janitor's daughter was gross.

"Forget the past." Rachel waves a hand. "What matters is that you pounce on Conor before someone else does."

"I'm sure he has his pick of women—he's like everyone's biggest crush at headquarters, you know that. Why would he choose the most prickly girl of the bunch?"

"Maybe because he kissed you like he was going to die if he didn't give it his all?"

I roll my eyes. "He's an athlete. I'm sure if it had been Kaylee instead, he'd have gone all out too."

"You don't mean that."

"I half do and half don't."

She snorts. "I don't see him looking at Kaylee the way he looks at you."

I can't help how I lean forward. "How's that?"

"Like there's literally no one else in the room and he doesn't give a shit if anyone catches him watching."

"Oh." My insides flutter and my heart's strumming a song I'm unfamiliar with. Something warm and sweet like a Christmas carol that is just for me. "Is... is that so?"

"Well, since I'm going to stop being your teammate soon, I have a confession to make." I brace myself in case she's going to say that she has a legit crush on Conor too, but instead what comes out of her mouth is, "The rest of us have a bet going over the two of you. Kaylee and I think you'll get together at some point, but the men think you'll never let that happen."

I hang my jaw.

"Of course, I'm not saying this because I'd take a two-hundred-dollar cut once Kaylee and I win, but just so you understand that you don't have to walk on pins and needles around the office if you decide to pursue something with him.

Which you should, in my opinion." She caps this off with a big grin.

"Richard too?" I feel my face scrunch up in mortification.

"I'm afraid he and I were the originators of the bet."

I groan and throw an arm over my face like the picture of drama. "Kill me now."

"What I'm saying is, there are no obstacles in front of you other than yourself. Get your man, Sierra."

CHAPTER 19
CONOR

"Okay, I have to admit I'm really excited about this one." I bounce my right knee because that's all I can do to release some of the energy coursing through my veins. Part of it is because I'm so damn hungry—I skipped lunch because I was stuck in a call, and I'm really looking forward for this taste test of the catering service to fix that issue.

The other part has no solution. Sierra and I sit together in what has to be the world's smallest booth with only a minuscule round table in it. I get that this caterer isn't a restaurant, so the floorspace can be minimal. But I'm 6 foot 2 and putting my arm in between us made her contort, so I've just taken to leaving it on the backrest. That means we're glued together, thighs, hips, and sides. Her curls tickle my nose if I turn to the left, and she smells amazing. I've been breathing as deep as I can, just so I can bottle up the scent in my cells.

The biggest challenge is how she feels. We removed our winter clothes because the place is too warm, so there's only a normal amount of padding between us. But her shoulders would be the perfect height for my arm, and she feels warm and soft in all the ways that make me think definitely not-safe-for-work thoughts.

"I hope everything's good." Sierra bites her left thumbnail softly. "We literally have no built-in buffer in the schedule for any emergencies."

"Don't worry, I have a backup plan," I say.

"Oh yeah?" She lifts her face up to mine and our noses brush.

I can't move, not even to breathe deeper. If I do, I'm going to lean down and taste the lip she's biting right now.

I swallow hard and my voice sounds alien to me as I speak. "Gramps makes a mean casserole."

Something bright and lovely flashes in her eyes right before she elbows me in the ribs. "Be serious."

"Oh, I'm dead serious. It's to die for." Like the feeling of her body against mine right now.

"Alright, here we have assorted samples," a different voice comes from nearby.

Turning away from Sierra feels like the same physical effort it takes to lift up an entire car with my own hands alone, but somehow I manage.

The owner of the catering service stands before us, lowering a tray twice as large as the table. "To the left, we have the savory options. Cheese and bacon dipped pretzels, pigs in a blanket with Italian sausage and flaky pastry, and three different types of mini quiches ranging from vegan to vege-tarian and carnivore."

My stomach grumbles loud enough to echo around the locale. Sierra stuffs her fist against her mouth, probably to stop herself from laughing.

Chuckling, the man continues. "And to the right, we have the sweet samples. Two options of churros, sugar and ginger-bread, with hot chocolate. Vegan S'mores with our homemade gingersnap cookies. And finally, a black forest gateau with black cherry compote."

Sierra offers him a delighted smile. "If everything tastes half as delicious as it looks, this is going to be a success already."

"Excellent, please enjoy." He offers us two tiny forks. "I have to prepare for another tasting that is happening any minute now, but please do let me know if you have notes on any of the items."

"Thank you," she says.

Before either of them are done with the conversation, I attack the mini quiches. I don't know what combination of flavors it is that I just put in my mouth, but they hit me with a wave of pleasure and relief that my whole body vibrates with a groan. Sierra stiffens beside me and the caterer chokes.

Fire consumes my face. "Sorry. This is delicious and I'm hungry."

"Well." He coughs into his hand. "I'm glad you—" The rest of his sentence dies off as the entrance door bell goes off. "Oh, if you'll excuse me."

"Oh my gosh, Conor. I told you to stop that," Sierra hisses the words in a low tone after he leaves.

"I dare you not to moan once you try these things," I say back.

Harrumphing, she pinches the twin mini quiche to the one I just gobbled up and gives it a try. She places a hand against her lips as she chews, slowly turning to me. "Oh."

"See? It's not my fault. These are damn amazing." I grab the pig in a blanket and before eating it, say, "Do you think they'll give us seconds if we ask?"

"If not, you can just eat more of your Gramps' casserole."

"I'm starting to change my mind. I don't know if it's really that great anymore compared to this."

She backhands me in the middle of my chest. "Don't be mean."

"It's just my stomach speaking."

Sierra smiles up at me as she chews, her cheeks rosy and I don't know if it's from the amusement, the amazing finger food, or the proximity to me. I hope the latter factors in at least a little.

"Sierra Fernandez? Is that you?"

We both turn to the voice of a stranger, and I feel Sierra take in a sharp breath that paralyzes her. I stay put in the act of taking a loaded piece of pretzel to my guzzler.

A blonde woman stands before us dressed in designer clothes I'm familiar with—expensive and tight. They were the kind of stuff I used to regularly gift to my ex for her birthday or anniversaries. It's like this woman goes to the same stylist, too, because her makeup, the artificial wave to her hair, and even the waft of perfume scream Nikki-look-alike.

There's a man next to her too, one of those corporate types who look bored being anywhere but outside of their office. I only know they're together because he keeps one hand attached to the blonde, while scrolling through his phone with the other one.

I don't have a lot of room for big movements, so I can only shift my eyes to Sierra. She's clenching her jaw hard enough that a muscle jumps, which immediately tells me this interaction isn't welcome.

"Brandy," Sierra spits back.

The other woman turns her attention to me. "How fascinating to see you here at all. Kyle and I are here for our wedding tasting—you do remember Kyle, right?"

"How can I forget? You two made my high school experience an unforgettable one." Sierra's lips stretch into a tight, humorless smile.

All at once I remember a conversation that feels simultaneously ten years ago, and also yesterday. Sierra mentioned that she had been bullied through school for being the janitor's daughter. I don't know if these two led the charge, but they certainly had a hand in making Sierra miserable.

Something lights up in my brain that activates my body before I can fully control it. One second I'm about to eat a morsel of food, and the next I'm nuzzling my nose behind Sierra's ear.

"I got you," I murmur softly against her ear.

Her body breaks into a shiver but she jerks her head into a nod and doesn't pull away. I do what I've been itching to do since we sat here: I rest my arm on Sierra's shoulders and bring her flush against me until she can feel how hard my heart slams in my ribcage. I place a hot, soft kiss under her earlobe and turn to the other woman.

"So, are you a friend of my Sierra?"

"Oh, um." She blinks fast. "I'm Brandy Jackson, the future Mrs. Kyle Montgomery. And you?" I ignore the hand she offers.

I tilt my head. "Still wondering about the answer to my question."

"I—I—" The woman gives an awkward laugh. "Yes, of course we're friends. We went to middle school and high school together."

"We're not friends," Sierra says with a deadpanned voice as she leans forward to pluck a churro from the plate. I'm close enough that I can see her hand shake slightly. "In fact, Brandy and Kyle here were the biggest bullies in school and they should feel ashamed at even showing their faces in front of me."

Damn. My chest swells with pride for her. Sierra doesn't really need me to play knight in shining armor when she herself is a shield and a sword all in one. I don't know why but I find that hotter than the chocolate steaming on the table.

The Kyle dude snorts and doesn't even look up to say, "Hey, babe. Can we just sit down? My feet are getting tired."

Just hearing his whiny voice is almost enough to ruin my appetite. It recovers quickly as the blonde stutters something and leads him to the booth next to ours.

I pull away slightly so I can face Sierra. She continues eating in silence for a moment until she meets my eyes. When she allows the silence to prolonge, I ask in as low a timbre as I can manage, "Are you okay?"

"Unsure," she admits with a shrug. "Can we hurry?"

"Say no more." I unleash my full hunger and polish my half of the food in the blink of an eye. Sierra's slower, but it seems like the brief encounter with her past tormentor has closed off her stomach and I end up eating the rest.

"Conor?" she asks after I'm done stuffing my face. "Would you please do me a favor now?"

"Anything."

She startles a bit at the vehemence of my answer, but recovers quickly. "Can you please keep pretending you're my boyfriend?"

"Sure." I lean closer to her so I can speak directly into her ear. "What kind do you want me to be? Whispering sweet nothings into your ear like this? Publicly handsy? Openly hostile to them?"

"Um, all of the above?" Her voice comes out like a squeak.

"Deal."

We get up from the booth and exchange a glance. We're doing this, all right.

I offer my hand to her and Sierra grabs it without hesitation. We march over to the counter to wait for the owner. His voice drifts over from the booth where the two shitty people are sitting, waiting for their little food. It could be just me but I feel laser beams on my back. Bullies hate it when someone else is the center of attention—I wouldn't be surprised if the real reason those two set their sights on younger Sierra was because she was smarter, cooler, and more beautiful. And I'm sure that at least the blonde woman is going to lose her shit seeing someone else prove this.

Letting go of Sierra's hand, I place mine on her opposite side, right at the curve of her waist and hip, and slowly travel it lower as I pull her flush against me. Sierra gasps and blinks up at me, but doesn't stop me as I move my hand lower around her, until I'm sliding my hand into her front pocket.

Her face is red like a streetlight, though.

"Um, good acting." She lowers her eyes.

It's not acting, though. If I really was her boyfriend, I'd be desperately seeking skin right this second.

"You might want to reciprocate for the audience," I murmur.

"You're right." Clearing her throat, Sierra twists in my embrace until she can free one arm. Next thing, her hand slides into my back pocket and gives my ass a little squeeze.

I'm proud to repot I manage to keep a moan in check. Somehow.

The caterer meets us at the counter, takes one look at how Sierra and I are suddenly fused to each other, and fortunately decides not to blow our cover. "So, how did you like it?"

I like it. Very much. I don't even want to drop the act.

"The food was even better than advertised," Sierra says smoothly, if a little throatier than usual. "No notes from me. What about you, Conor?"

"No, it was perfect. The eggnogs from earlier too," I manage to add at the last second. We sampled the drinks first since they contained alcohol, and I'm driving us back to the office after this.

"Fantastic, then we'll proceed with the order as we agreed."

After a few more pleasantries and handshakes, we head out of the store still touching. Her walk squeezes my hand slightly in the crease of her upper thigh and hip as she walks, and I'm pretty sure the palm of her hand has a perfect map of my gluteus maximus now.

At the door, I pause to glare over my shoulder and sure enough, the blonde woman is gaping at us like she's never seen a more shocking sight in her life. The man beside her is stuck in a conversation and if that's the level of attention he typically gives her, I figure she's already got the punishment she deserves.

It physically hurts to tear myself away from Sierra so we can jump in my truck. The silver lining is that since the walk was basically non-existing because we parked right out front, I didn't need to put on my jacket and the freezing air keeps my boiling blood in check.

Still, since Sierra is deathly quiet inside the truck, I ask, "Are you okay?"

"Yeah, I guess." She props up her elbow on the window and glances out of it as I drive us out of the parking lot. "I'm just annoyed at myself that I had to drag you into it just so I could save face."

"Er, don't worry about me." Especially not when I enjoyed it so damn much, which actually makes me a complete douchebag. "I'm sorry, though. I feel like I took it too far."

"You didn't." She expels a big breath. "In fact, you saved me from leaping over that tiny table and pulling at her hair. How did you know exactly how to get her to back off?"

"I know her type. I dated one just like her." Sierra whips around to stare at me and I'm glad that traffic keeps my eyes off what no doubt is disgust on her face. "I know, I'm not exactly proud of myself."

"Huh. How did that even happen? That's not the kind of woman I'd picture for you."

It's just on the tip of my tongue to ask her who she imagines me with, and see if her answer matches mine. But this isn't the right time to feel her out. She's obviously hurting and eager to steer the conversation away from that.

I'm happy to oblige, even if it's at my expense.

"I was young and naive once," I say, wrinkling my whole face in distaste at myself. "This hot, blonde woman approached me—and not any other player—and I caved right away. Ignored all the red flags waving in my face like the shithead I was."

"Yikes."

"That's putting it mildly." I tap the steering wheel with my thumbs as I keep driving. "She dumped me right after the accident, when it was clear I'd never play again."

"Oh, wow. What a dirtbag. I'm so sorry, Conor."

"Me too, especially because Gramps could see all along what kind of vain creature I was dating." I clear my throat, embarrassed as hell. "Anyway, this Blondy or whatever reminded me of Nikki, and all Nikki ever cared about was showing off, so…"

"Well, thank you for thinking fast." She makes a pause and speaks quietly, "Although I'm really sorry you had a Brandy in your life, too."

We're stopped at a red light, so I turn to her. I lick my lips, bracing myself for what I'm about to say. "You know, I used to be real sour about her but this whole thing made me realize something."

"What's that?" Sierra blinks in confusion.

"That I can now recognize who's worth keeping around and who isn't." I search her face for any clues that she understands the meaning behind my words, but she gives me nothing. She could win a poker tournament on her expression alone.

I decide not to push it further. There are other ways to show her I'm going wild about her. I just need to have patience.

CHAPTER 20
SIERRA

Am I worth keeping around?

This question has plagued me since the catering tasting yesterday. I'm pretty sure my eye bags reach my chin after a whole night of tossing and turning in bed, the question running circles in my head.

Two months ago, when I was still acting like a tool to him, I'd have said yes. Absolutely. I wouldn't know anyone more worthy—or so would my pride have led me to believe.

My answer right now is no.

I've been horrible to Conor for two years, just a nightmare to work with. And last night, under the suffocating weight of my conscience, I realized I've never properly apologized. I've acknowledged my behavior, but never said I was sorry and that I won't do it again. Except an apology now is going to look so self serving when what's behind it is that I want to go out with him.

I don't want to pretend to do couple stuff with him like we did in front of my school tormentor. I want the real thing. The drives around town together, but holding hands while no one's watching. Eating together with his grandfather. Talking about horrible exes. Going shopping for stuff that isn't work related. Kissing well outside of the range of mistletoe.

But I don't deserve any of that.

I drag my feet into the premises of Conrad's Rink. My backpack is loaded with masking tape to mark the spots where the booths will go. It bounces against my back as I walk through the entrance and the small concessions area loaded with vending machines and a fountain for drinks, before heading over to the wide hallway by the seats.

Faint swooshing and slapping sounds echo along with different voices, some children's squeals and adult laughter. I pause to check the time, and only now figure out I'm too early and Conor's still in the middle of class. I take the nearest seat I can find at the top, far from the moms watching the session.

"Did you see that?" One of them points toward a toddler at the front. "That's my son. Future McDavid right there."

I slide my hand into the pocket of my coat and use my phone to look up the name. All I glean is that this McDavid guy is some one-of-a-kind talent, so I guess the mother's comment now makes sense. This must be how all of them see their offspring even though to me they're little balls of chaos on the ice. There's a cluster of like five kids smacking their sticks against the ice, I assume looking for a puck... except the rubber disc is actually clear across the ice.

Conor is in the middle of that, wearing black training clothes for winter, and hockey gloves to carry his stick with. He glides smoothly between the future superstars, voicing instructions that go completely unheard. I stifle a chuckle against my fist.

If it were me, I'd have lost my patience already but not Conor. He stops for a moment to explain something to one kid, who then takes off skating with difficulty in his oversized padding. Then Conor sees another kid making snow angels, except there's no snow. I can tell by how his chest rises that

Conor sighs in a what-can-you-do way, but he bends down and picks the kid up by the jersey with one hand, until the kid's skates find the ice again and off he goes.

Something happens then. The world tilts off its axis and sends me hurtling down in free fall into a void. I put a hand on my chest, willing it to calm down the frenetic beat of my heart. With the other hand I grab onto my seat's armrest tight, needing a reminder that I'm not actually falling down a cliff. I'm still sitting here, watching Conor show the patience of a saint among a gaggle of unruly kiddies.

Except, this is the moment I know for a fact... that I've fallen in love with my former foe.

I don't just like him. I love everything about him from the way he's no nonsense at work, to how sweet he is with his grandfather and these kids, to the way he looks at me when I say something important—like there's nowhere else he'd rather be than listening to me. Including how he seems to know what I need without me even saying it.

Conor Mahoney is such a good person, and I've been such a fool.

I exhale a shaky breath. This can't be happening. We haven't even gone on a date. We just kissed once and it wasn't even organic, we wouldn't have kissed if there had been no mistletoe above us. I all but hated him until just a few weeks ago.

And yet right now, he's all I can see. He keeps me awake at night and makes me dream during the day. He's been the sole topic of every conversation I've had with Grammie the past few days. I even wish the company event would never come— even if it means no ten-thousand check or promotion—just so I can keep working closely with him every day including weekends.

"Ugh." I drop my face into my hands and groan. I'm so screwed. The event's in seven days. I can't undo two years worth of acting like a turd in seven days. I should just start by genuinely apologizing today.

But then it'll be Christmas break and new year's. Should I wait until January to see if the feelings are still there? If these strange past few weeks haven't played games with my forever-alone heart?

Except, what if the distance from the holidays makes him even less eager to give me a chance?

What then? What do I do with myself?

Obviously… I won't insist. I'm not entitled to him. But something deep inside tells me that I won't find anyone better than Conor. The loss would be entirely mine.

He blows the whistle twice, it's as much as it takes for the toddlers to roll and tumble around him. I can't hear what Conor is telling them between the animated chatter of the moms and my own furiously beating heart. I just glean that it's the end of the class because Conor claps his gloved hands and some of the moms start getting up.

A few give me curious glances and one of them giggles at me. Like maybe I already have a giant billboard over my head advertising that I have the hots for the hockey instructor.

I wait until every single person has filed out, sinking in my seat in hopes that Conor won't notice me yet. We're still fifteen minutes from the time we agreed to meet here, and Conor hasn't seen me from the stands. The benches are opposite of me, and he skates toward one of them to drop off his gloves and replace his stick with something that looks like the cousin of a broom. While skating, he uses that thing to collect the pucks scattered here and there.

It's when he skates by my side that my ruse is up. Conor brakes hard enough to splash the boards, and as the slush slides down the glass, I see a smile stretching his lips in a way that makes my heart lurch toward him.

I want more smiles like that, please and thanks.

"Hey, stranger. How long have you been there?" he asks, casually hanging his hands off the end of the weird broom's stick.

Long enough to work myself up into a heart issue. Instead, I squeak, "Like, fifteen minutes?"

"Oh! Shit, did I give you the wrong time?" He checks his watch again, a wrinkle appearing between his eyebrows when he realizes he's not wrong. It's me.

Isn't that a metaphor.

"No worries. I got here early by accident." Clearing my throat, I decide to pick myself up from my seat and approach. Conor watches me walk down the steps until I stand before him, the wet glass in between. "So."

"So." He tilts his head.

Don't worry, Conor. I too wonder where I'm going with this. Your pretty eyes are addling my brain.

"That was you in your element, huh?" I ask, grasping at straws now. Any straws.

He leans an arm against the glass, his forehead coming to rest against it. "What did you think?"

"It looked pretty cool." It's kind of a lie because all I could pay attention to was him, and he's something better than just cool.

"I was way cooler back in the day," Conor says with a toothy grin. "Just zipping up and down the ice at a million miles per hour, battling it out with big dudes who didn't care about losing teeth."

I narrow my eyes. "You seem to have kept them all."

"You're right, that's definitely a silver lining of retiring early."

"How about you show me?"

His eyebrows pop. "My teeth?"

I bark a laugh. "No, you silly goose. Your zipping up and down, like when you were allegedly cooler."

"Allegedly? Those are fighting words, woman." He grumbles before pulling away from the boards and skating backwards. "Fine, I'll show you."

"Yes, please," I murmur into my scarf. And I don't even mean it in a pervy way, I just want to see every facet of him that has been out of my reach.

I sit at the front row now while he retrieves his stuff from the bench, and once he's outfitted, Conor transforms. The stick becomes an extension of his body as he picks up speed and turns, taking one of the pucks along with him. Powerful thighs pump hard against the ice and he eats terrain faster than I can blink. Conor is a blur as he skates past me, somehow not dropping the puck for a second.

My breath hitches in my throat and I jump to my feet. He's going way too fast and the net is too close. I don't even care that the puck hits the back of the net because he's about to freaking crash!

But he doesn't.

He bends his legs and that changes his direction. One second he's hurtling at the boards and the next he's gliding along them, stealing the puck off the net to start all over again.

I plop on my chair, my heart racing just as fast as Conor zig zags around the ice, not even losing steam even though I'm tired from just watching him. How amazing was he during his career, if this is what he can do now that he's retired and not conditioned?

Abruptly, I remember something Richard said before Conor arrived for his first day at *SPORTY*. "I saw this guy tear up the ice at Madison Square Garden two years ago, I can't believe he's joining our team now. Life is wild, huh?"

"Qué si no," I tell myself.

"How's that for *allegedly*?" Conor asks as he brakes across from me once more. He's breathing slightly harder, though not in great guffaws like I'd be. His cheeks are rosy and his eyes are bright behind his glasses. But the part that kills me the most is his hair—it's a spiky mess at the top of his head that is begging for my fingers to comb it.

"I stand corrected," I admit in a breathy voice. "You're still amazing."

His lips part as in surprise. "Still?"

"Yup."

He traps a glove between his elbow and ribs, and uses the free hand to brush his hair. "Well, thanks. I still skate on my own so I'm glad to know I haven't lost it."

"Does it make you happy?" I lean forward, eager for the answer.

"Yeah." His eyes crinkle at the corners.

"Then you'll never lose it."

Conor stays quiet, although his face is still smiling. It's like he needs a moment to marinate the words, use them to reach an answer of some sort in his mind. And then he asks, "Sierra, do you want to skate for a bit before we start working?"

Like a… like a skating date?

But I shake the thought out of my head hard. Dates aren't a spur of the moment thing, so that's not it.

"Um." I hide further behind my scarf. "I actually don't know how to skate."

Wrong thing to say to a former professional hockey player. Conor's eyes widen and when he picks up his jaw, he says, "That's it. We'll pull an all-nighter if we have to, but first I'm going to give you some lessons."

And you know what? Screw work. I offer exactly zero protests at this new plan.

CHAPTER 21
CONOR

My heart is beating at a million miles per hour because I just skated as hard as I did during practice drills for my former professional hockey team —*not* because this is a skating date with Sierra Fernandez. Because this isn't a date. We're here for work.

Except it feels a whole damn lot like one.

The nicest pair of size eight rental skates hang from my hand as I walk the tunnel, every step making my body thrum with more and more energy. It wasn't even like this when I made my way out to the ice for the winter classic game I played in my rookie year. That's the chokehold this woman has on me already.

I hit the ice, my eyes immediately seeking her figure. She sits on the bench glancing around like she's trying to memorize this view, until her eyes find mine. She smiles so wide that her cheeks turn pinker.

Meanwhile, I feel like I'm being checked against the boards and my lungs lose all the air.

That's it for me. There's no going back now. If anything, I need to find a way to move forward with her. I need to tell her the truth—that she's driving me wild and I need her to give me a chance.

"Hey." I'm breathless as I brake in front of the bench.

"Welcome back."

What's the German word for when someone's smile increases your blood pressure, but at the same time you don't ever want to look away from it? I'm sure there's one.

Clearing my throat, I say, "Found you some semi new skates. Do you know how to lace them?" I lift them over the boards and offer them to her.

"How hard can it be?" But the way she eyes them warily and doesn't take the skates tells me everything.

I straighten up and glide over to the door, still carrying the skates in my hand. I tower over her and Sierra has to crane her neck back to keep meeting my eyes. My voice is a throaty, raspy mess as I tell her, "I'll help you."

Sierra's eyes widen as I lower myself to my knees. I hook a finger around her shoe laces and pull.

"Conor!"

"Hmm?"

"I can take my own boots off!" She tries to pull her foot away but I'm faster. I clasp my hand around her calf and that freezes her.

"I'll be much faster, trust me. Besides, I have to make sure that the skates are laced right so you don't hurt yourself."

"What if my feet stink?"

I lift my face, biting my lips so I don't laugh. "Do they?"

Sierra folds her arms, face scrunched up in a pout. "I don't know. I don't think so, but you seem to have a dog's nose and now I'm nervous."

I chuckle. "Well, I appreciate the concern but your feet can't possibly smell worse than a locker full of sweaty men and their gear soaking up all that juice."

"Eww." She pretends to gag. "That's not the mental image I needed."

"Sorry for ruining any fantasies you may have had." I remove the first of her boots and pause. Her feet don't stink but I think her real worry was this—her Hello Kitty socks. I lift my eyes only, looking at her over the rim of my glasses. "Cute."

I enjoy the way her cheeks explode with heat. "Not another word, Mahoney."

"Didn't know they sold these in adult sizes—ow!" She smacks me hard on the shoulder.

"I warned you." Her eyebrows crash into a fierce frown that would've cowed me months ago.

I'm still laughing as I fit her with the skate. She has to shift closer to the edge of her seat for her foot to go in all the way, and I stiffen as she puts her hands on my shoulders to prop herself. Too soon she removes them, and I trap the skate between my knees to work on the laces, testing with my fingers for the right fit.

We repeat the same process on the other side and I have to bite the inside of my cheek so I don't quip about her fluffy, pink socks again. I never would've pictured tough as nails Sierra Fernandez having a weakness for cute stuff like this, but then again this is why I want to go out with her. To discover what else lies between a perfect baseball throwing technique and Hello Kitty socks.

Once I'm sure she's not going to twist her ankles out there, I put my hands on my thighs and meet her eyes again. "Ready?"

"I'm not sure." Her shoulders rise toward her ears. "This seemed like a fun idea fifteen minutes ago, but now that I have knives under my feet I'm not so sure."

Slowly, I rise to stand on my own knives and offer my hand. "I won't let you get hurt."

Sierra stares at my hand for a moment, until my skin starts

to itch. Finally, she places her gloved one on top. "And you won't make fun of me?"

"That, I can't promise." I grin.

After a long sigh, Sierra pushes herself off the bench and stands. She wobbles slightly and I hold tighter onto her hand, but that's all the help she needs up until she's right at the edge between the flooring and the ice. There, she pauses like she's deciding whether to jump off a cliff.

"I wore braces in high school," she says in a mumble out of the blue. "If all that effort goes to waste tonight, I'll hold you financially responsible."

I snort a laugh. "Is the great Sierra Fernandez chickening out?"

"Absolutely not." She lifts her chin, slides one skate on the ice, and promptly loses her balance.

I catch her in my arms, easily pulling her against me. Her hands clasp on my jacket at my sides and she keeps her face buried in my chest. I leave my hands wrapped around her arms, trying my best to behave like a gentleman. No doubt she can feel the rapid slamming of my heart against her face, though.

"You okay?" I whisper.

Sierra's response is muffled against my chest. With a deep breath, she pulls away enough to look up at me. Her eyes are wide, lips parted in surprise. "Oh my gosh, this is so much more slippery than I expected."

It takes my brain a moment to process what she's saying, where we're at, and who I even am. "Ah, yes. You uh, get used to it."

"Will I?" She cringes.

I move back carefully, still keeping my hands on her arms as anchors. "If I can do it, so can you."

"Says the guy who was probably born wearing skates." She looks down at her feet and that makes her tense even more.

"Look at me." For once, Sierra obeys. "First of all, that would've been too painful for my mom. Second, I had to learn like everybody else. Third, you don't need to be a professional of any sort to have fun. Loosen up, Sierra."

Her eyes widen almost comically. "Have you met me? I'm the most wound up person in the planet. I don't know how to do that."

"Yes, you do." My eyes lower to her lips as she bites them. She's loosened up in my arms before, when we made out under a mistletoe as if nothing else mattered. Or even when she threw felt-wrapped baseballs at a velcro tree. "You're capable of so much more than you think."

I skate backwards, pulling her along. Sierra gasps and clutches at my forearms with all her strength, but she doesn't let go. She doesn't fall. For a blissful moment, it's just the two of us gliding down the ice. I'm happy to do all the effort as long as she doesn't let go—and she doesn't, even as I slide my grasp down her arms to hold her hands.

"Doing okay?" I ask.

"Better than I expected."

"We'll have you shooting pucks in no time." I run my thumbs over her gloved knuckles but stop when she says my name.

"Conor…" Sierra bites her lip and I'm afraid I might've shattered the moment, but then she asks, "Do you miss it?"

"Huh?"

"Hockey." Her eyes tear away from mine, fixing on a messy pile of pucks I didn't finish picking up earlier. "You looked like a completely different person when you were skating. Like that was who you really are…"

Shit.

My chest twists in a painful way. Somehow, she managed to see right through me in minutes.

I stop us near a faceoff circle, noting how she's able to

balance herself well enough, and I cling to the pride I feel to have helped her get to that point. Just like I do every time I teach the kids how to play the sport that has been a part of my life from the beginning.

"Yes and no," I respond in all honesty. Sierra tilts her head in confusion. "Not being able to play feels like… like having lost a family member. But it's kind of weird, because the grief fills that empty spot so they're still kind of with you all the time, right?"

Her eyes soften and she surprises me by squeezing my hands. "You've lost a lot, Conor. Your parents, hockey…"

I swallow down the lump in my throat and avert my eyes. The last thing I want to do is start weeping like a freaking baby in front of the woman I want. "It's not all bad. I, um, I've gained stuff too."

"Yeah?"

"I have a new dream now—teaching the next generation of professional hockey players. And other silver linings, like…" I turn back to her and pull her slightly closer. I inhale deep, the subtle scent of the ice mingling with hers, and I bury them in my mind forever. Two of my favorite things.

"I'd still be trapped in a toxic relationship. I wouldn't have started working at *SPORTY*…" My heart races, trying to tear out of my chest as I say, "I wouldn't have met you."

Sierra's lips part in a soft gasp, shocked as what I'm implying sinks in. I stay still, waiting for a sign that she's okay with this, that I can kiss her again and whisper how I can't stop thinking about her, about her body pressed against mine, about how her clever quips make my soul sing, and how her dark eyes have the power to make my entire existence thrum with music.

Or not. Or a sign that she doesn't feel this way at all. Or that she doesn't welcome anything more than a friendlier work relationship than we had before.

Sierra runs her tongue through her lips and says, "Conor, I—"

"What are you two kids doing there?"

We both jump away from each other. Sierra flails her arms, yelping as her weight shifts. I rush forward and wrap my arms around her before she tilts too far.

"Gramps." I breathe hard. "How long have you been there?"

Did he hear what I just said? Because if so, I have to prepare myself to find the nearest cliff and jump from it.

As usual he ignores my question, though. "Are you planning to suffocate the young lady?"

"What?" I glance down. I have Sierra pressed tight against me and when I tear away, she takes a big gulp of air and her face is beet red. "Sorry, I—"

"It's okay. Maybe, erm, we should start doing some actual work," she mumbles.

The way she evades my eyes doesn't bode well. And even though there's a serrated knife slicing off a chunk of my heart because of what that means, I don't let go of her hands as I help her to the bench to remove her skates.

CHAPTER 22
SIERRA

I must be running a fever and this is all a hallucination. That would explain everything from the chills running through my body, to the heat all over my skin that makes my clothes feel too scratchy, to what just happened.

Did Conor Mahoney just allude to feeling something for me?

I'm not delusional enough to convince myself he'd say something like that to any other coworker. It was too pointed. Too sweet. Too much like something straight from my deepest fantasies. That's the part that trips me up and makes me wonder if this is all a figment of my imagination.

As I sit back on the bench, staring at his bent down head as he loosens my skates, I pinch my cheek hard just to make sure. Wincing, the pain confirms I'm very much awake.

A grumble sounds nearby, and it's from Gramps. He walks over to us, shaking his head, but instead of coming to the bench, he keeps going until he hits the ice with way steadier legs than mine. "Have to do everything around here. Too distracted."

His grandson's ears are as red as can be. I have to sit over my hands so I don't run them through his hair and tilt his head back so I can kiss him. I have something important to say to him before that.

"I got it from here," I say as Conor's about to put on my boots for me.

"Okay." He sits back on his haunches and his eyes avoid mine. "Guess I'll go change, too. Meet you out in the corridor."

"Ah, yes." I watch him rise with the agility of a gymnast and he walks away even faster, carrying the skates I borrowed in his hand. The back of his neck is burning too, and I have to press a hand against my mouth so I don't squeal or laugh or something embarrassing like that.

He's so damn cute, I could die.

Quickly, I put on my boots again and run out of the arena, somehow expecting him to be ready and waiting for me at an inhuman speed. I pause just beyond the last row of seats and take several deep breaths. Conor just put himself out there and I'm about to do the same, big time.

I've never done this. I've never met a guy that made me want to take an Olympic swan dive into his arms. No one has ever made me feel this safe, while at the same time making me burn up with just a glance. I didn't even think it was possible, especially for someone like me. And that's why I have to make sure that Conor knows what he's buying into, because my name is not quite on the nice list.

Conor appears through the doorway that leads to the offices, one hand in the pocket of his training pants, the other one rubbing his beard, eyes cast down like he's deep in thought. And if I go by his hunched over shoulders, I can't imagine they're the happiest thoughts right now.

I wring my hands, nerves fluttering as he approaches. I open my mouth but he speaks faster.

"Shall we start taping?"

I close my mouth so fast that my teeth make a sound. Then I remember leaving my backpack with the supplies behind. "Right. Let me get my backpack."

I rush back to the stands and find it on the original seat I took while I watched the class. As I pick it up, I observe Gramps dumping pucks into a basket and his shoulders shake, like he's either crying or laughing.

Laughing, I confirm as he turns to take the basket over to the bench. I don't need two guesses to know whose expense it's at.

I skip back out to the corridor, where Conor's using a measuring tape to check the span of a booth from the corner nearest to the entrance. "Got the tape?" he asks, his back to me.

"Yes, sir." I unzip my backpack and grab the first roll of masking tape I can find. "Let's do this."

He keeps the measuring tape in place as I crouch down to mark the spot. Conor removes his hand right before mine brushes it and I freeze. But he's already standing back up to run the measuring tape out, tracing the perimeter of the space the booth will take up in the hallway. He lifts his eyes to mine when he finally notices I'm not moving.

"Sierra?"

My ears roar and I can't hear what he says after my name. Slowly, I get back up and walk over to where he stands, unfurling the masking tape as I go. My mind races back through what's happened, like a film montage in rewind, until I reach the exact moment when his mood shifted.

It was when he kind of admitted that he might be into me, and I panicked a bit before Gramps interrupted.

Did Conor take that as a rejection?

It's okay. I can fix this. I guess I won't have to wait until January to hash this out. I just need to find the right words to do this correctly.

We work in silence for a while and successfully tape up the blueprint of the first booth. He's the one who breaks through the quiet. "Wait, which booth is this one going to be? Maybe we should note that down too so we don't have to think on the day of."

"Good idea." I tear a strip of masking tape and put it on the wall where it'll be most visible. I shrug my backpack off to search for a pen or marker. "Since this is the welcome booth, what do we want people's first impression to be?"

"Alcohol?" I see him lift a shoulder from the corner of my eye, and he's still looking at the floor like it's the most interesting thing.

"We could even cordon it off to keep the rest of the hallway off limits, and direct everyone from booze to getting fitted for skates, then to hitting the ice to find their group for the activities," I say in a firm tone of voice, pretending that I'm actually paying attention to the work we're doing, and not like my every cell is tuned up to him.

"Good idea." He slides over to stretch the tape from wall to wall. "Do we cordon off here?"

"Looks about right." I finally find a marker at the bottom of my backpack and uncap it to scribble over the tape. "Would that be safe, though? People skating right after hitting the booze booth?"

"It's okay, we're capping the amount of drinks per person for each round. Besides, they'll have to do the full course of games to reach the booze booth again."

"See? We're a great team." I offer him a smile that morphs into a bit of a grimace when he just blinks at me without any further reaction. I cap my marker back up and let the strap of my backpack slide down my arm, until I just toss it on the floor. "Hey, Conor?"

He clears his throat. "Yeah?"

"Remember when we *weren't* a team at all?"

"What?"

I uncap the marker and cap it again. "I still do. I was super rude to you and it wasn't even once or twice. It was two solid years of acting like total a jerk around you up until virtually yesterday."

He runs a hand through his hair, watching warily as I take a step closer to him. I fiddle with the marker in my hand, biting my lip until I can speak again.

"I've been meaning to apologize properly but…" I force myself to lift my chin and meet his eyes, even though what I really want to do is pull my beanie down until it hides my entire face—or my whole body, if it could. "The thing is, I had a plan in my head to first, tell you how truly sorry and ashamed I am at my own behavior. And then, take my time to show you that I'm worth keeping around with concrete actions."

Conor's eyes widen slightly, like he recognizes the words as his own. "Wait, what?"

I don't think I need the marker as a clutch anymore, so I stuff it in the pocket of my coat and take a bold step closer to him. It brings me so close I have to tilt my head all the way back.

"I wanted to make sure that this, all the sparks between us, weren't just because we once kissed under the mistletoe. That they're there beyond the Christmas season."

"Sierra, I—" His hands slowly rise to clasp my arms, and then he pulls me flush against him. Conor's forehead rests on mine as he whispers, "I guarantee what I'm feeling for you isn't just Christmas magic."

"Oh, good. Then I won't have to hang this over you two."

We both turn.

Gramps is just a few paces from us, close to the main entrance, and in his hands he holds a bunch of mistletoe wrapped in ribbon. He gives a big sniff. "And I'm really glad, because this thing gives me allergies."

My jaw drops.

"Gramps!" Conor's hands abandon me to cover his red face. His voice comes out muffled. "Are you going to keep interrupting?"

"Sorry, sorry. You're just stressing me out with how damn slow you're moving. You had so many chances to kiss the girl out there on the ice, you fool."

Conor drops his hands to glare at his grandfather. "And I'm glad I didn't, because I'm not going to kiss Sierra in front of you."

"Bah." Gramps waves a hand. "Do you think I don't know how it goes? I produced your father, in case you—" He's interrupted by a thunderous sneeze. Gramps shakes his head hard and runs the back of his sleeve across his nose. "You two carry on, I'm going to go toss this wretched thing."

With that, he turns around and leaves out the front door.

I feel Conor's fingers lace between mine and he tugs at me. "Come with me, before he returns to keep inflicting severe embarrassment on me."

Chuckling, I follow him across the corridor and into the office area. Conor pulls me into the main office and leans his back against the door, locking it behind him with his free hand just in case.

My pulse pounds in my ears as I take him in, his shoulders wide enough to almost span the width of the door, the lock of brown hair falling over his forehead, those whiskey colored eyes boring into mine.

I pull my hand from him, but only so I can step closer until my legs are between his and our bodies flush. I splay the palms of my hands on his chest and that activates something in him, the part that makes him cinch his hands around my waist.

Conor leans down and my eyes flutter closed, lips parting

to welcome his. But instead of kissing me, he whispers, "Sierra, I'm a bit freaked out right now."

"What?" My eyes snap open. "Why?"

His teeth rake over his lower lip. "Because I'm falling for you so fast and so hard, I'm scared I'll crash into pieces."

"You won't." I run my hands up his chest, to his neck and jaw, mapping the sheer size of him, his heat, the softness of his skin, willing it to imprint itself into my muscle memory. I pull him down until our lips brush, and I feather my words against his. "Not when I'm on a free fall too."

Conor holds the back of my head as his lips close around mine, molding perfectly as if our mouths were made for each other. My chest vibrates with a satisfied little sigh like it does every night when I crawl into bed after a long day. But this is different, because being in Conor Mahoney's arms feels like I'm waking up to life.

I rise on my tippy toes, trying to get as close as I can but it's not enough. Nothing feels enough. I rake my fingers through his hair, trying to pull him closer. Conor takes the hint and works his jaw a little harder, his tongue caressing my lips to coax them open. It feels like a lick of fire down my body and I gasp for oxygen, stoking the heat even more when it gains him deeper access to my mouth.

His tongue finds mine and Conor lets out one of those moans that turn my legs into jelly. Luckily, his arm is around my waist to catch me before I physically fall.

The figurative one has already happened. I've fallen for him—which I don't question, he's absolutely adorable.

But why did he even fall for me?

"Conor." His name comes out like a groan against his mouth. I'm panting as I pull away slightly more. "Why do you like me?"

"What?" His chest rises and falls against mine, and it takes him another moment to be able to open his eyes.

"All I've done is show you the worst of me these past two years." My eyes stay glued to his wet, swollen lips as I lean away from him. But his arm doesn't let me go far.

Conor pinches my chin between his fingers, lifting it until my eyes meet his heated gaze. His voice is gravel thick as he says, "All you've done is show me you're an honest person. You live your truth, whatever it may be, regardless of who likes it or not. I find that so damn hot, Sierra."

I take a sharp breath. If his words weren't enough, he lifts his thumb to run the pad softly against my bottom lip. The friction sends a shock of electricity all the way down to my toes.

Keeping his thumb on my lower lip, Conor leans back down to close his lips on my upper one, sucking it slightly and coercing a shiver out of me. "You're so damn hot," he says while still savoring me. "It's driving me wild."

"Why didn't you kiss me in the elevator, then?" I ask, letting out the last of my insecurities.

"Because of this." He slides his hands up my back, past my shoulders and down my arms. Holding one of my hands, he places it back on his chest where I can feel the frenetic beat of his heart. My other hand he brings up to his face, making sure I can feel just how absurdly hot his red skin is. Conor's chuckle is low and throaty. "I didn't want this to happen in the middle of the office. I would've given us away."

"Oh, I see." I swallow hard and brush my nose against his. "That would've been embarrassing."

"Very."

"So you did want to kiss me." I nibble his bottom lip gently.

Conor expels air so harshly it almost sounds like a growl. "Desperately. I'm trying to make up for it. Is it working?"

"Very much." I smile against his lips. "And this time we didn't even need mistletoe."

CHAPTER 23
CONOR

On Monday afternoon, I catch Sierra yawning for the nth time, and switch tabs on my work computer to go from a budget sheet in Excel, to the messaging software for employees. These days, her name is pinned at the top and I could find it with my eyes closed.

MAHONEY, CONOR - 3:48PM:

Can I bring you a cup of coffee?

FERNANDEZ, SIERRA - 3:48PM:

Appreciate the sentiment

But I don't want these gossipmongers to start running their mouths

MAHONEY, CONOR - 3:48PM:

I can pretend the cup is for me and leave it at your desk without anyone noticing

FERNANDEZ, SIERRA - 3:49PM:

Everyone will notice. I bet they've already noticed something

In fact, I should randomly glare at you for old
time's sake

I snort because a second after sending that message, Sierra pops her head over our monitors and offers the mightiest frown. It wrinkles her forehead and lips in a way that is more adorable than terrifying. She looks like the cutest grown woman trying to pick a fight. Not to mention, the dark circles under her eyes throw the whole vibe off too.

I have to duck my face so I don't laugh, but hopefully that makes me looks scared of her? Old time's sake, indeed.

MAHONEY, CONOR - 3:50PM:

Sorry for keeping you awake last night

FERNANDEZ, SIERRA - 3:50PM:

Oh my gosh, Conor! You can't say things like
that, what if someone reads over our shoulder
and takes it wrong?

It takes me a second to reason why. This time I hide my face from any prying eyes because I'm sure it's burning.

MAHONEY, CONOR - 3:51PM:

Geez

Sorry, I didn't realize

What I meant to say is SORRY FOR KEEPING
YOU LATE WITH WORK RELATED TOPICS

Is that better?

FERNANDEZ, SIERRA - 3:51PM:

You know what?

Go get me coffee

Anything so you stop

MAHONEY, CONOR - 3:51PM:

That's not what you were saying last night

FERNANDEZ, SIERRA - 3:51PM:

Conor!!!!!!

Chuckling, I lock my computer and stretch my arms, really selling the whole need for coffee even though I'm buzzing with electricity.

Last night was something else. One second, I'm trying to teach mini mites that the way to play hockey is forward—toward the net, and not clustering around each other—the next I'm making a fool of myself in front of the woman I've been most attracted to in my entire life—many thanks also to Gramps for that. And then the next, she and I start making out like teenagers until Gramps needed to close the place and kicked us out.

If it hadn't been because we had to come to the office today, and because there's literally only days left before the big Christmas event, Sierra and I might've gone on our official first date.

Alas, all we could do is spend the entire night texting back and forth. We're both equally guilty of not wanting to sleep, trying to catch up in one night about everything we didn't allow us to learn about each other in two years.

I now know that her favorite color is what she calls soft peach, but to me is cream. That's why her beanie and gloves are that color. Christmas is her favorite season of the year, and it's why she's looking forward to spending this one with her Grammie so much. She particularly loves Christmas music, anywhere from the commercial stuff that plays in stores, to the carols sang by a choir at church. Her childhood dream was to play professional baseball but had to give that up when some-thing called puberty hit her and revealed to the world that she was a girl. Yes, she has a weakness for Hello Kitty, although she personally feels like Gudetama represents our whole generation —and I had to Google that on the side because I had no flipping clue what she was talking about. She also prefers coffee over chocolate, but the combination is superior, and since her family hails from a coffee *and* cocoa country, she's extremely sensitive to bad quality stuff. I already put an order for high end chocolate truffles with coffee bean centers to gift her for Christmas.

There were so many other details, jokes, movies, seemingly unimportant things that kept the conversation going until dawn. But I filed each one of them in my memory bank, because even if she mentioned them just to pass the time, they must be important enough to be at the forefront of her mind.

So I guess we did have our first date, it was just an unconventional one—especially because we skipped around and kissed well before it. And even though we didn't talk about any of the important stuff, like where are we going from here, how serious this is, when do we make it public… I don't care.

I'm not in a rush. Sierra will tell me exactly what she wants when she wants it, and not a second earlier. It's her world and I'm just living in it, happy to spin circles around her if that's what she wants. Like the lovesick fool that I am.

I push myself off my desk, casually casting a glance around the office to see what everyone's doing and calculating the likelihood that they'll see me bring Sierra coffee. Rachel's not at her desk because, now that she's moving to another team starting January, she's been splitting her time with them to train in advance. Richard's gone off to a meeting in another floor. Stephen's in one of the soundproof booths on the opposite corner. Dave is still suspiciously sick at home.

The ones to watch out for are Kaylee and Lewis. The latter's sitting at his desk beside mine, headphones on as he listens in on a meeting. Kaylee's perusing a *SPORTY* magazine displaying the ace pitcher of a rising baseball team on the cover. I've seen her spend hours reading the articles and dissecting every minutia allegedly for research—A.K.A. checking out the hot athletes featured on the issues—so I guess this is as safe as it's going to get.

I stuff my hands in the pockets of my jeans and whistle All I Want For Christmas Is You as I head over to the kitchen. I can practically feel Sierra's laser beams pierce the back of my head.

There's a sliver of old coffee in the pot, and I can't give her that. I pour it down the sink and set out to clean out the machine's filter to start a brew from scratch. As I wait, I lean my hips against the counter and scratch my beard.

What's a good place for a date around here? The last time I went out on one while living in Mapleton, I was in high school. And back then, going to the mall cinema was the biggest deal. Obviously, that's not gonna cut it this time.

"Wow, I'm rusty," I murmur to myself. But also, it's not like this is New York City, where there's always something going on. My dating scene over there used to be fancy parties thrown by sponsors or by one of the other WAGs, or some celebrity events my former manager scored me tickets for.

None of that is available now. I also have a feeling Sierra wouldn't gravitate to those things, which makes me like her even more.

I pull up my cellphone and type *good places for a date in Mapleton, CT.* I'm about to click on a blog result when someone speaks right beside me.

"Are you finally dating someone?"

I jump and put my phone against my chest. "Lewis. Has no one told you that reading other people's phones is rude?"

"You looked so engrossed, I figured it was something good." He grabs a new mug from the rack and stares at the coffeemaker as if that would hurry it up. "So, who's the lucky girl? Is it someone at *SPORTY*?"

"Her name is none of your damn business, last name get lost."

He snorts. "She must be, then, if that's the response I get."

"Don't make me ask you if you're dating someone at *SPORTY* just to get you off my back."

"Low blow, man." His eyebrows pinch. Everyone and their mom knows that he has a giant flaming torch for Kaylee, but he also knows—just like the rest of us—that she only has eyes for Stephen. The real mystery is Stephen, because he gives zero indication of whether he's interested in her or anyone at all. Hence, the never ending stalemate.

And also why Kaylee and Lewis would love to get their hands on the breaking news that Sierra and I are… doing whatever it is that we're doing now. It would be a reprieve from their own drama.

"Not sorry. You started it," I say as the machine finishes the cycle and I reach over for a clean mug with the company logo.

"Anyway, you could try that fancy new restaurant on Main," he says as we walk out of the kitchenette with steaming mugs in hand.

"The one with the huge windows overlooking the street with the most traffic in the entire town?" I snort a laugh. "You tried."

Lewis grins. "What can I say? I'm just curious to see who finally snagged the most eligible bachelor in *SPORTY*."

"The what?" My eyes bulge.

Sierra swivels on her chair, her jaw dropping.

And of course, this is the one thing that tears Kaylee's attention from the magazine. "Ohh, is Conor off the market?"

I look anywhere but at Sierra as I head back to my desk and sit down with a huff. "Can you guys keep it down? I have to hop into a meeting with a client now."

"Sure, sure. But you have to tell us all the details afterward."

I ignore Kaylee by making a big show of putting on my headphones. Said meeting isn't a lie, but it's not for another ten minutes. So I key in my password and find the chat with Sierra again.

MAHONEY, CONOR - 4:03PM:

Sorry. I think I'll have to keep the coffee

I'll treat you later when we head to my place?

But that gets me no response for the rest of the day. Until I'm driving us to my house.

*

"Okay, now tell me what the heck happened to make Lewis think you're dating someone in the company in a matter of like, five minutes." Sierra's arms are folded tight and she glares straight ahead at the road.

I turn my attention to it because it's snowing pretty hard. Sighing, I say, "I was looking up places to go on a date."

"Anything good?" she surprises me by asking.

"I don't know yet. I couldn't even click on the link before he started trying to fish for information." After a beat, I add, "Sorry."

Sierra turns to the window. "It's okay. Eventually everybody will find out, right? It's just that right now it's so…"

"New?"

"Yes. And different."

"That too." I tap my steering wheel. "A month ago we were exchanging barbs in every conversation. I guess they'll pass out when they see us holding hands or something."

"Or not," she says with more calm than I'd have expected. "Conor, there's something you should know."

"Uh-oh, that sounds bad."

Sierra clears her throat and because I stop at a red light and traffic is light, I allow myself to look at her directly. She's biting her lips in a way that lately makes my blood boil, and that makes me miss the first words she says. "…about us."

"What?"

"They have a whole bet running about us."

"*What?*" I ask with more force.

"Yeah, half of our team thinks we'll eventually end up dating. The other half says it's never gonna happen. Apparently, it's running for a few hundred dollars."

My jaw drops. If it wasn't because someone honks behind us, I'd have stayed frozen there until I turned into an old man. I get us going again before I dare to speak. "Uh, so who all is winning?"

"Rachel and Kaylee. They saw the potential before we did."

"Huh, and here I thought I was the captain of this ship," I say with a snort.

"So, about that date…" Sierra trails off and I tense, waiting for whatever comes next. "When is it going to be?"

I shift a little on my seat. "Maybe this weekend after the event?"

"Hmm, sounds good."

I bite my lips so I don't hoot like a frat boy or something, and we spend the rest of the drive in a weird silence where it's tense with all the things I'm not saying, because I'm busting at the seams. I want to tell her that being with her makes me feel just as happy as when I was smack in the middle of a gritty hockey shift, like deep down I have this certainty that it's what I'm supposed to be doing with my life.

Sierra jumps out of my truck the second I park it, but she grabs my hand as we trudge over the snowy gravel to my front door. The house feels colder inside than the air outside, and I hurry to get a fire going so it can warm up. Tonight we have to wrap as many presents as we possibly can. They'll be the ones we throw in the ball pit for people to fish around, and we intend to be generous. It will definitely help the process if our fingers are not falling off with frostbite.

"Come here." I motion at her to join me by the fireplace and she skips over. This isn't the first night of overtime work where this has happened, but it's the first time I pull her close against me and hug her from behind.

Sierra sinks against me with a sigh that does something to me. I'm pretty sure my whole body is as hot behind her as the heat radiating off the fire in front of us.

"Can we stay like this the whole night?" she asks with a sleepy voice.

"If it was up to me, yes. A thousand times yes." I tuck my chin over her head and hug her just a bit tighter. "But maybe laying down on the couch instead."

"Ugh, don't tempt me, Mahoney." Slowly, she extricates herself from my hold and turns. She blinks slowly at me, more because she's tired than anything else. "Let's get to work before I fall asleep and start snoring in your presence. It's way too early in this relationship for that."

So, it is a relationship? I tuck my tongue against my cheek, voicing nothing to that effect and just basking in the win.

"Okay. Let's turn this place into a gift factory."

I make us two cups of coffee as strong as tar and she sets out the layout in the living room. It gets toasty pretty quick, so we discard our outerwear and sit on the carpet around the coffee table. We get to wrapping and it goes well maybe for an hour or two, we start collecting a decent pile of presents wrapped in clear cellophane with curly ribbons.

But then all of a sudden I blink, and my eyelids don't lift again. The last thing I'm aware of is something soft falling on my shoulder.

CHAPTER 24
SIERRA

It smells amazing. Line pine, cinnamon, steaming hot chocolate with little marshmallows floating on the surface. Like the warmth of a cozy fireplace and cheer and happiness. I inhale deep, trying to absorb as much of it as I can, and that's when it clicks in my sleep addled brain.

What it really smells like is… man. Laundry detergent, clean skin and deodorant.

I keep my eyes closed, just letting my other senses paint a clearer picture. The next thing I notice is that I'm rising and falling ever so gently, which makes absolutely no sense until I finally understand why I'm so warm. It's because I'm lying half on top of Conor. My head rests on his shoulder and I have one arm over his chest. In fact, my hand is curled around his neck. Most problematic is that I have one of his thighs trapped between my legs all possessive-like.

And I can tell this is my doing, because Conor is still out cold on the carpet, his arm trapped between the base of the couch and my back. His steady breath fans over my face, which is what buoys me every so often. His free hand holds my arm in place.

I shift my head back by minuscule increments, but my nose brushes with the beard at his chin and it makes him twitch. Conor squeezes his eyes behind his glasses—which somehow managed to stay put—and after a deep breath, he opens his eyes.

And they keep widening some more after catching sight of my curly hair so close to him.

"Um, hi," I say with a voice raspy with disuse. Conor doesn't even move an inch, which also makes it impossible for me to guess whether my breath stinks or not. That's something I've never had to worry about until this literal moment.

"Hi." He blinks fast, maybe not yet processing but certainly not making any effort to let go. "What time is it?"

I haven't the foggiest clue nor the slightest interest in moving so I can find out. All I do is cast a glance around. Bright light streams in through the windows, which is not at all what I expected. The last time I remember closing my eyes, it was nighttime but early. Maybe around eight? We had only been wrapping presents for a little while.

Crap, did we sleep like twelve hours?

Groaning, I push away from his chest and sit back. Conor hisses and I freeze. "I'm sorry, did I hurt you?"

"No." He snorts. "The problem is that I like it too much."

It being that I'm straddling his thigh. As I jump away, I echo what I said last night. "Oops. Definitely too early for that in this relationship."

Or is it? Because as I watch him sit up, how those wide shoulders of his stretch the fabric of his clothes, and I realize that I just had my head lying on one of them… I kinda want to backtrack and say it's perfect timing. That we can definitely keep snoozing or…

Conor lifts the knee farthest from me and sets his arm on it, propping himself up with the other one. Does he know how good he looks that way? With his hair a royal mess from sleep? With his brown eyes staring at half mast?

My eyes catch on something I hadn't noticed before. The T-shirt under his open flannel shirt has bunched up, showing a sliver of his hip muscle. My tongue is a lump in my mouth but somehow I manage to swallow and not salivate in front of him.

"You keep saying that word." Conor's voice is velvet wrapping around me. I have to shake my head to make the words fall in the right order in my mind.

"What word?"

"Relationship."

I lick my lips to stall, but I don't know how to navigate this. Every guy I've dated has approached me first, but they've also left me before things could really become official. In contrast, I have yet to go on a formal date with Conor, but I already know I don't really need to. He's more than I ever dared to dream about and for some reason, he has bad enough taste to like me back.

"Is… is that an issue?" I wait with bated breath for an ax to fall.

But this former hockey player turned lumberjack says, "Nope. But I didn't want you to feel pressured into labels if you didn't want to." He runs his free hand through his hair, messing it up even more. "Besides, this hasn't been quite, uh, conventional."

"Does it have to be?" I shrug and run my hands over my thighs, trying to shake off the last of my nerves. "Who said we have to follow a formula to be together?"

His eyebrows rise. "Does that mean you don't want to go out on a date with me after all?"

"Not on one, but I'll settle for hundreds of them. Maybe thousands." I scoot over the short distance back to him and grab a fistful of his T-shirt to pull him closer. "What I mean is, I don't need to go to some overpriced restaurant with you and make small talk to figure out that I want to be with you."

Conor holds my neck, applying delicious pressure to the back of my head to bring me closer. His eyes singularly focus on my lips as he says, "How funny, I feel the same way."

"Wait." He freezes, eyes lifting to mine. "Does my breath stink?"

The corner of his lips lifts. "To be honest—"

"Oh, no." I slap a hand over my mouth.

Chuckling, Conor shifts to free his other hand so it can remove the barrier. "You could spend a whole month without showering or brushing your teeth and you'll still smell better than a locker full of sweaty jocks."

"Oh, okay." I nod my head. "I guess that means you're up for a stinky morning kiss, then?"

"Very much up for it, yes," Conor responds with a solemn nod. "You? I mean, I haven't exactly spent the whole night eating peppermint candy."

I crash my laughing mouth on his and I decide it's a waste of time to worry or to even try to brush my teeth, when I can better spend it like this. In Conor's arms—well, not exactly. I'm just leaning over him. But as the kiss gets more intense and my hands on his shoulder and chest aren't enough to keep me upright, I feel him grab my hips and lift me onto his lap with no resistance from my end.

A gasp escapes from my throat as he settles me down easily and even wraps my arms around his neck. "How's that?"

"Me gusta." I shake my head again. "I mean, I like it. How about we don't move for the rest of the day?"

"If only." He leans closer to trap my lower lip between his. One of this hands stays firmly on my hip as the other one travels, first going backward to the curve of my butt, inching up towards my back and leaving a trail of tingling fire. "This is way better than wrapping presents."

I'm about to suggest maybe unwrapping each other when buzzing starts from somewhere nearby. I ignore it in favor for another kiss, this time rising on my knees so I can control it. I run my fingers through his hair and it makes his chest vibrate with a groan of those that shut my brain off.

Or would, if it wasn't for the incessant buzzing.

Our lips make a loud smacking sound as I tear apart. "That's a phone, isn't it?"

"Maybe?" Conor squeezes his eyes shut, his nose wrinkling in an adorable way. "Can we keep pretending we're in a secluded cabin in the woods?"

"We *are* in a secluded cabin in the woods." I chuckle and peck him in the lips. I love that even though we're very open about what's going on between us now, his face is still as red as a tomato. It makes me wonder if the rest of his skin looks just the same under his clothes.

"Right." Sighing, he opens his eyes. "How about this, if it's nothing important we keep making out for a bit and then get back to work."

"Sounds perfect." I drop another little kiss on the tip of his nose and Conor squeezes my hip in return. One of the saddest things I've ever done is crawling away from him right now.

Our movements are equally as lethargic as we look around for our phones. Conor finds his first among the cushions on the couch and shakes his head. It must mean that the buzzing was from mine, and when it starts back up I locate the offending device face down on the coffee table, under a mound of unused wrapping paper.

I pick up my phone and two things register at the same time. First, it's eight thirty in the morning. Second, the one calling is my mom. I connect the two dots in an instant.

I've been missing in action for about twelve hours.

"Mom, I'm okay!" I say as greeting the second I pick up the call.

"Sierra Fernandez!" Her screech is so loud that even Conor shrinks. "Where the hell have you been? Your father and Grammie and I are freaking out—"

"Grammie?" I gasp. "But her hypertension—"

"You come home right this second and explain yourself!"

Then the line goes dead. Which means…

"Oh, I'm so dead."

"Quick. Let's take you home." Conor jumps to his feet in a second and starts gathering around my stuff strewn about his living room, starting by the one shoe I managed to remove in my sleep, and even my purse.

I whimper.

Conor's lips twitch but he manages to stay serious. "Get up, Sierra."

"I know I have to, but that's the start of my death march."

He sets all my stuff at the end of the couch and starts putting on his winter layers. "It's going to be okay."

"No, you don't get it." I've lost all desire to live, but somehow pull myself to my feet and start donning my outer layers. "Latin American parents are… Even more specifically, my parents are really old school. They're going to leap to conclusions I have no way of proving otherwise."

Conor stops by the door. "I'll be your witness, then."

I choke in the middle of wrapping my scarf around my neck. After thumping my chest hard, I say, "Do you have a death wish? If you so much as pop your head into the discussion you'll lose it."

"Worth it." He shrugs. "Let's go."

"Conor!"

"I assume the more we tarry, the more they'll theorize?"

"Shit. Let's hurry."

We tumble out of Conor's house and the hurrying ends right there. The outside has become a field of white blanketing the pine trees, the ground, and more importantly, Conor's pickup truck that brought us here.

He rubs the top of his head over his beanie. "New plan, I'm gonna start shoveling and in the meantime, you call your parents to let them know we'll be there within the hour."

"Okay, and then I help you." We nod to each other and get to work.

*

"Stay in the car," I say as I unbuckle my seatbelt.

"Nope." But Conor's faster and he's out of the vehicle before I can even process.

Yelping, I try to move faster. Except, I slip as I get out of the car and latching on the door gives him enough time to walk around it. I watch as if everything was happening in slow motion—Conor rushing over to help me at the same time as Mom and Dad open the front door.

"Sierra Fernandez!"

This is when Conor catches me in his arms, legs spread wide to balance our combined weight. We both turn to my parents.

Dad's face is purpler than I've ever seen it and he's gnashing his teeth in a way that looks painful. Meanwhile, Mom holds up her cellphone like she's taking a picture of us. Our front yard isn't very long, and the nearness helps me catch a tinny voice coming from the device.

"¿Grammie? ¡Estoy bien!" I scream from the sidewalk.

"No. You. Are. Not!" Dad grouches back and points a finger at the porch floor. "Come here right this second."

"I'm going to let you go slowly," Conor whispers in my ear. "Ready?"

"No. Yes." I grab onto his arms until my feet are firm on the frozen path. To my family, I say, "I can explain."

Dad turns his index finger into the house. "In! Now."

Goodness. I've never heard him speak in syllables alone. I'm really done for this time.

I shrug my purse strap higher and trudge at a snail pace.

"¿Y ese quién es?" Grammie asks from through the phone, and that's when I see Conor following after me.

"I said stay in the car," I half hiss, half whisper.

"No." The set of his eyebrows is as stern as I've ever seen it and I figure I can't help a man who is bent on marching to his death.

No one says anything until we're secure inside the house, away from our snooping neighbors. I didn't see anyone openly watching, but I have no doubt they were.

Once the door is closed, Dad rounds on me. "¡Explícate, señorita!"

I draw in air and explain, "Conor and I were working on the office event but we were so tired from everything that's been going on, that we fell asleep and woke up with Mom's phone call. That's the honest truth, cross my heart and hope to die."

"Fell asleep?" Dad's eyes bulge.

"Is that how kids are calling it these days?" Mom grumbles, still holding the phone up.

"Que alguien me diga qué pasa," Grammie says from her end.

Mom starts translating for her, but Dad's not done with this. He lifts an accusing finger at Conor. "You! Who the hell are you and what are your intentions with my daughter?"

"Um, I'm sorry for greeting you this way but my name is Conor Mahoney and I'm..." He blinks at me. "Whatever Sierra wants me to be?"

I press my lips tight so I don't laugh, groan, or intone any epithets that could get me in further trouble. Dad shifts his angry gaze between Conor and I, and I can practically see the gears in his mind churning.

"Her chauffeur?" Dad asks.

My jaw drops.

"Yes." Conor is nonplussed.

"Organ donor?"

"Hopefully we don't get to that point but sure."

I snap my mouth closed and look at Mom, asking for help. But she's busy translating for Grammie in real time.

"Bank account?" Dad folds his arms.

Conor bobs his head. "I'm not super wealthy, but yeah."

"But after marriage," my dad has the nerve to say and I've had enough.

"Stop, Dad." I step in between them, even though they weren't about to come to blows or anything. "Conor and I literally started going out two days ago. Why are you talking about marriage?"

"Because that's when couples can have sleepovers," he says back.

Heat travels up my neck and settles in my face. "Yeah, okay. This was an accident. I—I assure you nothing like that happened." The slip is because something did happen, just not what Dad fears most. Even then, he probably wouldn't be glad to imagine his one and only daughter climbing some man's lap to eat his mouth for breakfast. "Can we please stop this and move on with our lives?"

Dad's finger travels in the air between Conor and I. "If this happens again, I won't be this kind." With that, he turns around and stomps toward the rooms.

Mom starts giggling. "Grammie, tu nieta tiene su primer novio."

I hide my face behind my hands.

"Hmm." Conor hums beside me. "I take it we live to see another day?"

"You do, I'll get killed the second you leave," I respond, muffled by my hands.

"Then should I stay?"

Sighing, I lift my head. "No, it's best if you go back home and get a head start on the gifts. I'll… I'll join you from the afterlife later."

"Go." Mom nods at him. "It's all good now."

But I know it isn't. Conor gives me a sweet hug I'd have loved to linger in, and Mom, Grammie, and I watch him head back out to his truck.

Grammie breaks the silence. "Se ve grande ese muchacho."

My face steams even more as I explain that he looks big because he was once an elite hockey player, and then the two of them launch into a barrage of questions that truly send me to the next life.

CHAPTER 25
CONOR

"**B**reathe."

"I'm breathing," Sierra says in a squeak.

"Deeper." I order, giving her hand a little squeeze. In return, she clutches at my hand in a death grip. I lock every muscle in place not to wince. "Are you sure you're breathing?"

"No. I've decided it's best to pass out right here and have you carry me away. That way neither of us has to be subjected to this torture." She turns a toothy grimace my way.

"I have bad news for you." My voice is a soft whisper that echoes in the hallway, just outside of the conference room at the top floor across from the CEO's office. That's where all the company's executives currently sit. "We've postponed this until the literal last minute. If we don't do this now, it's never."

"Would that be so bad?" Sierra blinks up at me, a little wrinkle appearing on her forehead. "Like, the whole event won't be ruined just because we don't convince the executives to do this. So, why are we even trying?"

"For fun."

"Whose? Because I'm shaking in my Uggs and you're bathed in sweat."

"It'll be fun when everyone's drunk at the party." I wipe a bead from my brow. "Maybe we should've taken a couple of shots of liquid courage before this."

"I wish," she grumbles.

"In any case, it's too late to run. We already got a spot in the agenda to talk about this and it was announced to them, so…" I swing her arm gently. "Just remember you're not alone in this."

"You better not let me talk all by myself, Conor Mahoney, or else." She narrows those dark eyes of hers that make me feel like she can see right through to the core of me, promising a world of pain if I don't do what she says. I'm pretty sure this is going to be my life from now on, and I don't mind it one bit.

"I won't." I lift her hand, bringing the back of it against my lips. I want to linger in the moment as long as I can, my eyes lost in hers, my lips on her skin, inhaling the soft scent that is only hers—something like a warm, spiced vanilla.

But then the door opens and we jump apart.

Richard's still laughing along at something that must've happened a second ago, and when he turns to face us, Sierra and I are at a respectable distance. "Hey, guys. You ready?"

"Of course."

"Totally."

We're both all smiles and fake bravado—that's how you survive in marketing anyway. It's not that exceptionally brilliant people are required to pitch wild ideas to customers while at the same time gathering intel from them—we're just really big practitioners of the fake it till you make it doctrine, mixed with high levels of determination. I feel it's not that different from being a professional athlete.

I motion for Sierra to walk ahead of me and join her in facing all ten executives, plus Martin Richter, *SPORTY*'s CEO.

Individually they're all pretty chill, except for Camila Puig. But together, they're ten Camilas. This is why this executive team has taken the brand to worldwide stardom, competing toe and toe with the top European and Asian brands of sportswear and equipment.

A trickle of sweat travels down the middle of my back and I stand stoic against the itch.

"Hi, everyone. Thank you for granting us a few minutes of your time," I start just as Sierra and I rehearsed earlier. "This is Sierra Fernandez, and I'm Conor Mahoney. We work for Richard in marketing and today we'd like to request your support for the annual Christmas event that will take place this Friday."

Our boss nods, which is a little hint for everyone else to be amenable to this. Meanwhile, Camila looks at us as if she couldn't believe we just wasted thirty seconds of her life introducing ourselves to *her* again.

Sierra takes it from here, seemingly unfazed by the glaring executive. "Now, I'll preface this by clarifying that it isn't a request for further budget. In fact, we've optimized expenses to reduce twenty percent of our allocated budget."

Richard gives us a discreet little thumb up. At the same time, the body languages in general improve. I decide it's best if I ignore Camila altogether for my own mental health.

"What we'd like to ask you is…" I make a strategic pause until I lift a shopping bag and place it at the end of the long table. "That you stick to a very specific dress code."

Martin's eyebrows rise. "Oh?"

"We thought the best way for the employee base to relax and get in a festive mood, aside from spiked eggnog, would be if our executives lead by the example." I put my hand in the bag and grab a fistful of velvety fabric, knowing exactly what I'm about to pull out because I literally packed this bag myself.

I take a bracing breath and take out a very familiar looking garment. "Martin, we're thinking this should be your attire."

I hold the red fabric up with my other hand, in case it's not clear to everyone that it's the top half of a Santa outfit.

"And for everyone else…" Sierra repeats the same motion, this time pulling out a green garment. "Santa's helpers."

You could hear a pin drop in the ensuing silence.

How come this doesn't feel like an out of body experience at all? That would make this so much funnier, or at least I wouldn't be so aware of how fast my heartbeat is, or that I'm pretty sure I've soaked through every clothing layer under my armpits.

From the corner of my eye, Sierra appears composed and regal. No one would guess she was five shaky rabbits in a trench coat just a few minutes ago. She has this way more down pat than I do—maybe because she has two years more work experience than me, or because her personality is generally more kickass than mine. She'd have made a fine hockey goalie, to be honest.

But then Andre, the CFO, blows a raspberry that ends in guffaws. "Oh, wow. That's just amazing. I'd have paid big money for this and I'm going to get it for free? Sign me the hell up."

"Did you get my size, you guys?" Richard grins.

I respond solemnly. "Yes, sir. Size L at the top, M at the bottom. One second—" I rummage through the bag until I find Richard's outfit in a smaller package. "Here it is."

"Perfect, throw it over."

I toss it in the air and it lands right in his hands.

Martin slams his hands on the table and stands up, making everyone freeze. His eyes narrow on Sierra and I, and after a long moment he says, "I'll only do it if there's a beard and hat too."

Sierra's face breaks into a brilliant smile. "Of course. We can also get you a fake beer belly if you want."

Lindsay, the boss of procurement, says, "I didn't know there was beer in the North Pole." She extends her hands out, waiting for her package, and Sierra takes it as the hint to start passing them along. We did our best to estimate the sizes based on eye measurement alone, and it seems to have worked for the most part based on the light conversation around the table.

That is, until Camila Puig receives her outfit.

One by one, all the voices and laughter are snuffed out. We all watch her, waiting for her reaction. I don't think anyone else will drop out just because Camila may be the only odd one out, but it'd definitely make the whole thing weirder.

"Do I really have to?" She sighs.

Sierra and I exchange a glance and I can glean that we're on the same wavelength. That wasn't a firm no.

Before either of us ventures a say, Martin speaks. "Well, it's not mandatory and neither is attendance. However, like our marketing colleagues said, we do lead by example."

"Fine." Camila drops her outfit package on the table and leans back on her chair. "But I'm only wearing the top and I'm ditching the ridiculous hat."

My eye twitches. That's the only reaction I'm brave enough to show, even though I almost feel like doing the celly I favored when I scored a goal—one fist in the air, arm folded as if I were showing off my bicep.

"Excellent, I'm looking forward to getting drunk in this thing," says Felix, our legal exec.

And with that, we win by shutout.

*

Unfortunately, the elevator was packed on our way down to the sales and marketing floor, including our boss, which means

Sierra and I couldn't celebrate by giving each other a loud, sloppy kiss the kind that accelerates our cardiac rhythm. Alas, all we can do is sit at our desks, passing along messages on chat and avoiding each other's eyes.

MAHONEY, CONOR - 11:21AM:

You were amazing

FERNANDEZ, SIERRA - 11:21AM:

So were you

Thank you for not leaving me alone

MAHONEY, CONOR - 11:21AM:

Never

You didn't look nervous at all, how did you do it?

FERNANDEZ, SIERRA - 11:21AM:

Easy, I was dead on the inside

I snort and duck my head, in case anyone's watching me too closely.

CONOR, MAHONEY - 11:22AM:

Well, now that that's done, it should be smooth sailing from here

FERNANDEZ, SIERRA - 11:22AM:

Don't you dare jinx it, Mahoney

CONOR, MAHONEY - 11:22AM:

Let's see

Music — check

Catering — check

Props — check

Gifts — wrapped

Execs — festived

FERNANDEZ, SIERRA - 11:23AM:

That's not a word

My phone pings and I type the next message in our chat quickly.

CONOR, MAHONEY - 11:23AM:

Let me ride this high, woman

After hitting send, I grab my phone and it's still ringing. I tap the green button and bring the device to my ear. "This is Conor Mahoney."

"Mr. Mahoney, it's Joe Malone from Malone and Sons."

That's the carpenter we hired for the booths, so I sit up straighter. "Hi, Mr. Malone. How are you doing? Are the booths coming along?"

Sierra's head pops over the edge of her computer monitor, dark eyes attentive.

"That's precisely what I was calling about," the other man says, clearing his throat. "I'm afraid we have a problem."

"What kind of problem?" At my question, Sierra jumps to her feet so fast that her chair slides backward a few feet. Our other coworkers start looking up like meerkats.

"That big snow we just had stranded one of our trucks with the rest of the wood we needed for the project. I tried to shift around supplies from other jobs but it's not enough. We're short by three booths."

I take a sharp intake of air through my nose.

"Conor? What?" Sierra rounds our desks until she stands right next to me. "What's happening?"

I run a hand through my hair, my attention trained on her

as I speak with the carpenter. "Does this mean you're certain that you can't complete the job?"

"That's right." I can tell by the man's voice that this pains him just as much as it does me. "Of course, I'll offer you a refund."

"I—I understand, thank you. If you don't mind, I have to talk with my colleague now to come up with a plan B."

"Right, sorry for the inconvenience."

"No, thank you," I grumble and we disconnect the call.

"Conor!" Sierra grabs my shoulders and gives me a shake. "You're killing me, what happened with the booths?"

"We're going to be short by three." I explain the situation through gritted teeth. "Sorry, it looks like I jinxed it."

"I didn't know you had the power to make it snow." She cries, throwing her hands in the air and letting them fall on her face. "Ugh, this ruins the whole plan. What are we going to do now?"

Sighing, I get up and pull her against me, wrapping my arms around her. It works, because she immediately relaxes against me. I bury my face in her curls. "We could call every carpenter in town."

"The lead time is too tight, I'm sure they're full booked by now," she mumbles against my chest. "Or they're all on holiday already."

"What if we go to a hardware store, buy some plywood, and make the booths ourselves?"

"I know you like chopping wood but have you ever worked with it before? Because I haven't."

"I'm afraid not." I run my hands up and down her back. "Are there any booths we could transform into simple tables?"

"Sure, but where's the magic in that?" She sounds deadpanned at the suggestion. "If only there were Christmas booths just laying around that we could borrow."

I lift my head, blinking hard without seeing anything. Then

Sierra does the same, and a microsecond later we pull away and speak at the same time.

"The Christmas fair!"

I snap my fingers. "That's it, Christmas is saved."

"Don't jinx it again, Mahoney." She twists out of my arms to palm her pockets until she produces her cellphone. "First, we need to see if it's still open."

"If not, I'm sure someone at the convention center can give us a lead." I grab my car keys with one hand and my coat with the other. "I'll drive until the end of the earth if it means I can come back in time for the event with three damn booths."

"Let's go." Sierra nods at me and rushes to her side to pick up her things.

That's when someone else clears their throat.

We both freeze in midair and I guess Sierra is having the same realization as me—which is that we got so wrapped up in the disaster, we might have forgotten that we weren't on our own.

All our colleagues, including our freaking boss, watch us with equal levels of interest. Except for Rachel—she seems more amused than surprised. I guess Sierra must've told her we started dating already.

"What just happened?" Lewis asks with his mouth hanging open.

"I think…" Kaylee starts slowly. "That y'all just lost a bet, suckers!"

"Hah!" Rachel jumps to her feet and claps her hands. "Pay up."

Sierra's expression grows sour and she mumbles something in Spanish that I have no hope of understanding from my Duolingo skills alone. As she finishes shrugging her coat on, she says, "Let's deal with this later. We have more pressing concerns right now."

"Right." I clear my throat and give her a wide berth as we head over to the elevators.

Except right before we're out of our colleagues' sight, Sierra slips her hand in mine and the stooges explode in hoots and hollers. I turn to Sierra but she's smiling like she did it on purpose.

And that's how the entire company finds out the formerly bitter rivals are now an item.

CHAPTER 26
SIERRA

"Was that okay?" Conor grips the steering wheel harder as if trying to anchor himself. I don't understand why his sudden nerves, though. A quick glance at me has him adding, "I mean, that I blew our cover in a moment of panic and now basically the entire universe will know we're dating?"

"Oh." I lean back against my seat, fiddling with the strap of the seatbelt. "Um, it's earlier than I anticipated revealing this but it's fine. It's not like we're just fooling around." I pause. "Or are we?"

"Nope." His lips make the p pop loudly. "I'm dead serious about you."

He has to keep his attention on the road, but I'm free to stare at him all I want. I gnaw at my bottom lip, wondering if to share what's on my mind or keep quiet. But I'm not very good at secrets anyway, so here it goes.

"It's just, I'm nervous about how this will reflect on me."

He shifts his pretty brown eyes to mine for a second. "What do you mean?"

I take a deep breath and turn to the window. "The scary

part about an office romance is that, if it doesn't work out, it's usually the woman with something to lose. That's why I wanted us to be a bit more, I don't know, firm, before we said anything."

Suddenly his hand's on my knee. "I get the theory," Conor says, "and I will crush whoever dares to talk shit about you."

"Thanks." I snort through my nose and pick up his hand between mine, observing the straight fingers, the tendons and veins showing in the back. "But even if *SPORTY* has a pretty decent environment, it's just how things are in this crappy society. Besides, my reputation is just a few levels below Camila's in light of how I used to treat you, and I'm sure a few of your fans will be very annoyed to find out you like me anyway."

"The solution is for me to scream it higher, then." He shifts his hand until he's lacing his fingers with mine. "Say, maybe we should have a date in front of the whole company."

"What?"

"At the Christmas party." His lips stretch into a grin. "Let's kiss under the mistletoe."

My jaw drops. "You're kidding."

"Not one bit. And based on what you're saying, we need to mark each other's territory pronto."

"That sounds so caveman." I scoff and after a moment, I say, "Deal."

Conor chuckles, and the sound is enough to dissipate that worry from my belly. Another one stays roiling in it, though. "Now, all we need is for these booths to work out and we'll be on track for ten grand each and a promotion for me."

"Hah! That's a good one. You mean ten grand each and a promotion for me?" Conor teases back.

"Don't be mistaken, dating hasn't changed the fact that I'll be the one on top."

He bobs his head all nonchalant for someone who just got

thrown a major challenge at him. "I admit I do like you on top."

"Conor!" I still have hold of his hand so it's easy to smack his arm.

"What?" he asks all innocent like, not even bothered by my smack. "I was pretty sure you liked sitting on my thighs and having my hands all over you this morning."

Heat rushes not just to my face, but everywhere else, and I'm not sure what I can do with it while we're strapped inside the cabin of his pickup truck going forty miles per hour. I drop his hand on his own lap and say, "Ugh, is this what dating you is going to be like from now on?"

"Yes." But then he shakes his head. "No, I'm probably going to get worse, actually." For a brief moment, he turns to me while licking his lips in a way that makes the heat in my belly turn positively volcanic. "You're making me lose my mind, Sierra. I've been dreaming about you every night since we kissed the first time."

I suck in all the air in the space, which makes me choke. All the little prick does is laugh with that husky voice of his while he drives us the rest of the way downtown at a snail pace.

Thing is, my shock isn't because of what he said, per se. It's because I've had the exact same problem the past few nights. Like just a few kisses from him have awakened my hormones to a level I'd never felt before. I've leapt the stage of *I find him hot* straight into *I'll mark my territory soon* like a freaking cavewoman —and soon can't be soon enough.

Finally, we arrive at the convention center and we hastily exit the truck. We grab hands as we dash across the half empty parking lot, leaving plums of breath in our wake. It only clicks with me that something's weird when Conor and I make it to the entrance.

"Wait." I breathe with difficulty, and it's not because of the run. The ticket counter is closed and the gaudy decorations we saw last time are gone. The sign welcoming us to the Christmas market fair is missing and there's literally not a soul in sight. "Oh, no."

Conor pushes through the inner door leading to the convention floor, and holds it open for me. As we walk in, all that's missing is the tumbleweed to make the scene even more devastating.

The whole thing is empty.

The only proof that there ever was a Christmas fair is a few strands of golden tinsel strewn on the carpet here, some red glitter there, a few green leaves over there. Even my harsh breathing echoes in the vast emptiness.

"What are we going to do?" I whine.

Conor tightens his hold on my hand. "We won't give up yet. Let's see if we find anyone."

"What for? Everything's been cleared. We're screwed." I drag my feet after him and at first, it feels like we're walking aimlessly until I realize he's following the overhead signs that guide the way to some offices beyond a corridor.

It's warmer here, which is the first sign of life we've found since we arrived. Conor struts like he owns the place, I don't know if it's because he's been here before or if he's just that determined to make this work. It must be a hardcore athlete thing, that of not giving up easily, and I'm so glad I have him to snap me out of my spirals. He did the same thing earlier when I was freaking out before talking with the executives, and if it hadn't been for his encouragement I'd have collapsed under the weight of my own fear of failure.

The wall on the right opens to a counter and behind it sits an older lady clicking away at a computer keyboard.

At last, human life.

"Excuse me, ma'am," Conor says with his most polite voice. "We work at *SPORTY* and we're interested in talking about an event we need help with."

Succinct message loaded with keywords that should get us some results. I could kiss the guy for his brilliance right now.

Slowly, the woman tears her attention from what we're interrupting and she blinks up at Conor. "Wait, aren't you Conrad's grandson?"

"Uh, yes." He glances at me, as if checking for any clues as to whether this is good or bad news.

"He did say his grandson works at *SPORTY* one time at bingo." She rummages around on her desk behind the counter until she brings up a clipboard with a pen. "Fill in this interest form. Although you didn't have to come all the way here, you know? You could've set an appointment online."

"Actually, ma'am, um…" I clear my throat once her pointed stare turns to me. "I'm afraid we're on an aggressive time schedule. We were hoping we could talk with someone now… or today. Any time today is fine."

She scowls and pushes her glasses higher by the corner of one lens. "You're lucky that today is a slow day, but I won't guarantee anything until I talk with the boss." Grunting, she pushes to her feet and turns away saying, "Be right back."

"Right. Thank you." As she disappears behind a door, I say to Conor, "I could kiss your grandfather right now."

"How about you kiss me instead?" He tilts his head and taps his cheek right above the trimmed edge of his beard.

I shake my head. "How are you so calm?"

"Me? Calm?" He scoffs. "I'm about to pop one extra anti-anxiety pill."

"Does this help?" I pull him lower by his arm and peck his cheek right where he pointed before.

The rascal turns his face right before I lean away, and steals a quick taste of my lips that makes my toes curl in my Uggs. "Oh, yeah. That's the best medicine." Conor smirks as he pulls away.

Fortunately—or unfortunately—that's when the receptionist walks back out. "You're in luck. The boss is between meetings and she'll see you now. Follow me."

Conor raises a fist in celebration and I send me most heartfelt thanks up to the heavens. We all but skip after the older woman as she takes us down a narrower hallway, until she stops at an office door embossed with a woman's name and the title Event Center CEO below it. She knocks on the door and a voice sounds from inside.

"Come in!"

The receptionist opens the door and motions us in. This time I lead the charge pulling Conor by his hand, and I stop in the middle of a nice office that overlooks the parking lot. The biggest contrast is that the inside is decked in so many Christmas decorations, this space could be its own fair.

"Please, take a seat." The boss points at the chairs by her desk, and Conor and I scramble to do as bid. "What can I do for you?"

"Right, we—" My words die in my lips when I zero in on the woman's face. Blonde hair, crimson lips, dark eyes, a heart-shaped face… somehow she rings a bell but I can't pinpoint where I might've met her.

She's the one who snaps her fingers. "Oh, I know you two! You were the cute couple who refused to kiss under the mistletoe. I take it you've changed your minds since?" She points at our joined hands.

My mind plucks the memory of her in a revealing Mrs. Claus costume a few weeks back. "You were at the fair."

"That's right." She tosses her hair over her shoulder.

"I thought you were a booth owner," Conor says, eyebrows raised.

"Nah, that's what I let everyone think this year. I'd rather change out of these boring clothes and into something more festive," she says, motioning at her red cardigan. "But I assume that's not what you were here for. *SPORTY*, huh?"

Conor switches back to business faster than I can. "Yes, we actually need your help for the annual Christmas event that our company puts together."

"Hmm, we're a week away from Christmas so I assume your event will be happening in the next few days. The problem is that we're already booked with a Christmas themed art exhibition that we'll start installing tomorrow."

"It's not the venue we need," I say, leaning forward. "It's the booths you had during the market fair."

She blinks her perfectly made up eyes. "The booths."

"Yes, we need to rent them for our event. Our supplier had some issues and we're fresh out of booths."

"And it doesn't matter if the owners live far away," Conor adds in a rush. "We have a pickup truck and we can just go get them if you help us contact them. We're more than happy to compensate everyone generously."

That's right, screw our twenty percent budget savings.

The woman waves her hand. "That won't be necessary—"

"But—"

"Because the booths are ours."

Both Conor and I gasp.

"There's only one problem," she continues saying. "They're already in storage along with five million other props and equipment, and they're also fully disassembled already."

"We're more than happy to find them and assemble them ourselves," I say.

"That's great, but we'll need our facility manager too and he's… kind of particular." She picks up the receiver of a landline phone, and presses some digits on the pad that eventually connect her to this guy. We can hear the droll of his voice from the other end, but the conversation ends quickly and if it wasn't for her nods, I'd fear he isn't willing to help.

However, some ten minutes later we stand next to the facility manager inside a large warehouse that is packed with floor to ceiling shelves. In turn, they're brimming with junk in all sizes from shoeboxes to whole crates.

The guy is less nice than the CEO, because he slaps some work gloves on our hands and walks off without even telling us where he stored the booth parts in the first place.

I glare at his retreating back before turning to Conor. "I guess we don't actually need his help. How hard can it be to find those big, super festive-looking booths?"

"So long as they're not wrapped, we should be able to find them easy enough." Conor tucks his winter gloves in the pocket of his jacket and replaces them for the neoprene coated ones. "Should we divide and conquer?"

"Good plan or midnight will catch us out here. I'll take the next aisle over and you check this one."

"Roger that." He salutes and I swivel on my heels. "Wait."

His hand closes around my arm and he pulls me towards him. My back lands against his chest and before I can react, his fingers tilt my chin back and his head obscures the overhead lights. His lips aren't perfectly aligned with mine but for some reason, that shoots tendrils of sensation down my entire body.

"For the road," he says as he pulls away.

I gape after his back, and it takes shaking my head like a dog to snap out of the desire to push him against one of these shelves and have my way with him.

"This freaking guy," I grumble as I march over to the next aisle. "He's going to give me a heart attack one of these days."

Anyway, I better get to work if only to distract myself from the tornado of hormones whipping my insides. I'm not sure how disassembled booths even look like but I remember that they were painted brown, with uneven white trimming and decorations that made them look like oversized gingerbread houses. I ignore everything that looks too small or has too much volume, and find a crate with a pile of flat sheets. I rush over to it, but it looks like a bunch of tables instead.

"I think I found something," Conor announces from the aisle behind mine.

"Oh?" I pick up speed around the shelves. "Should we call the facility guy?"

"No, I think I got it. All I have to—"

But right as I round the corner, his voice cuts off and the shelf rocks dangerously.

I gasp—that's all I can do as I watch Conor take a step back to look up. But the movement causes whatever he's been pulling to come loose, and as it slides down it sends more junk tumbling.

"Conor!"

He puts an arm up but that's not enough. The piece of booth knocks a big box over and it falls on Conor's head.

The same head he once told me was a ticking bomb.

And down he goes.

CHAPTER 27
CONOR

Groaning is the only thing I can do for a hot moment.

I don't know what hurts more, if my freaking head or the shoulder I landed on. I hear my name over and over, and it only registers that it's from Sierra when I feel her hands on my chest, on my face, on my arm.

"Conor, please tell me you're okay."

"I'm okay," I slur, turning over to my back. I try opening my eyes and the white overhead light stabs them in a way that tears another pained noise out of my throat.

"Open your eyes, tell me how many fingers you see."

I squeeze them instead. "The light—"

"Conor, please!" The desperation in her voice forces me to try.

This time her head is right above mine and the light doesn't stab my head anymore, but part of her face is blurry and the one thing that's clear to me is that there are tears streaming down her cheeks.

"Are you hurt?" I lift my hand towards her face, but she traps it in hers.

"Are you freaking kidding me? You're the one who got hurt! Do you see my fingers?"

"Two," I rasp the word out.

"Any dancing lights?"

I squint. "Kinda?" There are some popping flashes here and there, nothing worse than the throbbing on my temple.

"That's it, we're going to the hospital."

"I'm fine, I just need a second to get my bearings."

"No." Her voice is harsh and brokers no argument. "We're going. Can you move?"

I tighten my jaw to not make a single peep as I haul myself up to sitting. I stretch out my hands behind me to balance myself, and one of them falls over a familiar object. My glasses. I feel like I sway slightly as I lift them up for inspection. They're fine, just like I am.

As I put on my glasses, I say, "Sierra, it's not so bad. My bell's just a bit rung but I'll be fine in a moment and then we can get the booths."

"Booths my ass, we're going to get you checked out by a professional." She grabs both of my arms and makes a brave attempt at pushing me to my feet, except I have at least fifty pounds and about a foot on her.

Sighing, I slightly turn on my side to pull myself up. It takes a lot more effort than it should, but no one would be fully functional after almost getting conked out.

Once I'm on my feet, Sierra slides my arm around her shoulder and walks me out of the warehouse. The more steps we take, the clearer my head starts to get, which would be a great sign if it wasn't for my noggin throbbing like a toothache.

We stop by the receptionist and Sierra's the one who speaks. "I'm so sorry, I'm afraid my partner just had an accident in the warehouse and I'll take him to get checked out. May I please have the CEO's card so I can call her back?"

"I'm okay, she's just being overly cautious," I say.

But one look at Sierra's face and the receptionist decides to go for Sierra's side rather than mine. We walk out of the convention center with only a card in Sierra's pocket, instead of the props we came for. She pushes my body to the passenger's side and I expel a heavy breath.

"Are we really doing this?"

"Yep, I'm not taking your safety lightly. Duck your head," she commands as though I didn't know how to get in my own vehicle. But fine, I can appreciate her concern for me.

After I'm safely strapped in, Sierra walks around the the driver's seat and climbs on. She wipes at the moisture on her face with the back of her work gloves, and extends a hand to me. "Key."

I fish for it and offer it.

She snatches it from the air, sniffling in a way that makes her nose wrinkle adorably. I lean my head back against the headrest and watch her the entire ride. Another good sign is that I'm not getting sleepier, even though the sky's growing dark and the pain in my head stays strong. But I keep quiet. I don't think she'd believe anything I could say right now because she's so damn worried to the point of shaking.

Hopefully, this doesn't mean I'm an asshole but... my chest feels all warm about it.

We get to the emergency room and even though I walk in of my own free will, I'm already regretting the amount of money from my bonus that will go into paying for this visit. But Sierra's probably right in that I should get checked, because my head isn't exactly in mint condition.

I drop a quick kiss on Sierra's temple right before I get sat on a wheelchair and we're separated.

*

The staff take this just as seriously as Sierra did, and they run enough tests to prove it. Aside from the huge bump toward the left temple, there are no other side effects. The blow didn't open a gash so there's no need for stitches, and the verdict is that I don't even have a concussion. In fact, the flashing lights have completely cleared from my vision and my pupils are responding normally to a beaming light.

However, I'm cleared some three hours later after a healthy dose of painkillers and a new gaping hole in my pocket. I complete the paperwork and follow the signs to return to the lobby, and that's where I find Sierra and Gramps.

I lift my glasses to rub my eyes but they didn't deceive me, those are really them sitting together. Gramps has an arm around Sierra's shoulders, his hand patting her arm sporadically. She's still sniffling the way she was when I left her, as if maybe she's spent all this time crying intermittently and she's now just calming down again.

I swallow hard, my chest squeezing at the sight. She didn't leave, even though I didn't expect her to stay this long. And she called Gramps, even though this shouldn't have been a big deal.

But now it is. This is the biggest of all deals.

I put one foot in front of the other until they take me before them. Their stares, lost among the spots of the granite floors, finally lift to me.

"Conor!"

They jump to their feet and Sierra launches herself at me with such force that I retreat a few steps. I wrap my arms around her and breathe in the shampoo scent of her hair.

"Hi," I whisper in her ear. As response, her arms tighten around me.

"Kid, are you okay?"

I look up at my grandfather. "Yeah, I'm fine. Just needed some industrial strength ibuprofen and I'm brand new. Ish."

"I was so worried," Sierra says, sobbing against my chest.

"I'm gonna have a word with Maeve," Gramps says and I have no idea what he's on about. "How could they let you in their warehouse unsupervised? Is this how they normally operate? Bunch of fools."

"It's my fault." I cringe. "We were in a hurry and I didn't think to ask for help."

"It could've been so much worse, Conor. You can't get hurt when we just started dating after years of me being a jerk to you." She smacks my chest pretty hard.

Chuckling, I catch her fist in my hand just in case she wants to use it again. "Hey—Hey, look at me." Ugh, look at her. Her eyes are swollen and her entire face, but especially her nose, is as red as a tomato. Her lips arch downward, chin still trembling with emotion. She's the most beautiful sight my three eyes have ever seen. "I'm fine. I'm right here. I'm not going anywhere, okay?"

"Are you sure?"

"Dead sure."

"Stop saying you're *dead* anything." She sniffs.

Smiling, I press my lips against hers for a quick kiss. "I'm not dying soon if I can help it."

"Good enough, I guess." Sierra pulls away. "Let's get you home."

Sierra offers to drive us home and take an Uber to her place, but I adamantly refuse. It's already late enough that her parents must be worried. After much canoodling, I convince her to drive my truck home and call an Uber for Gramps and I. She'll pick me up for work tomorrow.

I slump against the backseat of the Uber, exhausted now that this bizarre day is over.

"I nearly keeled over on the spot when the pretty miss called me crying her little heart out." Beside me, Gramps's voice grows gradually gruffer until he has to clear his throat. "I thought something horrible had happened to you, something worse than three years ago."

I rub my sweaty palms on my jeans. "Sorry, Gramps. I hate that I made you both worry."

"Worrying me is normal. I've done that everyday since you were in your mom's tummy. But that young lady…" He shakes his head, and I'm not sure if the flash in his eyes is just from the streetlights or if there really are tears in them. "She was just as bad. Like she already loves you and can't stand the thought of losing you."

My breath hitches in my throat. "I—I—"

"She's the stark opposite of your ex, Conor. So, don't screw this one up."

Gramps just verbalized what I've been feeling all evening, as the doctor and nurses tested my head and my eye—that Sierra cares for me in a way I haven't felt outside of my only blood relative.

She didn't leave. She could've waited only until Gramps arrived and then gone home. She could've decided right there and then that dating a guy with a permanent sports injury is too much hassle, and called it a day. She could've been Nikki two point zero but she's Sierra. And Sierra will do whatever it takes to make sure I'm okay.

Something larger than me surges from deep within me. I grab tight onto the door handle and a fistful of my jeans, squeezing my jaw to contain it. It's something primal and nameless, but somehow I understand it.

I too would move a mountain for her if I had to, because I love her.

"I won't," I finally respond to Gramps, firmer than it should be possible after this day. "Because she's the one for me."

CHAPTER 28
SIERRA

After enough drama to last me a lifetime, the annual *SPORTY* Christmas event is finally underway. The spiked eggnog is flowing, the canapés are vanishing into ravenous mouths, the games are being played, the gifts are being taken, and I finally have a moment of seclusion and peace all by myself in Gramps's office.

Do I feel bad for leaving Conor to the wolves? A little, but I just need five minutes to gather myself. I feel as if parts of me were scattered all over the place and that's why I can't function.

After securing the three booths from the convention center after Conor's accident, we spent the next two days installing them and decorating this place along with the help of some part-timers. Last night blended into this morning with all the finishing touches, and Conor and I took a nap in his truck before showering in the locker rooms, changing into our party outfits, and receiving the caterers.

That was when I realized we forgot to hire out the ginger-bread cookie baker so we could have cookies to throw Conor's axes to in one of the booths.

After a moment of panic, I had to run around town visiting

bakeries and supermarkets until I collected enough cookies to destroy tonight. By the time I came back to the rink, the first few guests were already arriving.

I couldn't even describe what all transpired after that. It's been a blur since of passing along information brochures but still having to explain everything anyway, to running around putting out figurative little fires here and there. I put on my comfiest sneakers for today and my feet are still so sore I can barely feel them.

I'm sure Conor feels just as tired and would love a respite, but he was surrounded by tipsy people the moment I found myself free, and so I ran for my life. I'll apologize with kisses when I can move again.

I groan to my heart's content as I place my feet on the coffee table and lean my head back on the sofa. I'm just closing my eyes when the door opens to a familiar voice.

"Has anyone told you that groan should be illegal?"

I crack an eye open. Conor doesn't look any less hot just because he's wearing a sweater with a massive reindeer at the front, complete with a red light-up nose. In fact, somehow enhancing his dork side makes him look even better. Not to mention, he somehow carved some time yesterday to trim his hair and beard and it's doing things to me.

"Has anyone told you that your face should be illegal? It makes a girl have naughty thoughts."

His eyebrows rise. "Oh yeah? Tell me more."

"Sorry, I don't have the energy to flirt more than this right now," I say with a weak laugh.

Clearly, he's not as drained as I am because he takes one look at the empty space beside me on the couch, and instead of joining me he offers a hand. "C'mon, save the adrenaline crash for the weekend."

I whine. "But, but…"

"We didn't put together this massive party to not enjoy ourselves too, right?"

"Kind of? I'm having tons of fun right now—ugh." There's nothing I can do but be hauled up to my feet by the power of his hands, although it's not so bad to land against his chest. I free my hands to wrap my arms around him like velcro and inhale the manly scent of his cologne. "Scratch that, I'm definitely enjoying myself *now*."

His chest vibrates with chuckles and he runs those big, warm hands of his up and down my back in a quite respectful way. What a bummer.

"You do know that if we're gone too long people will start talking, right?" he murmurs against my hair.

"Let them talk."

"I thought you were annoyed by all the gossip about us this week."

I nod, which rubs my cheek against him. "I was until this very minute."

"Don't make me carry you on my shoulder."

"You wouldn't." My words come out in a mumble because one of his hands has found my nape and is giving it a little massage that is short-circuiting my brain.

"I would. You make me feel very neanderthal."

"Hmm." That's good to know, but I'll have to make use of that information later and for a completely different setting. "Fine, let's go." Sighing, I separate from him as slowly as I can.

Conor slides one hand down my arm until twining our fingers, and keeps me on the spot as he observes my sweater. A corner of his lips lifts. "Ironic."

My sweater is the body of a gingerbread cookie, its arms running down the sleeves and my head acting as its head. I snort. "I know, it was what reminded me that we had forgotten about the cookies."

"It's like we were on the brink of disaster everyday without realizing it." He tugs me out of the office and shuts the lights as we go.

"That's kind of how the past month has felt," I counter, swinging his arm. "Except some really amazing stuff has come out of it."

"Like what?" Conor wags his eyebrows, no doubt hoping to hear his name from my lips.

Instead, what I say is, "Like ten grand and a promotion for me."

He groans. "I thought love was more important than money."

"Love, huh?"

I stop us at the end of the hallway right before the sprig of mistletoe we hung in the morning. Just beyond us, the party's roaring with hundreds of *SPORTY* headquarters employees and their plus ones. As Gramps is the owner of the venue and that allows him free pass, Conor gifted me his plus one ticket so that both of my parents could come. They're hanging out with Gramps somewhere, either skating or tasting the catering goods together as if today wasn't the first time they were meeting. As if the relationship between Conor and I wasn't moving at warp speed because it's so right. As if Conor and I weren't perfect for each other, in all our imperfections and our desire for the same promotion.

"Uh… Too soon, right?" He's rubbing the back of his neck, his cheeks growing pinker the more I stare at him.

"Nope. Right at the Conor and Sierra pace." I grab a fistful of his sweater and drag him right under the mistletoe. We're both pulled by the same invisible string that tugs smiles on our faces right before we kiss, my arms around his neck and his circling my waist.

The people nearby break into hoots and hollers like they've been doing all night every time a couple finds themselves under the sprigs we tied here and there. I can't believe I was ever so against it when it found me what I didn't know I was missing.

Conor breaks apart enough to speak, though he keeps his forehead against mine. "So, you too?"

"Conor." His name comes out as a whine. "I'm pretty sure I was already halfway there when I thought I hated you."

"Let the record show I never hated you."

He lifts me up in the air and swallows my yelp with another kiss, this one open mouthed and so hungry that it makes my face flame up because there are still people cheering us nearby. I pull away with a gasp and Conor has the nerve to grin up at me.

"Never mind me, just marking my territory."

"Cave troll." I smack his shoulder but grin. "Let's go find a different mistletoe to make out under."

Laughing, Conor slides me down back on my feet and it's when someone starts wolf whistling that I figure we better get ourselves occupied with something other than each other, or we're going to start giving a show that will get HR on our case.

"Good job," one of the sales guys palms Conor's back as we pass. The wink he sends Conor's way suggests he's not exactly referring to the event.

"Ugh, that could've been me," a woman from accounting says with a glare directed at me.

I raise an eyebrow at Conor, who's not missing a thing but is pretending like he is. The only tell is that he keeps biting his lips to contain the laughter dancing in his eyes.

"You're enjoying this, aren't you?" I ask under my breath.

"Oh yeah, I want everyone to know that you're mine."

Then he does the same move from the catering test, when we pretended to be together for a moment. He circles his arm around my back, his hand settling at my hip in a very possessive way. I enjoyed it then as much as I am now, and only because this is a work event I don't slide my hand in his back pocket. I just hook two fingers on his belt loop.

We're following the circuit in reverse, stopping here and there for a quick chat with coworkers. Questions are still the main topic, but we keep being held up by people wanting to know how the biggest rivals in the company got together all of a sudden.

Conor takes care of those. He's really good at joking around without actually saying anything incriminating or useful, and still leaving smiling people behind him. It allows me to just rest my head against his chest and rest, and I admit this is way better than Gramps's office couch.

Eventually, we make it to the start of the circuit, which is the booze booth. There are tens of people lining up for a repeat attempt of the so called Guess the Spike game. It's basically just sipping from different eggnogs and if you guess what kind of alcohol they were spiked with, you win a ticket for more time at the ball pit to fish for gifts.

When it's our turn, the part-timers recognize us right away and I say, "Skip the spiel and pour me rum eggnog."

"The brandy one for me," says Conor.

We step aside after gathering our goods, clink our themed paper cups, and take hearty swigs.

"I have something for you." Conor leads me down the seats towards the ice rink.

"Huh?" I stay confused until he sits me on some chair at the front row, except it's not random because he pulls out a nicely wrapped box from right under it, and places it on my lap. "What?"

He's kneeling on the floor and motions at it with his chin. "Open it."

"I know we've moved quite fast but it's too early for a ring." I joke, knowing full well there isn't a ring this ginormous in the world. The box is kind of heavy and I won't try to shake it, but

I hesitate to open it. "Conor, I didn't think about getting you a gift."

"Don't worry about it, this one is for my own selfish purposes." He tilts his chin toward it once more.

I'm the kind of monster who takes her sweet ass time unwrapping gifts, trying not to tear the paper. I can tell Conor's losing his ever loving mind on the inside by the way his eyes keep widening with impatience. Chuckling, I decide to free him from his misery and tear the paper the rest of the way.

"Hah!" I lift up the box and laugh now that I can see what it is—a brand new pair of skates. "I get it now."

Grinning, Conor reaches under the next seat and pulls out a sports bag. When he unzips it, it reveals his own well loved pair. "Now we can have tons and tons of skating dates whenever we want."

"You ice dork." I lean to place a peck on his lips. "Guess I know what to get you for Christmas now."

"Something baseball related, isn't it?" he asks as he does much quicker work of changing out of his shoes and into his skates than I possibly can.

"You know it. I'll make you the best beer leaguer in town. We start training next week."

"Looking forward to it."

Conor helps me finish my laces and then doesn't let go of my hand as we set out for the ice.

A group of tipsy people tumble into each other like bowling pins and one of the part-timers immediately skates over to assess the situation for any damage. We watch as the part-timer collects their names and after they go, he feeds them into a walkie talkie for the booze booth part-timers to ban them from further spiked eggnog. Assigning people for this duty was a stroke of genius from Conor after the incident with the booths, when safety became of the utmost importance.

Said genius gifts me a bright smile after that whole little episode. I elbow him gently. "Good job, Conor. Without you, this whole thing would've been a disaster."

"Oh." He blinks as if taken aback. "Well, I wouldn't have managed any of this on my own to begin with."

"We both deserve the ten grand and this." I curl my finger at him and he takes the hint right away, sliding closer and leaning down for a kiss.

Except someone else clears their throat and says, "But only one will get the promotion."

Conor and I jerk away by reflex. Thankfully, the boards are right behind me and I don't fall flat on my derriere. Richard, our boss, has a smile on his face that makes me nervous. Given that he's been a strong supporter of this relationship before it was even born, I'm not too concerned with what he just heard or almost saw. It's more about what he just said.

"Oh, hey, Richard. Having a good time?" I ask as I recover my balance with the help of Conor's arm.

"Absolutely, you both truly put together the immersive experience you promised. Thanks to the eggnog and the games, I feel both like an adult and a child at the same time."

"That's great." Conor smiles with way more ease than I feel. "We're so glad it met your expectations."

"And then some." Richard makes a pause. "Both of you did. And I really wish HR had approved two promotions instead of just one."

"We're sure we can't split the promotion?" I joke but at the same time I wish it was possible.

Richard shakes his head. "Alas. Now, do you want me to tell you who's getting it now, or will that spoil the night's fun?"

Conor turns to me and I look up into his eyes. He's serene, and I don't know him to be the kind of person who masks his thoughts or feelings. This must mean he's fine either way and, surprisingly, so am I.

The Sierra of a month ago would be dishing out barbs to relieve the panic rising on the inside. Right now I feel nervous for sure, but I'm not scared. If Conor gets the promotion, I'll be thrilled for him because I know how hard he's worked to put together this event. It's opened my eyes to understand that's the same mettle he's given his job at *SPORTY* ever since he started.

I'd be sad for myself because I've worked damn hard too, but that wouldn't take away from his accomplishment. His success doesn't take away from mine. In fact, if it makes him happy, I'll be happy too.

I hug his arm tighter and turn back to Richard. "I think we can hear it now."

"All right." Richard takes turns observing Conor and me, and finally opens his mouth to announce who's getting the promotion.

CHAPTER 29
CONOR

"Actually, can I please say something first?" I ask right before Richard can even form the name in his mouth.

The two of them stare cartoonishly at me, as if they can't believe I'd dare to interrupt this significant moment. But it's for the best reason, so I make that little noise from my throat that is like a question on its own, until Richard snaps out of it.

"Very well, if you must." He folds his arms across his chest.

"I was just telling Sierra how I couldn't dream of doing all of this on my own." I motion around us. "In fact, the whole thing was her idea from inception."

Sierra interrupts with a shake of her head. "That's not true. You're the author of classics such as Throw the Ornament at the Velcro Tree, and CEO Santa and his helpers. Not to mention you almost died for those booths."

I snort and squeeze her hand. "I was riffing off your ideas and you know it. You masterminded this whole thing, expertly blending in the holidays with what we do at *SPORTY* and who we are. And look, everybody's having a blast."

Serendipity is saying that and pointing right at Camila Puig as she skates by in her half elf costume, laughing her head off at whatever Rachel Leon is saying next to her. The three of us aren't the only ones who have stopped to stare at such phenomenon.

"Indeed," Richard says with his eyebrows up to the roof.

Sierra shakes my arm and casts a fierce scowl in my direction. "If you're trying to get me the promotion, I will kill you, Mahoney."

"There'll be no bloodbath tonight because I'm the only one with the decision power," Richard chimes in and we both ignore him.

"No, I'd be completely wrong if I said I deserve it more than you." I shrug. "I have two years less experience, yet in the past month I've learned more from you than those two years combined. I'm just stating facts here."

Sierra blows air in an exasperated way. "It has to be a fair and square game for it to mean anything."

"It is. It has been. You deserve this." I smile down at her even when she continues to glare.

"As fascinating as it is to see how drastically the dynamic has changed between you two, I have to remind you again that I'm the one who decides." Richard shakes his head at us, amusement oozing from his pores. "Can I finally make the freaking announcement now?"

"Yes, sorry." I clear my throat.

"Please," Sierra says in a begging tone. "Put us out of this misery."

"Is me giving you well deserved compliments a misery?"

"Conor." She smacks my stomach.

"Anyway, I actually agree with Conor," Richard says, which shuts us both up right away. "Sierra, I didn't forget that it was your haphazard pitch what started this whole thing. I certainly noticed how you put aside your biases to team up with Conor and shape the pitch into something tangible. He just said it in a nicer way than I intended—you really captured our essence with this event, and it feels leaps and bounds more memorable than skiing in Aspen. But don't tell Lewis I said that."

"We definitely won't," I respond because Sierra's jaw has dropped and she's not giving any other signs of life. Even bringing her closer against me isn't snapping her out of it.

Richard continues, "Anyway, this has really shown me that you're ready for more responsibility, so congratulations, Sierra. You're getting promoted."

"Uhhh…"

I burst into a laugh. "I thank you on behalf of my speechless girlfriend."

"I'll take it." Richard shifts his attention to me. "And you."

"Yes, sir," I say, as if this were my days of being ordered around by a coach.

"Don't think I didn't notice how hard you worked on this as well. I'm genuinely impressed by your work ethic and your brain."

"My brain?" I frown.

Richard does a double take. "Have you never heard yourself when you're trying to deliver a pitch? I'm glad you use that talent for marketing and not for evil."

"Me too," Sierra grumbles.

Richard clicks his tongue at her. "You stood no chance, Fernandez."

"I know." She sighs.

I scratch my head. "Am I being praised or shaded?"

"Both," they say in unison.

Richard slides over to pat both of our shoulders. "Excellent job, you both. Now, enjoy the party or yourselves. If both, keep it PG, okay?" He chuckles at his own joke and with that, our boss skates away.

I shudder dramatically. "Oh, wow. I just saw a glimpse of

our office life starting January and it scared me. I don't think they'll let us even look at each other without teasing us."

"Shush, I'm still annoyed at you." But she squeezes my waist hard enough that I'm forced to turn into the hug. Into my chest, she says, "Thank you for caping for me."

"Happy to." I kiss her head.

"I'm sorry I didn't think of doing the same. I feel like garbage that I was just going to hear the verdict and that's it." Sierra pulls away and this is when I notice her eyes are watery. "I honestly would've been over the moon if you'd got the promotion instead."

"Hey, hey." I run my thumbs across her cheeks, clearing the trickle of tears and again when they fall once more. "I didn't mean it like that. I just truly think you deserved it."

"You're a much better person than me, Conor Mahoney, and I don't understand why you like me."

Holding her face in my hands, I lean lower to nuzzle her nose with mine and then kiss her softly. And twice for good measure. I pull away just a smidge to say, "That's not how I see it—or how I see you. You're competitive and determined and honest to a fault. I'm just a little more laid back, and I think that's the perfect complement to each other." Sierra sighs and drops her head right over my heart, which is beating like a fast drum. "Besides, there's a different promotion I got that I'm more interested in."

"Hmm?"

I whisper, "Your boyfriend."

Her arms tighten around my waist. "Congratulations, you are the winner."

"That's right, baby."

"We'll have to workshop the cutesy nicknames, though."

I hum from deep in my throat. "Bebé? That's how you say it in Spanish, right?"

She shifts her head until she's looking up at me. "Did you Google that in advance?"

"I may or may not have downloaded Duolingo after our first kiss in the hopes that I could ask you out in Spanish."

Sierra shakes her head. "You are a danger to society, Mahoney. I'm so glad to be the one taking you out of commission."

Grinning, I extricate myself out of her hold and offer just my hand. As she takes it, I lead us for a leisurely skate along the boards so Sierra can grab onto them as well. "So, your grandma arrives next week to spend Christmas with your family thanks to the bonus. Now that you're receiving a promotion, does that mean you'll be moving into your own place like you mentioned?"

"Why?" She cocks an eyebrow at me. "Do you have a particular interest in me living on my own?"

"A curiosity, more like."

"I'm thinking I'll save money for a while," she says in a breezy voice. "Maybe splurge on some dates with my boyfriend and see where that takes us."

"Sounds like a great plan to me." I lift her hand to my lips. "Ready to hit the booths?"

"Oh yeah, let's see who can collect more tickets for the ball pit."

I smirk. "You're on."

We make a stop to change back into our shoes and I tuck away our skates. Gramps knows where they are and he'll get them tomorrow after the dust clears.

Sierra and I race around the booths, heckling the shit out of each other like we would've done months ago. I try to sabotage her ornament pitches by hugging her from behind, but she somehow still manages to land more ornaments on the velcro tree than I do. She tries to take revenge while I'm throwing axes at gingerbread cookies, and I don't know how I manage to not drop an ax on my foot while I have her curves pressed up against my back. We even turn eating churros into a competition even though there are no tickets being handed out at the food both, and then make a pit stop to make out under the mistletoe while our mouths still taste of sugar and cinnamon.

And then, we finally make it to the ball pit. "After you," I say, standing in line beside Sierra. We spent big dime on this inflatable ball pit guaranteed to be ten times stronger than average, but I don't really trust it.

"Don't tell me ax throwing doesn't scare you but this does." Sierra tilts her head.

"I'm not scared, woman, but it'd really suck if my weight deflates it."

"Listen, if a hundred people didn't burst it before you, you won't." Sierra offers her hand, palm raised up. "Let's go together."

"You're making it sound like we're about to bungee jump or something."

"Oh, Conor. I didn't know you were such a scaredy cat." She pouts cutely.

I roll my eyes and grab her hand. "Fine, let's go."

I clench my jaw tight as we climb the unstable ramp, ready to catch Sierra the moment this thing goes. But it doesn't. We make it to the entrance without incident and seeing the massive pool of plastic balls tears a laugh out of me.

"See? It's fun." Sierra's eyes shine with joy as she swings my arm. "Ready?"

"Ready."

"Let's go!"

We jump together. I'm too tall for how deep it is so I immediately bounce once my feet connect with the bottom. Meanwhile, Sierra sinks all the way in as if she were a child. I'm still cracking up as she resurfaces with an exaggerated gasp, and I don't know if my eggnog was extra spiked or if I'm the one who's spiked now because I can't stop giggling.

Neither of us are interested in the gifts, so we just toss balls at each other and wade around, pretending that we're swimming, until Sierra finds me sitting in a corner and comes to join me. I find her hips and shift her around until she sits between my legs, her back resting against my chest.

She sighs as I hug her tighter. "It's finally over."

I push her curls away with my face until I find her neck and kiss it softly. "Almost."

"But not us," she says, angling away to give me more access. While I take advantage of it, she runs her hands up and down my outer thighs as if mapping them.

"Not us," I murmur against her skin. "We're just getting started."

"Merry Christmas, Conor."

"Merry Christmas, Sierra." I smile against the crook of her neck. "The first of many together."

CHAPTER 30
SIERRA

Without a doubt, this has been the best December of my life. First, I get the previously unthinkable gift of a boyfriend. Second, I get the gift of a bonus and a promotion—although, are they really a gift if I worked my ass off for them?

Anyway, third, I get the gift of Grammie coming over for Christmas.

"You look like a kid on Christmas morning, mija," Mom says from the passenger seat of our truck. "Are you that excited?"

"More." I can't stop moving. During the drive from home to the airport I've fiddled with my seatbelt, the window, my phone, my hair—which I've put up in a ponytail and then down again—and my phone again, texting every minutia to Conor and shockingly not making him sick of me yet.

"Good thing I'm the one driving," Dad says with a snort and glances at Mom. "Am I the only one who feels jealous that she doesn't get this excited to see me?"

"No, clearly there are favorites." Mom laughs.

"Oh, please." I huff. "You were the ones who basically

decided to redo the guest room and even came up with the idea of installing guardrails in the bathroom."

"Really good idea, mi amor." Mom places her hand on Dad's arm.

"Thank you, I saw it on the 'Gram."

I don't bother hiding my cringe. "And also, you've been playing guarachas non stop for a week already because it's Grammie's favorite music." It's this old, really fast cousin of salsa with somewhat spicy lyrics that was all the rage during Grammie's youth. It was all well and good except for every time that my parents left me alone to clean, because they needed to have an impromptu dance session in the kitchen.

Cute, but really annoying. I look forward to being that obnoxious with Conor one day.

Speaking of, my phone buzzes in my hand.

CONOR THE BOYFRIEND

Did you make it to the airport okay?

ME

Not yet. So close yet so far

CONOR THE BOYFRIEND

Don't forget to breathe

I send him a sassy emoji because this isn't the first time he says this. Apparently, when I feel an emotion too strongly, I tend to hold my breath. I wonder if that lack of oxygen flowing to my brain is what has caused me to make bad decisions, such as when I determined that Conor was going to be my enemy. Clearly that was wrong.

But I'm feeling magnanimous today, so I take a few deep breaths and find that I'm fidgeting a lot less. I'm about to text this man about the curious calming power he has on me even when he's not around in person, when I feel the truck slowing down. We're finally entering the airport's parking lot.

Welp, so much for calming down. My heart rate skyrockets.

While Dad finds parking, I check the airport app on my phone and it shows that Grammie's plane hasn't landed yet. That's great, because we definitely want to be waiting for her when she clears security. I'm sure the trip has been exhausting and the language barrier overwhelming.

Unfortunately, that also means that I have to do a lot of pacing back and forth in the terminal as we wait. Mom and Dad have camped right at the travelers' exit, a couple of shopping bags at their feet with all the welcome paraphernalia we prepared. I wish I could be like them and could be excited but calm. Alas.

"Are you sure you want us to come over today?" Conor asks me over the phone. I had to call him, desperate for a distraction.

I officially broke the news to the family last weekend, right after the *SPORTY* event, and their reactions were so funny. Mom couldn't stop repeating the words *I knew it*. Dad sat on the couch as if he'd lost all strength and, spent the rest of the day on the exact same spot just staring blankly at the floor. But Grammie's reaction was to say she didn't care about meds or doctor appointments, what she wants out of her visit to the States is to meet my boyfriend.

"El mismo día que llego," she said, folding her bony arms and jutting her chin with stubbornness.

"Yes, it's Grammie's orders," I respond to Conor's question. "You've taken the top spot in her bucket list now."

"Well, okay, no pressure." He jokes at his own expense. "Should I wear normal clothes or a tuxedo?"

"Got a happy in between?" After a moment, I grow more serious. "No, really. I can make up an excuse if this is too early."

"This is important to your family, so I'll see you in an hour, okay?"

"Yeah, thanks," I say more with air than with voice, because this is the moment I know that this is the man I'll marry.

I had classmates who bullied me for my accent or even because my homemade lunches were completely different from theirs, but Conor doesn't dismiss these cultural differences or gets uncomfortable by them. I only had to explain to him how Latin American families are *everything* and *always there*—even if they physically aren't—for him to get it and respect it. I'm sure any other guy would be running for the hills if he had to formally meet his girlfriend's family like just two weeks after getting together.

We finish the call and I'm grinning from ear to ear as I rejoin my parents to really set up the welcome banner and balloons. No matter what scary things the future holds—and they're scary when one of your loved ones is elderly and sick— I know this is a special moment and I'm going to cherish every last second of it.

People start trickling out of the exit wheeling suitcases and carrying bags, but we're watching out for the wheelchairs. Of course, I made sure to book the assistance service for Grammie. She'd break her fast on caviar if she liked the thing and if I could have it my way.

The first sign that Grammie might be in sight comes from Mom, who lets out a squeal. I've been holding a flower bouquet for a few minutes and I lower it from my face, and there she is.

My frail little Grammie waving at us as an airport staff wheels her over.

I don't know who screams her name then, could've been Mom or me. All I know is that I'm bouncing more than I did in that ball pit a few days ago, and there are tears streaming down my eyes. When she's cleared the security area, I take off in a short sprint that ends with me kneeling in front of her and our arms around each other.

"Feliz navidad, Sierrita," she whispers above me and boy, isn't it?

Best. Christmas. Ever.

*

According to Grammie, things have changed drastically since the one time she visited when I was a kid. A strip mall didn't exist where there was an open field before, a bank was replaced by a fast food place, or some houses now used to be a parking lot. We drive by the convention center downtown and she says that one looks just the same, before launching on a tale about how the main market back in her hometown turned into the convention center once supermarkets became a thing decades ago.

I'm riveted more by the fact that she's right next to me, telling tales in person rather than through a screen, than by the tales themselves. My heart twists by the utter glee and sorrow warring in it. It's so hard to love someone this much, yet be mostly separated from them. Tale of an immigrant family, I guess.

Her hand has surprising strength for how slight it is, for the paper thin skin with a network of veins behind it. I think she squeezes mine much harder than the other way around.

She's talking about how pretty snow is, but that dies down as Dad parks the truck by the curb of our house and we spot two figures waiting on our porch.

"The boyfriend," Dad announces in a grouch.

"And the boyfriend's grandfather." My eyes widen. I guess this is going to be a full-on event, huh? Except, unlike last week's, I'm woefully unprepared for this.

We make quick work of getting out of the truck, and while Dad and I focus on helping Grammie out, Mom gets her suitcase from the trunk. The four of us make a slow walk up the shoveled path. I basically keep one eye on Grammie as I hold her by the arm, and another one on my boyfriend.

He's rocking on the balls of his feet, as if nervous.

How flipping cute is that?

Finally, we join them by the porch and for a long, quiet moment, it's like a standoff where everyone is staring at one another.

I'm the one who breaks it.

"Grammie," I say everything in Spanish for her benefit. "Estos son Conor, mi novio, y Conrad, su abuelo. Le dicen Gramps." Then I turn to them and speak in English. "Conor, Gramps, may I have the honor of introducing my favorite family member, Grammie?"

Dad blows a raspberry. "What am I now, the third most important person in your life now?"

"Fourth, honey." Mom pats his arm.

I burst into giggles and that dissipates the weird tension. Shoulders relax and eyes soften, until I translate all that for Grammie and she asks me to send everyone in and stay alone with her for a second.

Uh oh.

Mom and Dad aren't exactly the biggest fans of the cold, so they're happy to oblige. Gramps goes next and Conor hangs on for a moment, observing my expression to gauge if something's wrong. Problem is, I have no idea. After taking the hint, he places a quick kiss on my cheek and goes inside.

Grammie takes both of my hands in hers. "Ese muchacho te hace feliz."

"Sí."

"Y se ve que te quiere."

I nod, that's the most wonderful part of all.

"Y es muy atractivo."

I'm about to nod again when I do a double take. My small, sweet, delicate little grandmother gives me a sly grin.

"Y ahora que he conocido al abuelo, sé que tiene buenos genes."

"Grammie!" I gape.

"Así que está aprobado."

"¿Así sin más?"

The quick approval of my boyfriend based on qualifications such as the facts that he makes me happy, likes me, and has good genes, stops being shocking when she explains what we all know: she doesn't have a long time left. This is the reason why this visit was so important, and I'm just glad I get to share this with her at all.

Best Christmas ever, I think, even though I'm crying different tears now.

CHAPTER 31
CONOR

A beam of light pierces through my eye, making me moan in protest. I turn my head away but it's just as bright on the other side. With herculean effort, I lift a hand to rub the sleep off my eyes.

When I open them again, I see the mound of my pillow half obscuring the alarm clock. It's about an hour later than I normally get up for, but that's when I remember that it's Christmas and my gift to myself is no training today. My other gift to myself is the date Sierra and I will have later today.

That's all the motivation I need to get up, shower and do my hair, and put on clothes that don't look like I coach kids's hockey or spend a good portion of my leisure time splitting wood. The date will be low key, just sledding down the hill by Main Street in the morning and drinking homemade hot chocolate, followed by Christmas mass with Sierra's family and then brunch. But I'm more excited than on the day I got drafted to the pros.

I guess I'm an old man now, when being with loved ones is more exciting than opening presents under the tree.

Said tree catches my attention on the way to the kitchen to

make the hot chocolate. I can't quite pinpoint what about it made me pause, but it might be because I left my glasses in the bathroom. After retreating and putting them on, I march to my living room with purpose and stare at the tree again.

Same yay-high tree that I could put on a table because I don't really have enough footprint for the real deal—check. Same twinkling lights and hockey-themed ornaments—check. Two gift-looking things at the base, even though I definitely didn't put them there—also check.

One's a box with gold tissue paper and a red bow, jewelry size. The other one is a tube wrapped in the same colors, but opposite—red paper and golden bow. This smells of effort, and I wonder if it's from Sierra. But how did she even sneak them in? I haven't even thought of giving her a house key yet.

I take the box first and check the table, but there's no card under the things either. The mystery continues when I open it and find a nondescript key inside, also with no note.

Can't be Sierra's house key when she lives with her parents. Did she go ahead and rent an apartment in secret? But then, there would be a note.

Maybe it's in the other gift. This one's wrapped more painstakingly and it takes a longer moment to open. Inside, the tube is kind of like a case. I pull it open and find some papers rolled inside. But instead of an apartment rental contract, what I find is a property sale document.

For an ice rink.

"What?" I whisper in the quiet.

I blink hard, running my eyes across the words over and over until I'm sure that what I'm reading is right. That's Conrad Mahoney's name on the seller section, and Conor Mahoney on the buyer's, all right.

I rush out the door, halfway to my truck realizing that I didn't grab the car keys or a jacket. My breath blows plumes in the air as I run back into the house to grab my stuff and bundle up. I'm a ball of raw nerve as I drive through the country side, rows of snow capped pine trees flanking the road, a bright blue sky guiding me forward.

I don't think, I just drive straight into the parking lot of Conrad's Rink. I almost meet my maker when I slip on ice near the entrance, but the hockey thighs save me from that fate. I pump them hard as I run through the place, now clear of any vestiges of *SPORTY*'s party, stopping only outside the door to my grandfather's office.

"Come in, kid. I can hear you wheezing outside."

It occurs to me, hearing Gramps' voice from the other side of this door, that I didn't even contemplate the possibility that he might've been at home this morning—like everybody else. I open the door and stand still, opening and closing my mouth until I recover myself enough to talk.

"How can someone who loves this place enough to spend Christmas morning here, ever want to sell it and retire?"

Gramps snorts from his seat by the desk, fingers laced above his belly in the picture of serenity. "Maybe because, if you're the new owner, I can still come and go as I please without having any of the responsibility."

"Gramps—"

"No, I thought long and hard about this." He raises the palm of his knobby, wrinkly hand and it effectively shuts me up. "This is the way we both get what we want. I can finally retire and rest these old bones, you get to still use this place to pass on a legacy."

I swallow hard, trying to clear the lump that keeps growing in my throat but not quite succeeding. My voice comes out all garbled. "Stop making it sound like you're going to die tomorrow or something."

He shrugs as if this wasn't a big deal. "Probably not tomorrow but sooner than later, so stop looking like you're going to shit bricks."

"I—" Shaking my head hard, I say, "Of course that terrifies me, but right now I have a different concern."

"What now?"

I shake the papers in the air. "Ever thought that I might not be able to afford this? That's why I worked so hard for the event, because the ten grand will ease things a bit but not enough. It's nowhere near enough to buy the whole damn place."

"But it could make a decent down payment for, you know, a loan." He opens his eyes in a way that is the purest definition of sarcasm. I'm not tight lipped about my finances with him, and he knows I have a near perfect credit score. A loan is definitely possible.

"Fine, say I get a loan and buy the place. Then what? I still have a full time job."

"But you'd have the best part-timer you could dream of. This guy," he says, pointing both thumbs at his chest.

My eyebrows shoot up. "What about retirement?"

"I did say I thought long and hard about this, didn't I? Full retirement, just wondering what I'm going to do with my day everyday, or doing the same thing Monday through Sunday, doesn't really suit me."

That sounds about right, and I bet the one person he'd turn all that free energy on would be me. *That* is a truly brick-shitting concept.

I'm sold—or I should say, I'll buy. I'm now so on board with this idea that if my body were to produce a single ounce more of adrenaline, I'd shoot through the roof. If today wasn't Christmas, I'd turn back around and march into the nearest bank to request a loan. But I guess that'll be my plan for the new year.

"Can you give me a discount?" I ask, tucking my tongue against my cheek.

"No. This is how you'll fund my extremely low wage as a part-timer."

I break into a grin. "Thanks, Gramps."

"Merry Christmas, kid." Grunting, he waves a hand for me to leave. "Now, go get your other present."

"Huh?"

"Just go." He purposely shifts his attention to some random paperwork, and I have no option but to walk away.

There are no other wrapped boxes or suspicious looking things lining the hallway, other than the same stains that have decorated the wall paint for at least a decade. I walk out to the corridor behind the seats, where a few days ago we had booths teeming with people. Once I'm the new owner of this place, we'll have more events like to bring in more income—anything I can think of to sustain the hockey program.

I keep walking to the entrance when a sound stops me in my tracks.

Someone's skating on the ice.

I'm pretty sure the place is closed to the public today, thus no one should be out there skating. I change direction to take the steps down to the ice, and I immediately recognize the skater.

"Sierra?"

She tries to brake but doesn't have the chops to do it properly, and she comes crashing down. Before I know it, I'm tossing the contract aside and my car keys, not even caring where they fall as I rush to the ice.

"Are you okay?" I ask as I walk on the ice in my street shoes, trying to reach her as fast as possible.

"Yeah." Her nose is wrinkled, eyes shut tight as she sits up straight. One of her hands reaches for her butt. "Fortunately, I have really good cushion."

"You really do. I like your cushion a lot," I say as I kneel in front of her. "Does it hurt too badly?"

She opens her eyes. "Yeah, it hurts a lot. Maybe you should give it a massage."

I sit back on my haunches, snorting. "Flirt."

"You like it." Sierra reaches for my hand. "Speaking of, wanna start flirting back now instead of later?"

"Is this your way of asking me out on a date, Sierra Fernandez?"

"Yes." She nods solemnly. "Do you accept?"

"I do. But first, let's get you back on your feet." I reach for her.

CHAPTER 32
SIERRA

Maybe I'm being a neanderthal, but there's nothing sexier than when your boyfriend can lift you up onto your feet without breaking a sweat or even squeezing his jaw tight from the effort.

I squeeze him, all right. Once I'm vertical, I grab onto his arms and cop a nice feel of them. They're like granite, just like everything of his except for two things.

His eyes and his lips. Those are so very soft as he looks down and smiles at me. I sigh.

Taking advantage of the added height from my skates, I run my hands up his shoulders until I find his neck. "We said today's date would be nice and chill, so how about we stay just like this for the rest of the day?"

"I'm not wearing my skates," he says as if that was the most important thing here.

"Is it mandatory? Because I'm all nice and cozy enough right now."

As response, Conor's hands press just a little tighter around my waist. My lips part with a tiny gasp of delight. Maybe that's why he decides to travel his hands a little further—down, towards my erm, cushion. He pulls me right against him as he cops a little feel in return.

"Look at you, wearing waterproof pants," Conor whispers in my ear and I don't know why I shiver.

"Ahem." A raspier voice echoes around us. Conor and I separate enough to turn toward Gramps, who stands by the door to the rink with his arms folded. "I think I'm going home now. That way you two can be naughty or nice together if you want."

Conor groans. "Gramps, you're killing me."

"We'll be very nice." I grin, showing all my pearly whites. "Ish."

Gramps shakes his head. "Conor, be a gentleman to Sierra. And make sure to lock up when you lovebirds leave. Merry Christmas, Sierra."

This time my smile is for real. "Merry Christmas, Gramps."

Conor and I are still nice and snug as we watch the old man climb the steps back up, and we keep quiet until we hear the front door open and close.

Slowly, my boyfriend turns back to me and cocks an eyebrow. "So, I take it you and Gramps set this up together?"

"Yes. I wrapped your gifts and he sneaked them into your house. But then he sneaked me in here this morning. Were you surprised?"

"Very."

I brush imaginary lint off his chest. "But in a good way?"

"In an oh my gosh, I can't believe I'm able to contain this much happiness in my body kind of way."

"Good. Guess what will make you happier?" I ask.

Conor's expression turns pensive for a moment, eyes lost on a point somewhere above my head. "Oh, the hot chocolate I forgot to make this morning because I left in such a rush?"

"Something better," I say, only growing his confusion. I

reach into the pocket of my vest and pluck out a small bundle. His eyes latch onto it as I lift it up between us. "How's this?"

His warm brown eyes fall from the small bunch of mistletoe directly to my lips. "You're right, this is exactly what I needed for the moment to be truly perfect."

Conor holds the side of my face, tilting it with his thumb to get better access to my lips. I let my eyelids fall and abandon myself to the feeling of his hot, velvet-smooth lips caressing mine. Of his breath fanning my face and how he holds me so I don't fall.

But I've fallen, I've fallen so hard for him that I'm never getting back up.

At some point, the mistletoe has slipped from my hand in favor of feeling his hair, his neck, his jaw. If it wasn't getting harder to breathe, I'd be well on my way to feeling his skin under his sweatshirt. When we come up for air, I notice he did slide one of his hands under my shirt.

"Sneaky," I say among gasping breaths.

"I'll let you pay me back any time." He grins against my mouth, and I guess that's enough breathing for now.

I pull him in for another kiss, open mouthed and hot enough to melt the rink down, and I waste no time in getting my revenge. I slide my freezing hands against the taught skin of his back, enjoying how it makes him shiver just as much as I love the ridges of hard muscles up his spine, down his side, and the smattering of fuzz over his abs.

That's where he pulls away, grabbing my wrists. "Any more of that and I'm going to disappoint Gramps."

I mewl. "But…"

"Later." His gaze is intense and hot enough that I don't need any clothes to warm me up. "When we're not in a place where slipping down could send us to the hospital."

"Okay, fine." I roll my eyes. "I guess you can give me another skating lesson, then."

"I'm flattered by your disappointment." Grinning, he lifts my hands and places a kiss on the big knuckle of one hand, the kind that would've made a Regency era lady melt into a puddle. I can confirm it does the same to me, especially when he does the same on the other hand. "There's no need to rush, Sierra. We're in this for the long haul."

"We are." My voice is a throaty mess and I clear it. "We're sticking to the low key and chill date plan. High key and hot date to follow later."

Conor's laughter bounces back against the boards as he pulls me along toward the seats. That's when he discovers the extent of Gramps's and my planning, because the sweet old grump got me Conor's skates out of his locker and set them by the door, ready for this moment. And on the nearest seat is the enormous flask with thick, homemade hot chocolate that Mom and Grammie helped me prepare this morning.

Once he's done changing into his skates, Conor grabs my hand and slides onto the ice, and it feels like the beginning to the rest of our lives.

EPILOGUE

CONOR: CHRISTMAS ONE YEAR LATER

"Is it bittersweet?" Sierra asks, looking up at me even as she digs for the last kernels of popcorn in our bucket. She ate about one third of it by herself without realizing it.

What she did notice: that my stomach has been in knots. But it's not for the reason she thinks.

"Nope," I respond sincerely, looking into her eyes and not breaking the contact despite the two hockey players that smash into the glass right in front of our seats.

Sierra jumps so high that a few kernels escape the confines of the bucket. Her eyes are wide as saucers as the players grunt and push each other in their fight for the puck. "I have to say I'm kind of glad." She swallows hard. "I'd hate to see you getting hit like that."

That makes my lips stretch into a smile. "I looked pretty good when I was a little beat up, though."

"I think you look plenty good without injuries, Mahoney."

"And I think you look the best without any—" Abruptly she shoves popcorn at my mouth and doesn't let me finish the saucier words. That's too bad because they were just about to make me forget what's going to happen in a few minutes.

Now that I'm back to reality, I turn to the game right as Max finally wins the puck. While I was turned to Sierra, my left eye was the one on the side of the action and I hadn't noticed that he was one of the players going at it. Before taking off, Max flashes me a quick thumb up that I return.

The player from the opposing team that he was duking it out with was none other than our friend Nate, because hockey is a small world that way. But also, the two of them knew that Sierra and I were coming to this game, and just like we did with Max, they helped me prepare my private event.

Sierra has no idea I'm about to propose to her right here.

Okay, it's not an entirely wild gamble. She and I have talked about marriage and we're of the same opinion that it's what we want this relationship to head to. But the public proposal part is a bit trickier.

I couldn't ask her directly what kind of proposal she prefers —something just between us? At a destination? In front of family? In front of strangers?

So what I did is that I recruited her friends, Rachel and Camila. Apparently after a lot of boozy apple ciders over brunch, all they could get out of Sierra was "what I want is for everyone to know that Conor and I are wild for each other."

That could fit any scenario, but for some reason I decided to do it in public where I was guaranteed to freak out the worst.

I've spent basically the whole game with my right arm around her shoulders, my hand resting on her shoulder over her layers of clothes where she can't possibly feel how cold and clammy it is. My other hand I've kept occupied between popcorn and my drink, and away from contact with her.

The box with the ring is on my left pocket. Sierra hasn't

noticed how she's been kept to my right side the whole night so that she doesn't accidentally feel the box.

The ref blows the whistle stopping the play, and music blares around the arena. My heart kicks up violently once I recognize the familiar tune of the local team, but with a Christmas jangle twist to honor the season.

It's kiss cam time and also my show time.

The Jumbotron displays a first couple, an older one who have clearly been together for decades. They burst out laughing at the cartoon mistletoe drawn on the screen between them and the wife turns to smack a big kiss on her husband that gets the crowd going.

"That is so freaking adorable." Sierra grins up at the screen, unknowingly giving me hope that she won't hate this.

I don't even pay attention to the next couple because I know we'll be third and last. While everyone—including my girlfriend—are transfixed by the show, I dig my hand into my pocket and close it around the small velvet box.

Then the camera shifts to us, and someone's had the great idea of printing my name on screen along with the words former professional player. Now I don't know if the crowd's cheering is because we're about to kiss, or because of me, but it doesn't really matter.

"Oh!" Sierra laughs and covers her face, but with all the cheering around us she slowly peeks between her fingers at me.

I'm smiling, I know I am—on the inside I'm screaming, though.

"Oh look, it's mistletoe," I tease, my attention solely on her.

"Please, you don't need mistletoe for me to kiss you anymore." With another giggle, she leans over and presses her lips against mine.

My eyes close and for a moment everything is perfect. Her hand is in my hair and the noise around us drowns a moan from my chest that would've either made her scold me, or got her own engine revving. There's no in between.

Too soon Sierra pulls away and looks at the screen, expecting it to shift to another couple. Surprise registers on her face when she realizes that the camera is still on us. And she watches through it as I slide down the seat to my knee, taking the mostly empty popcorn bucket with me to set it on the floor.

That tears her eyes from the screen and back to me. "Conor, what's happening?"

Shakier than the five rabbits in a trench coat that she claims to be, I pull up the velvet box and present it to her. "This is happening."

Her eyes bulge. Her jaw drops. The crowd roars like the home team just scored the game winning goal.

I have to kind of scream for her to hear me at this point. "If I could go back in time and choose not suffering the accident and keeping hockey, but never meeting you, I would still choose you."

Sierra sucks in air and at the next blink, there's moisture in her eyes.

"And I would like you to choose me too," I ask, feeling red taking over my face.

It takes two tries to open the box but I manage, and another laugh gurgles out of her. I was a bit cheeky with the ring, setting three oval shaped diamonds over a smaller round one in an imitation of the mistletoe that got us together.

"So, Sierra Fernandez, will you please do me the honor of changing my status from former foe and boyfriend, to husband?"

She stays suspended in her surprise for a moment. Until her lips stretch into a wide smile that reaches her eyes and she throws herself at me. She knocks the wind out of my lungs—nothing new, to be honest—and I manage to catch her before we topple over.

Amid wolf whistles and clapping, Sierra says into my ear, "Consider yourself promoted, Conor Mahoney."

AND THEY SKATED HAPPILY EVER AFTER

*

*Thank you for reading **Mistlefoe**! I hope you can take a brief moment to leave a review on Amazon.*

Here are my other works if you're craving more closed door sports romance:

*Sign up to my newsletter at MARILOYAL.COM to read a **bonus scene** from the point of view of Camila, the heroine of my next Christmas romance to come out in 2025. You'll also get my free volleyball novella, **Set Me Up**.*

*The St. Cloud Hockey Series is fully available! Book one, **Faceoff**, is a rivals to lovers romance. Book two, **Overtime**, is a grumpy x sunshine romance. Book three and the last in series, **Shutout**, is a childhood friends to enemies to lovers romance.*

*Preorder **Wild Pitch**, book one in my upcoming Wild Baseball Romance series where the team's hot pitcher becomes our heroine's dating coach.*

Happy reading!

GLOSSARY OF SPANISH VOCABS

Chapter 2

- Mierda: crap or shit (see also Chapter 12, 16).

Chapter 4

- Tía Sierra: Aunt Sierra.
- Señorita: Miss.
- Bebé: Baby (see also Chapter 29).

Chapter 6

- Ya va: Hold on.

Chapter 10

- Mija: Colloquial way of saying "my daughter" (see also Chapter 10, 30).
- ¿Sí? ¿Qué pasó?: Yes? What happened?

- Que Dios te bendiga: God bless you.
- Tengo noticias: I have news.
- ¿Qué?: What?
- Que tengo noticias: I have news, I said.
- Me están dando un bono en el trabajo y te voy a poder traer para acá para navidad: I'm getting a bonus at work and I'll be able to fly you over for Christmas.
- ¿Qué pasa?: What's happening?
- Me encantaría pero es que estos días no me siento muy bien: I would love to but these days I don't feel well.
- Sierrita, no quiero que uses to dinero en mí: My little Sierra, I don't want you to use money on me.
- Ya hice la reserva de tu ticket. Te lo envío por email en la noche: I already made your ticket reservation. I'll send it to you by email tonight.

Chapter 12

- Qué va: No way.
- Duro: Hard.

Chapter 16

- Bueno: Good.
- No bueno: Not good in incorrect grammar.
- Cálmate: Calm down.

Chapter 18

- Pendeja: Dipshit (female).

Chapter 20

- Qué si no: As if.

Chapter 24

- Me gusta: I like him.
- ¡Estoy bien!: I'm fine!
- ¿Y ese quién es?: And who is that?
- ¡Explícate, señorita!: Explain yourself, miss!
- Que alguien me diga qué pasa: Someone tell me what's happening.
- Tu nieta tiene su primer novio: Your granddaughter has her first boyfriend.
- Se ve grande ese muchacho: That boy looks big.

Chapter 30

- Mi amor: My love.
- Guarachas: an old type of Venezuelan music.
- El mismo día que llego: The same day I arrive.
- Feliz navidad, Sierrita: Merry Christmas, little Sierra.
- Estos son Conor, mi novio, y Conrad, su abuelo. Le dicen Gramps: These are Conor, my boyfriend, and Conrand, his grandfather. They call him Gramps.
- Ese muchacho te hace feliz: That boy makes you happy.
- Sí: Yes.
- Y se ve que te quiere: And it looks like he cares about you.
- Y es muy atractivo: And is very attractive.
- Y ahora que he conocido al abuelo, sé que tiene

buenos genes: And now that I've met the grandfather, I know he has good genes.

- Así que está aprobado: So he's approved.
- ¿Así sin más?: Just like that?

ACKNOWLEDGMENTS

As always, I first have to thank the Lord. Contigo todo, sin ti nada.

Special thanks to Tamara Lush and Avery Keelan for all the extreme patience they show in the face of my chaos. And also for the cat memes.

To Enni at Yummy Book Covers who absolutely saved my behind *and* gave me the best cover a girl could possibly ask for.

To all my readers, ARC team, and to my cheerleaders for giving me a chance to take your minds away from the yucky real world and immerse you in this cute little Christmas romance. Thank you, thank you, a million times thank you for all your support during my first year as an indie author.

Last but not least, I want to thank my mom and my sister (who are both in a different continent this Christmas), and my dad up in heaven. Thank you for encouraging me to never give up. Los amo con todo.

ABOUT THE AUTHOR

Mari Loyal was born and raised in Venezuela, a baseball country that only cared about another sport, football soccer, every four years. As such, she decided to make hockey her whole personality because she had to make a point of being different. These days she no longer suffers from Not Like Other Girls syndrome and is very happy to be in the sports romance fandom. She writes closed door romance with a Latin American flair and an abundance of cinnamon rolls heroes. She also enjoys eating cinnamon rolls (the confections), in her spare time.

Sign up for my newsletter at MARILOYAL.COM